CALL OF SHADOWS

AIRSHIP 27 PRODUCTIONS

Call of Shadows
© 2012 David C. Smith

For Janine, with love

With thanks to the following for their assistance and comments. You helped me out: Susan Baim, Bronwyn Barrera, Joe Bonadonna, Ken W. Faig, Jr., Lewis Jenkins, Nancy Razzano, Rick Razzano, Tim Riley, Ted Rypel, Donald Sidney-Fryer, Mary Stanley, and David Stanley.

Published by Airship 27 Productions
www.airship27.com
www.airship27hangar.com

"Whatever happened to high adventure? It took flight with Airship 27."

Interior llustrations © 2012 Mark Saxton
Cover illustration © 2012 Bryan Fowler

Editor: Ron Fortier
Associate Editor:Charles Saunders
Production and design by Rob Davis

ISBN-13:978-0615618890
ISBN-10:0615618898

Printed in the United States of America

10 9 8 7 6 5 4 3 2 1

CALL OF SHADOWS

a novel by
DAVID C. SMITH

Lewis —
Thank you. You
helped me out with
this story, and I really
appreciate it.

Dave
April 3, 2012
Rosemont IL

Sorrow is knowledge.
Byron, **Manfred**
Act I, Scene I

1.

For five years, Trey Connors and his family and their friends had waited for justice to be done. For five years, they had sat patiently as lawyers in courtrooms, in Chicago as well as in Florida, met to file postponements and delays or whatever they were called, the paperwork needed to prevent a guilty man from being brought to trial. Five years. Meanwhile, one of Trey's uncles died, as well as a great-aunt. Children were born, including a little girl to Trey and his wife. And still the waiting, all of them waiting, Trey and his wife and their brothers and sisters, his parents, and the friends of other black men who had been damaged.

Damaged and murdered, too, because two of those black men were now as dead as Trey's uncle and great-aunt.

The justice they waited for, the trial they waited for, was that of a bad Chicago cop named Jim Burkey. In the late 1980s and early 1990s, Burkey, the commander of a detective squad on the South Side, had run an operation in which he and officers who answered to him detained and tortured black men. Only black men. Serious scuffles and lawbreaking had led to the deaths of several police officers, and in retaliation, Burkey and his officers bent the law, then broke it outright. Bring in black men, was Burkey's order; go after those scumbags. And the black men were clubbed, the black men were burned with cigarettes and electricity, they were choked with wet rags, and they were raped with sawed-off broom handles.

And what could anyone do about it?

No one could do anything about it.

Accusations were met with a cover-up. Finally, the crimes came to light when one of Burkey's cops who had helped with the electric shocks and the broom handles confessed, while he was dying of cancer, to what had happened. And so prosecutors had started looking into what they could do.

But by the time the cop with cancer confessed, Burkey had retired and was living well in Florida. A couple of his cop buddies, the specialists in the art of using water-soaked rags, had retired with him, and they and their wives now had homes outside Tampa. The statute of limitations had run out, but some of the attorneys in Chicago were determined to find other means of making sure that Burkey paid for what he had done.

It took them five years, fighting postponements and delays, filing and re-filing, but in the end, after five years, the clock had run out, their arguments did not convince the authorities in Florida, and Burkey and his cop friends continued to enjoy their retirement in Tampa, untouched and unapologetic.

This outcome hit Trey hard, him and his family and friends. Trey had suffered the least of any of them, but still, he now had to make do with a misshapen left wrist that had healed poorly after Burkey had broken it. Unable to afford a surgeon, Trey had had his friends set it as best they could, but it wasn't much of a wrist now, and he was clearly unable to use his left hand as well he had before Burkey had picked him up one winter night and used him for sporting purposes.

But at least Trey hadn't been murdered, which is what had happened to his friends Cornell and Rick. Burkey and his buddies had concocted a story about self-defense, how they had had to protect themselves against these two crazed black men who had attacked them in the station house, although it was evident to everyone that neither Burkey nor his buddies showed any signs of abuse, whereas Cornell and Rick's bodies had on them defensive wounds in numerous locations. Their arms and hands and wrists showed cuts and bruises indicating that each of the two had been attacked from several directions at once. The re-creation of the incident by attorneys in the courtroom was a scene in which Cornell and Rick, naked and with their arms raised protectively in front of their faces, had each finally turned to the side and curled into the fetal position, covering their heads with their hands. Cornell's hands had been beaten so badly that they had literally become jelly, and his skull had been just as severely damaged. Rick's neck had been broken.

Five years, and two friends dead, Trey with his wrist, and other friends of his now with pins in their legs or burned patches on their bodies, and the cops who had done it were enjoying life in Florida because the statute of limitations had run out and all of the other technicalities had worked in their favor, as well.

And Trey couldn't allow it. He couldn't, and neither could any of his friends, the ones with the scars and burned patches and pins.

They agreed on what to do. It wasn't a question of whether to do it but of how.

They asked around, and everyone recommended the same man, Dave

Ehlert. He even had a website, this Dave Ehlert. It consisted of one page with black lettering on a light green background. The lettering said, "Do you need assistance or help of any kind? Contact me. Complete discretion." With a phone number.

Trey had said, "This isn't right, this can't be for real," and he was told, "This man is not normal. He can do anything. Call him. Meet him. You'll understand."

Trey had done that, phoned Dave Ehlert and then met him in a public place two weeks ago, where Dave had told Trey, "I understand your problem. Do what I tell you. Get these things from Burkey, have someone in Florida help you, and when you have these items, bring them to me, and we'll talk business."

Now Trey was on his way to meet him again, the man who could do anything, the man who would give Trey and his family and his friends justice. Dave was not a lawyer, he had explained, and he was not a judge. Trey couldn't have told you what he was, but at the same time, he was not eager to pursue the matter. Dave was another white guy in a white shirt and slacks, although he spoke quietly, and he wore some strange kind of aftershave, and he didn't talk about what he did or how he did what he did.

All he'd said was, "When you have these items, bring them to me, and we'll talk business."

So now, after five years and two weeks, Trey was walking up South Michigan, heading into Grant Park, to give Dave what he had asked for.

Dave was standing close by Buckingham Fountain. Every time he saw big Buckingham Fountain, Trey thought of that old TV show, *Married . . . with Children*, where they have the fountain at the beginning of each show. Dumb.

As Trey approached, Dave turned to face him. He was a little above medium height and of medium build. Trey was taller than he by half a head, although he guessed they were about the same age, mid-thirties. Maybe Dave was closer to forty. Hard to tell. Nothing about him gave much away about his age. He might have been younger, or even older and in good shape.

It was warm today, almost hot for a late summer afternoon. The trees were beginning to change, just a few of them starting to show their golds and reds. Trey usually never paid much attention to things like that, the way the trees change color. Too much otherwise going on. But he noticed now because, as he had the first time he'd met Dave, he took it all in, the whole guy, and whoever this guy was, he made you notice the details all around you when you got within twenty feet of him.

Trey was not comfortable with that, but he'd started this, and he intended to see it through.

Dave didn't smile as Trey approached. He didn't offer his hand. He started walking and motioned for Trey to walk alongside him. So they walked.

Trey said, "I got it."

Dave nodded and said, "Good," but he seemed in no hurry to pursue the matter.

They walked slowly, Dave setting the pace. Occasionally he took in a deep breath, as though appreciative of the air and the sunny day.

Trey tried not to notice Dave's aroma. He had noticed the aroma the first time he'd talked with him, and now he recognized it again. Not a bad smell, not an odor, truly an aroma, but not anything that Trey could identify. Some kind of spice? What kind of man goes around smelling like a spice rack?

Trey tried again. "It was not easy getting this."

"I understand," Dave replied.

"It was his maid got it all. She was scared, though."

"He frightens her."

"I got to ask you something."

"What?"

"Is what you do evil? Like magic?"

Dave stopped and looked up at Trey. "Is that what you think?"

"I want to know."

"Why?"

"Because that shit is bad, and I'm trying to make sure my ass is covered on whatever the dealings are."

"I see." Dave started walking again.

Trey kept up with him. "You *see*? You *see*? I'm happy for your vision, but what the hell you got to say? Is it?"

"Yes, it is."

"Shit."

"It doesn't affect you. That's why you're asking *me* to do this."

"I don't want it coming back at me."

"It won't."

"You don't know how much I hate this mother and everything he did, but I am not doing that to myself."

"I understand. Let me have what you brought."

Trey took a legal-size white envelope from the back pocket of his jeans and handed it to Dave.

Dave opened it and looked inside. He saw two small plastic baggies, one containing human hair and the other, what appeared to be nail clippings.

"This is excellent." He folded the white envelope again and placed it into his own pants pocket. "Trey, don't be afraid."

"As many haircuts and manicures I had? This is the only thing that scares me, the fact that you can do hurt with shit like this."

"I tried doing a little research on our Mr. Burkey, but there's not much more than what was in the papers. Why did he retire to Florida?"

"Because the Virgin Islands only allowed virgins, and he already screwed over way too many niggas. How the hell am I supposed to know? He likes staying warm. Same way you like hurting cops."

Dave stopped again and looked up at Trey, stared at him coldly. His face darkened. "I don't like hurting cops."

"My bad."

"Where did you hear that?"

"Around. Somebody mentioned it."

"I used to be a cop."

"Look, man, I apologize." Trey moved back a step. Against everything he was familiar with, despite his whole life, his instincts told him to back away or say something inoffensive, to be careful not to anger this man confronting him. He said it again. "I apologize. Please. All we want is justice."

"You'll get justice."

"No more questions."

Dave told Trey, "Meet me here again tomorrow. Two o'clock. Bring the money."

"I will."

Dave started to walk away.

Trey said to him, "He's a dirty pig and he deserves whatever you do to him."

Not turning around, Dave replied, "He does. I know that."

The scent of spice or whatever it was moved away with him.

A breeze came up, and Trey looked at it move through the tops of the trees in the park.

Some little kids ran past him, chasing each other. He watched Dave go until he was well down the walk, past a girl standing at an easel, painting something.

Trey held out his right hand.

It was shaking.

"Is what you do evil? Like magic?"

"Is that what you think?"

Black magic. Some freakin' voodoo shit. He knew it. Had to be.

What had he gotten himself into?

Whatever Dave did, it worked. Either that or an amazing coincidence occurred. Trey saw it on the news that night. At his home outside Tampa, Jim Burkey had been entertaining his wife and some other couples, with Burkey tending the barbecue. In a freak accident, Burkey's shirt had caught fire, and he himself very quickly became a fireball. Channel Nine played some footage taken by someone next door with the video cam in his cell phone.

"Viewers should be warned," said Mark Suppelsa, the WGN anchor, "that although we've edited out the most disturbing material, the following contains graphic imagery." The handsome Suppelsa, a gray-haired news reader who had seen just about everything in his career as a Chicago reporter, typically was calm and self-contained, whatever sort of story he was reporting. But this material seemed to faze even him.

All that was visible on the shaky home video was a group of people on a large patio with a white stucco house in the background. Someone, a woman, was crying. For a moment, something large and black appeared stretched out near the bottom of the screen behind the sandals and shorts of the individuals on the patio. That was all.

Trey quickly moved to the computer he'd set up in a corner of the living room. Within minutes, he was watching the unedited footage. Whoever had taken it, this man in Florida, he'd posted it to his website and he already had ten thousand hits. The video showed Burkey on fire, moving slowly, a walking torch, so hot that at times the screen was pure white. Women were screaming and crying. Someone tried to throw a large blanket or beach towel over the walking fireball, but it, too, flashed on fire. Burkey collapsed. He appeared to fall onto his knees; then he rolled over and stretched out. The sandals and legs crowded in. This is where the

WGN editor had picked up the footage for the nine o'clock news broadcast.

Trey watched the video clip several more times. Maybe he was bringing to it more than was there, but a man on fire in his own back yard— Burkey deserved whatever came to him, but still, Trey was repelled by what he saw. That was the word: what he saw was repellent. Not simply video of an accident, more than just a man on fire, or more than just a normal fire. But what did that mean? Trey felt guilty; maybe that was it. And no one else in the world, or almost no one else in the world, knew that tomorrow he was going to give an envelope full of money to the strange man who had made this happen. Because he had, hadn't he? Strange Dave had done this.

Trey's cell phone beeped, and he saw that it was Anthony. Burkey had raped Anthony years ago with the infamous sawed-off broom handle and hooked him up to a car battery a couple of times. Trey flipped open his phone.

"It's all good," Anthony told him.

"You see it?"

"It's all good, Trey. Thank you, man. Dude is worth it. I am sleeping good tonight."

The next afternoon, in Grant Park, Trey and Dave took another stroll.

The day was cloudy. Still very warm, but muggy, and clouds were coming in. It would rain later that night.

Trey noticed something different about Dave. He found it hard to put his finger on it, but there was something . . . less intense, maybe. Less rigid. He didn't know how else to put it. He still had the aroma of being Spice Man, and, in fact, that was stronger than ever, now. Maybe it was like sex, whatever he did, and he had gone from needing to let it out really bad to where now it was accomplished, and so he was relaxed and feeling lighter. Maybe it felt good to him, too, doing that shit.

Trey drew in a long breath and stopped. He told Dave, "We're grateful. That's all. I seen a lot of shit, but I never saw anything like that."

"I understand."

"But this is enough for us."

"It's done," Dave told him. "Our business is done." He took a long sip from the large bottle of spring water he carried.

Trey watched half a dozen children playing in the grass in front of them. He said, "When I was like them, I used to think we could all get along. We can't, can we?"

"Not all of us. Do you have children?"

Trey looked at him.

"Don't be afraid. This isn't about you and your children."

"I got a daughter. Now, please . . . ." Trey reached into the pocket of his jeans to take out the envelope of money he'd promised Dave.

Dave told him, "Keep it."

"What?"

"Do something for your daughter."

"Are you sure about that?"

"Use it for your daughter. Or for some of the other children."

"What happened?"

"Nothing's happened. This is a whim of mine. I have whims."

Trey returned the envelope to his pocket. He said, "I take back what I thought about you. You make me scared. I have to say that. But you're a good man."

"No," Dave told him, watching the children as they played. "No. I'm not."

Fourteen hundred miles away in a motel room, a slender man with burns down the left side of his face and down one arm had his laptop open, and he was looking at the same video clip Trey Connors and who knew how many other people had looked at.

This man understood, however, what unnerved Trey.

Arthur Neely clicked Play and reviewed the clip several more times, then hit Pause at just the right moment.

For that one moment, deep in the flames surrounding the burning Jim Burkey, Neely saw a face, a face in the fire.

Dave Ehlert's face.

After staring at the face for some time, Neely hit Play again.

He said to himself, "Found you, you bastard."

2.

ave had two homes, one downtown, one in the far northwest suburbs, in semirural Inverness. His condominium in the North Loop was where Dave stayed when he was in the mood for fine dining or the theater. But he preferred the house in Inverness, deep in the woods, and spent most of his time there. This large house was built of old stone, and it filled two stories with many rooms, many things, and memories. Dave had almost no visitors here, and he kept no help. To live his life in this way, endlessly alone, was his choice.

The attic of the house was large, a wide and long single room without windows where he practiced his arts. The door and walls of this room were protected with tokens, talismans, signs, and spells. The remaining many rooms were free of such devices, although the grounds surrounding the house were charged with warding elements, and signs and objects were in the woods all around, as well, on tree trunks, attached to the branches and roots, to prevent malignant forces from intruding.

Still, Dave had few enemies, or so he thought. The many others who practiced the secret arts kept to themselves in small groups or engaged in the ways alone, as Dave did. The magical wars of a hundred years ago, the rivalries and contests of the first decades of the twentieth century, had long been settled. If those enmities continued, they did so on another plane, and only occasionally did that dark energy and anger intrude on Dave or the secret other sorcerers still alive from that time.

One room on the second floor of his home Dave kept dark. He did not turn on the lights in this room; the blinds and shades remained drawn. When he wished to see, he made a fire in the fireplace of this room, so that the waving flames and their cast shadows made the floor and walls take on movement the way any cave might have in primitive times, or the way the walls of a castle or hut might have, when the world was lit by fire.

Aside from a sofa and a chair and a few tables, the only ornament in the room was a large, gold-framed photograph hanging above the fireplace mantle. The photograph was that of a lovely young woman, a truly beautiful young woman. Her features were delicate; her skin was pale; her eyes were as dark and deep as the shadows Dave kept in that room. Her hair was as black as her eyes and in a tight marcel wave, perfectly done for this photograph, which the nineteen-year-old had sat for in 1931. The photograph was of Dave's daughter, made only a few weeks before he lost her.

He was staring at this portrait, thinking of his daughter and sipping whiskey, when the phone rang on the side table next to his chair. Dave listened as the recorder came on.

"I heard about you." The voice was not pleasant; this was an arrogant man. "You can help me, and we need to talk. Call me." He left a phone number.

Dave sighed and tasted some of the whiskey.

Very arrogant, indeed, this one.

People in need often behaved this way, he'd noticed. Demanding and petulant. Ashamed, perhaps, that they couldn't handle matters on their own, not even matters managed best in the dark.

Particularly matters managed best in the dark.

Dave finished his whiskey, stood, and left the room with its warm fire and its portrait of Miranda so that he could return the phone call from this demanding, petulant man.

Tony Jasco asked Dave to meet him in North School Park in downtown Arlington Heights, out in the northwest suburbs. This was convenient for Dave because Arlington Heights sits about halfway between downtown Chicago and Dave's home in Inverness. Arlington Heights is a prosperous village with a large population of men and women in professions. Many of these people moved in during the boom of the nineties, which had brought with it a renovated commuter train station and new condominiums and streets of many shops. Downtown Arlington Heights is charming.

"I come here to relax," Tony told Dave, when they met in the park.

It was a square block of rolling hills and a few trees and some modern steel sculptures. Dave had been here before. The park is particularly pleasant during the winter holidays, when it brightens with thousands of lights and attracts people attending craft shows and families bringing the children to see Santa.

Tony Jasco, on the other hand, did not seem the sort to be particularly pleasant during the winter holidays or any holidays. As Dave sat beside him on a bench in the park, Tony didn't even rise to offer his hand. He glanced at Dave and sat with his arms across his chest.

He was wearing a lightweight jacket emblazoned with a Bulls logo on the front and back and otherwise was in dress pants and a pair of black wing tips that hadn't been polished for a long time. He was not a tall man, shorter than Dave, but he was wide, strong in the chest, a bull, and he had thinning hair that had remained dark. Perhaps he was forty-five.

"I need help," he told Dave, squinting into the bright afternoon sun, "and I don't know where else to go."

"Describe the situation as clearly as you can."

"I need to know if you can be trusted."

"Everything you say is between us. I make no notes. I don't have a tape recorder. I keep it all up here." He tapped the side of his head with his right index finger.

"Good. Good," Tony said, nodding, and then wiggled his nose, looked Dave in the eyes, and asked, "What is that? Aftershave?"

"It's my own cologne."

"You smell like you come from a bakery."

"Well, I like to do my own baking and cooking," Dave replied, taking absolutely no offense, speaking as calmly as he ever did. "Now what's the nature of the problem?"

"I run a restaurant up on Dundee Road. Maybe you seen it; *Ava's*."

"I've driven past it, yes."

Dundee Road, near its intersection with Route Fifty-Three and for many slow miles east and west of it, is a long suburban stretch of strip malls, gas stations, apartment complexes, and mom-and-pop convenience stores and restaurants.

"You're having problems with the restaurant?"

Tony produced a pack of Camel Lights from inside his jacket, pulled one out, and lit it with an inexpensive Bic plastic lighter. He exhaled a long trail of smoke. "It was me and my partner's for more than ten years, only him and his wife were in a very bad car accident three years ago." He continued to look at the cement at his feet and flicked some ashes there. "My partner was killed, but his wife lived, God bless her, although she is still pretty banged up. Bad leg. Gets back pain."

"Go on."

"I told Ava, which is his wife, which is why we named the restaurant after her, that we should let it go. What's she need it for in her condition? Trying to be helpful, you know."

Now he looked Dave in the eyes, still squinting, and made a sort of smile.

"And she doesn't agree," Dave said.

"She won't let go, and we're losing money. We owe bills like out to there. I'm doing my best, but with the accident and the economy . . . . Just let it go."

"She still has half interest?"

"Sixty-six percent. I know I was dumb to do that, to let her and Steve have that much, but she helped a lot before she got sick with the accident, only she can't do much now, and it's eating me alive."

Tony finished his Camel and flicked it onto the cement. "Let me be frank about this. I can't afford to play games forever. I'm starting to get mad. All I want is for her to do the right thing. I'm trying to do the right thing." He stepped on the cigarette.

"And she's resistant," Dave said.

"This is what makes me real mad," Tony confided to Dave. "I've been giving her plenty of chances. It's getting old fast, okay? We sell it, we settle our debts. I know people that could do things with the place, and they want it, but not while I got all this hanging around my neck." He looked Dave in the eyes again. "I've done my best, but she's been holding out and she's starting to get cuckoo." He twirled his right index finger around his ear.

"Cuckoo how?"

"Get ready. She's saying I started all this and tried to cause the accident all along."

"Did you?"

Tony made a face and pursed his lips, and a sound something like "Fffft" came out. "I don't need to do that. Why would I do that? We were doing fine. Only not now. We're getting deeper in the hole every day."

"Do you want me to do whatever I can to convince her?" Dave asked.

For the first time, Tony slid his weight on the bench and shifted his hips so that he could face Dave. He threw his right arm over the back of the bench. "I think you understand that, right?"

"I think I do."

"If you can talk her into me and her finally selling the place, that's all I want. We go talk to the lawyers. Why won't she just do it? On account of 'cause of what happened to her and Steve? We were *friends*," Tony complained.

"Well, I'm not your friend and I'm not her friend, and I'll do whatever presents itself to me, if that's what you want. Is that what you want?"

"I want to sell the restaurant and pay off what we owe. That's what I want."

"Tell me about Ava. Is she in the phone book? Can I find her easily online? What's her full name?"

"Ava Beaudine."

"Spell both names, please."

Tony did.

"What does she look like? In general."

Tony described a rather petite woman, short, on the slender side, in her early forties, with dark auburn hair, who wore reading glasses and walked with a limp.

"Which leg?"

"Left leg. No, the right."

"Which one is it?"

"The right leg."

"From the accident."

"I guess. Yeah, from the accident."

"Any jewelry? Particular colors that she likes?"

"You know, I known her all this time, and I don't think I could tell you what her favorite color is."

"What kind of car does she drive? Does she like cats or dogs? Things like that."

"I don't know about any pets. She drives a silver Lexus."

"A coupe? An SUV?"

"A coupe."

"Anyone else she might be close to since her husband died? Mother, father, sisters, brothers?"

Tony shook his head. "She moved out here from someplace east. . . I don't know when. Long time ago. It was just her and Steve."

"She's not seeing anyone now?"

Tony said, with great exasperation, "Jesus Christ, I don't know! I don't know who she goes on dates with! She drives a freaking Lexus!"

"Fine. I'm just trying to establish anything you might know. Very often, it's the little things that make a difference, and those are the things we don't think about."

"Okay. Okay. What else?"

"I think that will do me fine."

"We shake hands or something?"

"Not necessary. I'll be in contact if I need further direction from you. The number you gave me—that's your cell phone?"

"No. That was at the restaurant."

"Should I continue using that number?"

"Yeah. Better than, you know, a cell. Anybody could be listening."

"Then that's the number I'll use."

"I want to know what this is gonna cost me. You ain't cheap."

"We can discuss that once I've learned a little more about things."

"I want to know now. Ballpark."

"Let's say that you pay me whatever this is worth to you once we see what happens. Fair enough?"

"Okay. Fair enough. Thank you." Tony stood and waited for a moment, then said to Dave, "The way you do this . . . if you have to use what you know how to do—" He stopped.

"If I have to call up the devil, you mean."

"Yeah. That doesn't include me, right?"

"You're safe from the devil, Tony."

"Yeah. That's good, then." He nodded to Dave and did a sort of wave as he walked off.

Dave watched him go.

He didn't believe a thing Tony had told him.

That wasn't entirely true. The car accident probably had happened. Maybe he did have people interested in helping him with the restaurant. And in all likelihood, Ava Beaudine did indeed drive a silver Lexus.

Dave kept his eyes on Tony until the Bulls jacket was out of sight. Tony turned once, looking over his shoulder as he left the park, to see whether Dave was still there.

Dave remained on the bench; legs stretched out and crossed at the ankles, elbows propped over the back of the bench, head down, thinking.

And when Tony at last was gone, Dave stood, then knelt quickly to the sidewalk to retrieve the Camel cigarette butt that Tony had dropped there.

3.

va's on West Dundee Road was one among many small restaurants and fast-food establishments interspersed with the requisite gas stations, tanning salons, and convenience stores. Their parking lots, side by side and one after another, saw constant rounds of traffic, cars zipping in and out in time to the lights at intersections. Their patrons passed each other, stepping inside or coming outside in the company of elderly parents leaning on quad walkers or quickly jumping and running children, all screams and dares.

Dave parked his Audi in a far corner of the restaurant's busy lot. At the entrance, he bought a *Daily Herald*, the conservative suburban paper, then stood back politely and waited for a small push of elderly women to exit. One of them, tiny and white-haired, could not stop trembling. She looked at Dave and smiled as she went by him. He wondered whether he had known her in another lifetime.

Inside, he was met by a small crowd of people standing in line to pay their bills. A large, bosomy young woman at the cash register took their money and handed back change, ignoring Dave. He noticed a business card holder alongside the toothpicks by the register and took a card. *Ava's*, in embossed blue ink on bright white stock, with the requisite address, hours, and phone numbers, but also an embossed silhouette of a bird in flight. Dave wondered whether there was any significance to the bird.

A middle-aged woman came toward him while wiping her hands on a cloth. Her name was on the plastic tag on the upper left of her blouse. *Hostess. Eileen.* She asked him how many. Dave raised an index finger. Eileen grabbed a large, laminated menu and led him between crowded tables to a booth in the back. The booth gave Dave a view of the entire small dining room as well as of the parking lot outside the large picture window across from him.

"Coffee," he told her.

She waved at a young Hispanic man making the rounds with two pots. He came by and poured Dave a cup of regular.

Dave looked at the room, and his attention immediately went to two men seated together at the lunch counter by the cash register. One was a white guy, in his early forties but very fit, blond, with a fresh haircut. He was in jeans but was also wearing a very expensive sport coat over a knit shirt of some kind. The other guy was a Hispanic man no older than thirty, dressed with nowhere near the care of the other one, simply in jeans and a stained tee shirt. The white guy had a bent nose; perhaps he'd had it broken in a fistfight and now his nose had healed that way, skewed. The Hispanic man had many tattoos coming up his neck and decorating both of his muscular arms. Dave noticed that the large young woman talked with the white guy as though she knew him, but not in a friendly way. No one, in fact, acted friendly toward either of them, not her, not the hostess, nor any of the busboys or wait staff. Still, they sat at the counter and made themselves comfortable there.

A young blond woman came by and Dave gave her his order for a slice of pecan pie. As she left, Dave saw the well-dressed white guy at the counter spin on his stool and reach for the hostess, Eileen. She pulled away from him, avoiding him, but then paused, relenting, and spoke with him. She shook her head. The white guy made a face, and the Hispanic man grinned. The hostess gestured with her hands out, a sort of pleading gesture or an I-don't-know, then moved on. The white guy said "Shit" audibly enough to cause patrons nearby to look at him and scowl. The Hispanic man smiled again, then reached for his wallet, removed a few dollar bills, and put them on the counter.

As they left, going by the cash register, they stood back to let a small, petite woman enter. The white guy spoke to her. She said something back, which upset them both. Tattoo Man seemed particularly upset, but Bent Nose slapped him on the shoulder and tugged him away.

Dave looked out at the parking lot and watched as these two characters walked to a shiny new Chevrolet Silverado, all big and red and smiley and with not a dirt spot on it. They climbed inside, the white guy behind the wheel, but he didn't start the engine. They sat there.

Dave's waitress brought him his slice of pecan pie, but he let it sit in front of him. He was looking at the petite woman, who certainly must be Ava Beaudine. She was speaking now with Eileen. They walked together toward one of the free booths just past the cash register. Ava moved with a noticeable limp in her right leg. She matched the description Tony had given him, right down to the auburn hair.

The two women sat and began talking. Their conversation soon became animated, although Dave couldn't overhear them. He took a bite of his pie and a sip of coffee. Ava Beaudine shook her head and tapped the table a few times, emphasizing whatever she was saying to Eileen. Then she rose and left.

Dave watched her through the picture window as Ava crossed the parking lot, walking toward a silver Lexus parked near the new pickup truck. As she came toward the pickup, Bent Nose and Tattoo Man both threw their doors open, hopped out, and confronted her, the white guy in front of her, and the Hispanic man to one side.

Dave got to his feet and took out his wallet. He dropped a five-dollar bill on the table, then moved quickly through the dining room and walked outside.

In the parking lot, as Dave approached Ava and the two men, he heard her say, very forcefully, "And if you find him, then *you* tell *me*, because he's avoiding me!"

The white guy said, "You're screwing with me. Do not screw with me." Then he looked up and over Ava's shoulder as Dave came up behind her.

"Why, Ava!" he exclaimed. "I haven't seen you since I don't know when!"

Ava turned and looked sharply at him. "What?"

Bent Nose told Dave, "Bug off."

Dave said to him, "Actually, I was hoping that you'd be the one to leave." Smiling, he stared at Bent Nose and then at Tattoo Man. He leaned forward a bit and said, "Bug off."

On a certain level, we survive, or at least avoid dangerous situations, because the animal in us, the primitive part of us, understands in the most elemental of ways what is behind the tone of a voice or in the light of an eye. We wear masks all day long; we create personas and live them; but when circumstances cause the masks to be pulled away and the personas to drop, we are left with the fundamental law of existence: fight or flight. A twitching muscle just before an opponent moves. The tone in a voice that registers just below the grade of conscious hearing. A cold smile that barely disguises the animal fangs. Pretense vanishes, and we are naked. The millionaire understands this as well as the gang banger and the street survivor.

And so Bent Nose, looking into Dave's eyes, hearing what was in his voice, said to Tattoo Man, "Let's go."

"What did you say?"

"*Let's go, asshole!*"

"Because of *him*?"

Bent Nose told Ava, "You just remember what I told you. You tell him."

She didn't reply. She watched them get back into their truck.

Dave touched her shoulder and steered her away as the white guy hit the ignition, gunned the engine, and jammed the truck into reverse, then squealed the tires as he steered across the parking lot.

Ava looked up at Dave. "I have no idea who you are."

"I know that."

"So what is this?"

✳ ✳ ✳

Rather than continue talking in the parking lot of the restaurant, Ava and Dave decided to go across the street, where they could sit on the patio of a coffee shop. They would be in public, which is absolutely where Ava wanted to be right now, but they could keep their voices down if they needed to.

Which they did. Dave was frank about why he had shown up as he had, even if he wasn't completely forthright about himself. "Your business partner," he said, "or you and your husband's business partner, wants me to convince you that he's serious about buying out your interest in the restaurant."

"He's told me that himself a thousand times. Did he tell you that I'm not interested?"

"I sense some tension between the two of you, or some bad blood."

"You still haven't told me who you are."

"I'm a freelancer," Dave told her.

"At what? What does that mean?"

"I was a police officer more years ago than I can remember. I retired. Now I take the cases that interest me."

"What on earth interests you about this one?"

"I don't think Tony is telling me the whole story, and before I go any further, I'd like to hear your side of it."

Ava made a gloomy face and sipped her coffee. She asked Dave, "Do you have a badge or something?"

"No."

"Aren't you supposed to have identification or something?"

"I can show you my driver's license. Will that help?"

"Not really."

"I have a Website."

She laughed genuinely. "I don't think that counts." Looking across the street in the direction of her restaurant, she asked him, "What do you know about those two? In the parking lot."

"Not a thing."

"You scared them off."

"I was bluffing."

"No, they were scared."

"Were they?"

"Oh, yeah. So who are you really, Mr. . . . ?"

"Ehlert."

"Frankly, I'm not sure I can trust you if you know Tony."

"Fair enough. Although I wouldn't say I know him. I'm here because he got in touch with me. All I know is what he told me. You and your husband and he started the restaurant. That's what he said."

"True. We bought out the family that used to own it."

"Your husband lost his life in a car accident, and you were injured."

"Did he tell you that he caused the accident?"

"Tony did?"

"I can't prove it, but I know he did it."

"Why? So that he'd get the restaurant?"

"That's right. Did he tell you why he wants it so badly?"

"You're deeply in debt."

"It wasn't when Steve and I ran it. He's into it deep with somebody, is what I think."

"Loan sharks? Gambling?"

"Any of the above. Tony thinks he's very clever and smarter than everyone else. He apparently needed the place bad enough to kill my husband, and he'd still like to see me dead and buried."

"So why not go along with it and sell?"

"It's my responsibility," Ava said. "I always wanted to have a restaurant, and I gave these people jobs. They rely on me. It's hard work, but you like running a restaurant or you don't."

"And you do."

"I used to." She smiled warily and asked him, "Did you ever dig in just because the other person was dug in, too?"

Dave replied, with more emotion than perhaps he meant to share, "Yes, I have."

"That takes control of the situation, doesn't it, doing that?"

"It can, yes. So it's a matter of being stubborn."

"In a way. It's my restaurant. It's my name on there. I know the economy's in a hole, but since Steve died, it's all I have. I honestly go back and forth on this, but I do it because Tony is making such a big deal out of it." She regarded Dave carefully. "So what else did he tell you? I mean, in your role as a freelancer."

Dave smiled. "He claims he's looking out for your interest because of your health. Also, either you're stubborn or a little bit nuts."

"Takes one to know one. Tell him that."

"I'll be sure to."

"And all he wants you to do is convince me to sell the restaurant."

"By any means necessary."

"Oooh, that sounds dangerous. That's the Tony I know. Big threats."

"Is that where the two young men in the parking lot come in?"

"I don't even know their names. I've seen them there twice before, that's it. Obviously it's something sleazy. I thought it might be drugs, but they're probably the ones Tony owes money to."

Dave said, "Anyone with cash right now can take advantage of people who need it. It's the economy."

"Exactly."

"Very enterprising of them."

Ava smiled again. "You're charming in your own way, aren't you?"

"I depend on it."

"Well, this is as far as it gets you."

"Maybe a little farther."

"And what is that supposed to mean?"

"Tony contacted me, and he told me his side of things, and I don't believe him. I don't trust him, either."

"Charming and intelligent, both."

"That's why I wanted to hear your side of it. What did you mean when you said that he'd still like to see you dead and buried?"

"Just that."

"Has he made attempts on your life?"

"That I can prove?" Ava said. "No. But do I think he has? Yes."

"Such as?"

"Such as a taxi almost runs me down, comes around a corner out of the blue and almost runs me down. That was a month ago."

"Did he try anything else?"

"I'm not sure. My power has gone out a couple of times, but I can't say he did it. But it makes me paranoid. I'm waiting for one of the Bowery Boys over there to pull some stunt if I ever give them the chance."

"I don't even know their names," Ava said.

"I see."

"Do you have what you wanted?"

Dave nodded. "But my concern is that you're not safe."

"Thanks for your concern," she told Dave plainly, "I could sign papers tomorrow and just let him have it, but he's not being honest with me, and that's why I'm not budging. All I want from him is the truth."

"That's understandable."

"When I was in bed, recuperating, I had a lot of time to think. Steve had made the comment a couple of times that Tony wanted to take over the business, even back then. Which is what made me think that he tried to kill us, and when I confronted him with it, he got nervous. I mean, really nervous. He couldn't lie well about it."

Dave nodded. "Interesting."

"He's been running things while I've been at home. It took me months to get out of bed, and then even longer before I could walk again. That surprised them. The doctors weren't sure how well I'd do with that, but here I am, walking around. And through the whole deal, Tony would come by and tell me encouraging things about the restaurant, how he was doing so good with it, and maybe I ought to just let him run it or buy me out. He's up to something."

"Maybe that's what I should be investigating, whatever Tony's keeping from you."

"It would be more interesting than trying to convince me to sell it. But you're a freelancer, and you have an agreement."

"Not if your life is in danger."

"And you think it is? You believe me?"

"Yes, if what you've told me is true."

"Oh, it's true, all right. So now what do I do? Here you are, and I have those two so-and-so's in the parking lot telling me to talk to Tony for them."

"What did they want you to tell Tony?"

"Something about how he was supposed to meet them, and he didn't. If you know where he is, then you can deliver the message."

"He told me that he phoned me from the restaurant."

"What was the phone number?"

Dave told her.

"He must have another restaurant, then. That's not the number for the phone in the back."

"Really? The more I hear, the less I like it."

"Welcome to my life, Mr. Ehlert."

4.

va relaxed that evening in a warm bath. This had become her habit since recuperating from the car accident, spending an evening this way. The warmth and the water helped with the pain that continued to pester her, and she was free, buoyant in the water, eyes closed, to let her mind go where it would. This is how she solved problems. This is how she helped herself. A warm bath did her more good than the help or advice of most of the people in her life.

She replayed Dave in the parking lot and her and Dave having coffee, and Ava remained dissatisfied. Who was he? He'd been truthful, she sensed, but what he'd told her was only part of the truth, and Ava still had a lot of questions. What was the rest of him about? What was the aftershave that he used, that cologne? Very odd. And frightening off those thugs of Tony's just by looking at them? What was that about? No one does that, stares down two creeps like that. Where did that come from?

Could she trust him? This was essential. It would be good to have someone on her side whom she really could trust and who could actually do her some good.

Ava wanted to trust him, and something told her that she could, but she resisted doing so, at least for now, for every good reason she could muster.

"My concern is that you're not safe."

Maybe he was sincere about that. Maybe he was honest enough that he wouldn't just write off the whole thing, Tony and her both. But why should he be concerned that she was safe? Ava didn't understand that. There was a mystery there.

Because Tony had lied to him? For the money, so that she'd pay him if he was able to solve the whole restaurant situation? Is that what he did for a living?

"My concern is that you're not safe."

Well, I'm concerned, too, Ava thought, and I'm not safe, but I don't understand why this matters to you all of a sudden.

"I had a lot of time to think. Tony would come by. He's up to something. When I confronted him, he got nervous. He couldn't lie well about it."

27

"Maybe that's what I should be investigating, whatever Tony's keeping from you."

Good luck with that, she thought, as she stood carefully in the tub, grabbed a towel and wrapped it around herself, and moved slowly to the rug on the floor.

Who was this man?

Who are you, Dave?

Her computer was in a spare room that Steve had set up as their home office. Ava was not a person to spend hours every evening at the monitor, but she went online occasionally, usually to keep in touch with the consultant who had designed the web site for the restaurant and to check her infrequent emails.

Also, she knew about googling, which she did now, sitting at the keyboard with her bath towel wrapped around her.

Dave Ehlert, she typed, and immediately got the address of his website. She went there.

It was a single page with black lettering on a light green background:

Do you need assistance
or help of any kind?
Contact me.
Complete discretion.

And a phone number.

That was certainly direct. His name, an ad, a phone number, and not another thing, not a clue, nothing.

She went back to the Google page and clicked on some of the other entries there for Dave Ehlert.

He, or someone with that name, had written a couple of articles in a literary journal. There were some pages tracking the Ehlert family from some town in Germany to western Pennsylvania and then out west. His extended family, maybe. And one other comment, part of a blog on a website about the supernatural and the occult.

Someone named Inquirer247 had posted a query two years ago, and apparently no one had ever responded. But what Inquirer247 wanted was information regarding a very intriguing problem:

I met Dave Elerht a year and a half ago and he helped me, but I know what he did was a form of magic or witchcraft and sorcery, and I would like further information on this aspect. I am not certain if what he did affected me but I have no one to talk to. If you have information please let me know.

Night, late at night, after one in the morning, and Dave in his windowless attic room lit tall candles, set out on a table the materials he would need, and removed his clothes, then stood behind the table.

The table was within a large circle, eight feet in diameter, painted on the floor. Dark blue paint. And at intervals around the circle were candles, their flames bright and still.

From a bowl on the table in front of him, Dave spread oil over his hands and over his body, oil mixed with spices, aromatic and earthy.

Over another bowl he crumbled coals, ordinary coals, and sprinkled the coals with incense, then with a single-bladed razor sliced the edge of his left hand so that blood dropped from him onto the coals and incense.

This was necessary, the blood. Nothing can be taken without something being given. The balance of all things requires it. As above, so below. We are reflected in the universe, and the universe is reflected in us, and the universe does not give without taking, just as it does not take without giving. Reciprocity. That is the one true law. So paying for wisdom with blood is necessary. Cleansing oneself with oil is necessary. Speaking with humility is necessary.

He sprinkled oil onto the coals, the oil mixing with his blood, and lit the coals so that a flame grew within them.

And then, into the fire, he dropped the cigarette butt of Tony Jasco's that he had taken from the park.

This is Tony Jasco, this cigarette butt. It was part of him, it remains him; it is him. This is the law of sympathetic magic. Whatever you touch, great or trivial, will always know you, will carry you with it. Just as your desires can be read in your dreams and your soul can be seen in your eyes, so your life can be touched by what you have touched.

As the cigarette butt was consumed within the hot coals, Dave spoke in Latin, which was his preference as he did these things, practiced his art.

"*Septime*," he said, "*suscita. Succurre me.*" Septimus, awaken. Help me. "*Suscita, Septime.*"

It did so, Septimus, this spirit, the seventh of Dave's spirits, opening before his eyes as a light just beyond the blue circle, a light in the dimness of the attic room, as though a hole were opening in the air or as though something that had been there, minute, suddenly grew to obvious dimensions, glowed, and returned Dave's attention by answering him with light.

"Septimus," he said, rubbing his left hand, which continued to bleed. "Tell me what you can of this man."

Open, darkness. Part, shadows. Speak, time.

Dave was given what he asked for.

✳ ✳ ✳

Dave phoned Tony the following day, and they met that afternoon in North School Park, a cool and sunny afternoon.

"I've looked into matters in more detail," Dave said. "I've met with Ava, and I've investigated you."

"Investigated me? What does that mean?" Tony asked him.

"Our agreement is over. I'm no longer interested in helping you."

"What?"

"Our agreement is over."

"The hell it is!" Tony angrily got to his feet, moving from the park bench, and faced Dave.

Dave remained seated, legs crossed, left hand raised thoughtfully to his face.

"You can't just do this!" Tony said to him. "This is business. We had an *agreement.*"

"I agreed to do whatever presented itself to me. That's what I agreed to, and that's what I'm doing."

"This is bullshit. You said you'd *help* me."

"And I promised that you'd be safe from the devil. And you are."

"This is so stupid."

"But you're not safe from me if you push it."

"What the hell am I supposed to do now?" Tony complained. "Huh? I called you in good faith. I met with you in good faith. I told you everything you needed to—"

"You lied to me."

"When did I lie to you? I did not lie to you."

"You killed her husband. And you tried to kill her."

"Really? And when did I do that? The *car accident*?"

"You know it as well as I do."

Tony wiped his face and sat on the park bench again. "It was an *accident,*" he insisted, and then, "Even if it wasn't, what the hell do you care? Why do you care? You do whatever people hire you to do."

"That's not true."

"That's what you told me."

"That is not what I told you. I do what I wish to do."

Tony pulled his hands into fists and got to his feet again. He yelled loudly enough to attract the attention of people walking nearby, "Who do you think you are? We had an agreement! Do what you said you were going to do!"

Dave rose, moving quickly, but he spoke quietly, and in a calm voice. "We are done. You don't tell me what to do." He turned to go.

Tony yelled at him, "You *kill* people, you asshole! Do what I told you to do!"

More passers-by looked at them, and quickly looked away.

Dave turned and faced him. "Do I kill people, Tony? Is that what I do?"

Tony looked at the ground, anywhere else. "We had an agreement."

"Based on certain conditions. You lied to me. You failed me."

He looked Dave in the eyes again. "Then what am I supposed to do? You tell me that." And then, "I know. You screwed her. Is that it? You screwed the crippled lady, and now you're on her side?"

Dave approached him.

Tony backed away. "You can't kill me here."

"I can kill you wherever I like."

"Is that what you want to do now, you twisted evil asshole?"

Dave looked him in the eyes. Looked deeply into him. Then spoke again. "Our agreement is over. You are not to be trusted. Walk away."

"Screw you." But Tony did it. Backed up, then turned, and went down the cement path, looking behind just once and saying one more time under his breath, "Screw you."

That night, when Tony received the phone call from Arthur Neely, he regarded it initially as a prank, then as a threat. He was sitting in the dark in the living room of his apartment, the only light that of the streetlamps outside the window, and was on his fourth beer, brooding terribly, when he picked up the phone in the middle of Arthur Neely's message.

"*Who* is this?"

"My name is Neely. I'm here because we have a mutual acquaintance named Dave Ehlert?"

"Jesus Christ. What about him?"

"I've been trying to find him. I understand you know him."

"I do not know him. And why am I even talking to you?" Tony hung up.

Immediately, the phone rang again.

Tony asked him, "How'd you get this number?"

"I phoned the restaurant. It took several attempts, but finally a woman there gave it to me."

"Then she's fired."

"Mr. Jasco, Dave Ehlert is not my friend, either."

"Then do me a favor and go kick his ass for me."

"I'd be delighted to."

"What?" Tony considered this comment for a blurred moment, then asked the man on the phone, "Do you know who he is?"

"I do."

"I mean . . . who he *is*? What he *does*?"

"I'm well aware of what Dave is capable of doing, yes."

Tony chuckled. "This is so messed up. Why am I in the middle of this?"

"What are you drinking, Mr. Jasco?"

"Beer."

"What brand?"

"I don't know. Old Style."

"I'll get some more and join you in a few minutes. I'm nearby."

"Wait a minute, wait a minute." Tony thought hard, then asked, "I'm supposed to trust you? Why am I in the middle of this?"

"That's a philosophical question. I have no answer for that. But you and I are both in the middle of it, believe me."

Think, think, Tony told himself, but it wasn't easy to do, he was frightened, he was angry. He was very angry. And not drunk, but relaxed enough to say to Arthur Neely, "Okay. Okay. I am probably kicking myself, but— You're nearby?"

"Yes."

"You know where I am?"

Neely gave Tony the address.

"Okay, that's right, you're right. Ring my number when you come in."

"Give me fifteen minutes."

In twenty minutes, Tony's buzzer rang.

He was hesitant to press the intercom button for the speaker in the apartment building lobby because he'd sat there for those twenty minutes wondering what in hell to do if this guy even showed up.

Ignoring the buzzer wasn't going to help, however. He didn't need to piss off another weird mother who operates by black magic for a living. So he let Neely in.

He heard the man's footsteps coming up the stairs outside, and the bottles of Old Style clinking in their cardboard six-pack, and then the knocking on his door.

Before opening it, Tony called out, "Mr. Neely?"

"Yes." Same voice as on the phone, only muffled.

Tony opened the door. He said, "Jesus."

"That's the reaction I typically get," Neely told him.

"What the hell happened to you?"

"I walked into a wall."

"More than one."

"May I come in? I have the beer."

"Yeah, yeah." Tony stepped away to let him pass but continued to stare at Neely as he took a seat on the couch.

Neely said, "I'm glad you don't have many lights on."

Tony closed the door. "Me, too."

Neely chuckled. "Dave did this to me."

"Then I can see why you might be pissed at him."

Neely reached for the bottle opener sitting on Tony's coffee table and took the cap off one of the bottles.

Tony couldn't take his eyes off him. The left side of Neely's face was in bad shape. Whatever it was, skin or muscle or scar tissue, had turned hard like lengths of rope burned together. Most of the hair was gone on that side of his head. Not much of an ear left. His eyeball was still in there, remarkably, but it was hugged very tightly by scar tissue all around the orbit.

And the ropy scar tissue continued down his neck and presumably down his arm, because what he was using as a left hand wasn't much of anything, pretty much a stump with parts of three fingers left.

However, Tony noticed that, as if to make up for what he lacked in looks, Neely was well dressed, in a nice pair of dress pants and a shirt and tie and a freshly dry-cleaned topcoat.

Tony said to him, "So . . . you called me."

"Yes."

"About Dave."

"I've been looking for him for a long time. I know what he did to the cop in Florida. I know that he has some connection to you, but I'm not clear what that is."

"And how do you know that?"

"I practice the same arts that Dave does."

Tony sighed. "Why the hell not?"

"It took me a while, but I've gotten this far. I intend to kill him, Mr. Jasco. If you can help me locate him, if you can help me kill him. That's why I'm here. I can make it worth your while."

Tony shook his head. "I don't want to be involved with people like you."

"I think you're already past involved. Is Dave helping you with something? Or are you helping him?"

"Not no more. He backed out."

"Did he?"

Tony finished the beer he'd been working on and set the empty on the coffee table. "He let me know that in no uncertain terms."

"Well." Neely lifted a fresh, cold Old Style from the six-pack he'd brought and passed it across the coffee table to Tony. "I say, let's talk, Mr. Jasco."

5.

She phoned Dave the next morning around ten, using the phone number she'd gotten from his website, and told him that it was important he meet her.

"Fine," he said. "Where? The same restaurant?"

Ava wasn't comfortable with that, but she wanted someplace public, and so she told him, "The library."

"The library?"

"In Palatine. Do you know where it is?"

"I believe so."

"I'll wait in front. It's enclosed. There's an entranceway before you go in."

"Ava, you sound worried. What is it?"

"I'd prefer to talk about it when you get here."

It took him the better part of forty minutes to reach the library. He parked in the small lot around the corner and up the hill from it and noticed that Ava's Lexus was there, as well, a few spaces down.

Dave walked down the entrance to the parking lot and around the corner to the sidewalk. The morning was drizzling and cooler than yesterday. Definitely a taste of fall, now, in the air.

Ava was waiting for him in the in the enclosed foyer.

"We could go inside," she said. "I thought we could walk, but it's raining."

"I don't mind the rain. What's the matter?"

She opened her purse and took out a sheet of paper. She waited until a woman and two young girls came through the automatic doors and passed them, entering the library. Then she showed the paper to Dave.

It was a printout of the comments made online by Inquirer247.

I met Dave Elerht a year and a half ago and he helped me, but I know what he did was a form of magic or witchcraft and sorcery . . . .

When he'd read it, he returned the paper to Ava. She put it back into her purse and asked him, "Did you know about this?"

"No. I don't spend a lot of time on the Internet."

"Who's Inquirer 247?"

"I have no idea."

"You have no idea, but you helped this person with some kind of witchcraft."

"I've helped a lot of people."

"Is that how you're going to help me? Is that why Tony called you?"

"Yes."

"He knew about that, and that's what he wanted you to do?"

"You should know that I saw him yesterday and told him that our agreement was canceled."

"You said that?"

"Yes."

"And what did he do? He's not going to like that."

"No. He didn't take it well."

"Why did you say that to him? Just because we talked?"

"You confirmed my doubts about him. He lied to me. I'm sure you're right, that he tried to kill you and that he really did kill your husband."

"You believe me?"

"Yes."

"But you have no reason to believe me."

Dave said nothing to that.

"You scare me," Ava said.

"Let's go for a walk."

"No. No." And then, "I knew a woman one time who read cards for me. What she said was going to happen to me, it happened. That was enough to make me never go back to see her. This stuff makes me uncomfortable."

"What do you want me to say?"

"I'm not sure."

"My concern is still that you might not be safe. I've angered Tony, now, and he'll take it out on you."

"Then I'll just sell the restaurant and put an end to this." She looked at him. "Should I do that?"

"That would be your decision."

"Why on earth do you care? What does any of this mean to you? Can you answer that?"

"I can try." He stepped toward the doors of the library. "Please."

She hesitated, but then went in front of him. The automatic doors opened, and they made their way across the lobby to the stairs leading to the second floor. There, Dave sat at one of the catalog computers, keyed in a few items, and reviewed the titles that came up. Then he stood and led Ava to the section on religion and mythology.

He found the books he was looking for and grabbed a few more. He carried all of them to a carrel, pulled the chair out for Ava to sit, and threw open the first book to a random page spread. She took it from there.

There were paintings of witches and demons, some of them very romantic images, others crude woodcuts or old engravings. There were black-and-white photos allegedly showing black masses in progress. Pages of Wiccan spells. Drawings of men wearing antlers and dressed in animal skins. Dreamy images of succubi and incubi. Men in robes standing inside large circles drawn of the old stone floors of crumbling medieval fortresses and castles.

Ava whispered to him, "What's your point?"

"Is this what you think of? Is this what you think it's about?"

"Yes, of course."

"Most of this is written by people who have no idea what they're talking about. They're an audience watching a play, that's all. They think I worship the devil and that I'm not human, and the truth is, I'm more human than they are."

"What does that mean?"

"They run around in circles claiming to know the truth."

"And what do you do that's so different?"

"I'm looking for something else. Or at least I started to."

"Like what?"

He looked at the shelves behind them, took down a book, and dropped it in front of her.

It was a book on the history of religion.

"God," he said.

"You're looking for God?" There was disdain in her voice. "And you haven't found him?"

"I've found him."

"Then tell me where he is, because he needs to start returning my phone calls."

"He's right here," Dave said, and tapped a finger on her head. "And here." He nodded to everyone in the library. "We're God."

"I don't find that very comforting."

"I don't find the idea of God very comforting. He feels like a lead weight. Do you think God laughs?"

"I have no idea."

"What use is God if he doesn't have a sense of humor? Have you looked out a window lately?"

Despite herself, Ava began to smile. "This conversation is way too strange for me."

"I can get serious again in a hurry."

"I think we'd better." She asked him then, "Do you want lunch? Or brunch?"

"I suppose."

"I'll buy you lunch if you let me. It was my idea to come here in the first place. Let me do that."

They were only a few blocks from a Bakers Square restaurant, Ava told him. Past some office parks on North Bank Drive.

"All right," Dave said.

But Ava could tell he still had something on his mind.

The young man with the pock-marked face had waited in the library parking lot until he was sure that Dave and Ava had gone in to stay for a while. Then he waited until the lot fell quiet. No cars pulling in. No moms with their kids coming around the corner to get into their SUVs. He crouched on the edge of the lot under some trees, pretending to tie his shoes.

He had an instinct for this, which was why Tony had hired him. "I need you to break into a car," Tony had told him. "Okay, what car?" he'd asked. Tony told him, "The guy lives in Inverness, but don't do anything out there. Wait until you can get to him somewhere else." And the young man had suggested, "I'll just break into his house." To which Tony had said, "Under no circumstances do you do that. This is very simple. Follow his car. When he parks it, break into the car. It's probably got an alarm. You don't even bother with that. You just smash and grab. You're done in ten seconds." To which the young man asked, "What do you want me to take outta the car?" And Tony replied, "Hair."

"Hair?" The young man had laughed.

"Human hair," Tony had told him. "You get yourself some of that big clear tape like you're gonna mail a package. Only you get into the car and you slap some of that tape around and then you bring it back. We want what's on the tape."

"This is a very weird request."

"Yes, it is. So what?"

But now here he was, doing it, in the parking lot of the Palatine Public

Library at eleven in the morning, and with nothing moving, he walked over to the Audi, smashed open the driver's side window with the weight he'd brought with him, reached in with the clear plastic tape, pressed it onto the headrest of the car and a couple of times on the back of the seat, and then walked into the trees.

The alarm had sounded immediately, but he'd ignored it. Now, under cover of the trees, he turned and looked back. The alarm finally went silent, and two or three people walking into the parking lot looked at the Audi with its broken window, but that was all.

He continued moving through the woods until he came clear of them, walking to the sidewalk in front of some office buildings, then jogged across the street to his car, which was parked in the lot of the Sears store on Hicks Road.

Tony's restaurant was twenty minutes away, and the young man phoned him while he drove there.

"I got it."

"That was fast."

"We got lucky."

"Well, bring it here and you win the prize."

In half an hour, he was in the office in the back of *Ava's*. He was shivering, as if he had suddenly caught a cold, and he had started to sweat. He showed Tony the wide clear tape with hair and lint on it.

Tony was seated at an old steel desk. He looked at the tape, then took it and handed it to a man sitting in the corner of the office behind him, in a wooden chair.

This man made the young man with the pock-marked face nervous. Half of the guy's face was bandaged; all you could see was his right eye, part of his nose, and most of his mouth. There were signs of terrible burns beneath those bandages. And he had no left hand to speak of, just a stump, sufficiently gruesome to make you wonder just how bad the rest of him was that you couldn't see.

The bandaged man said, "This will do."

"Good for you," Tony said to the pock-marked man. "Here." He reached into his wallet, pulled out three hundred-dollar bills, and handed them to him.

"Thanks."

"Go have a good time. Forget about this."

"Absolutely." He was still sweating as he went out by the back door, which led into an alley.

Tony swiveled in his desk chair and looked at Neely. "This is all happening pretty fast. Lucky you."

"Lucky me."

"What do you want me to do?"

"Nothing."

"You're not worried about the kid?"

"He'll be dead by tonight."

"What'd you do to him? I know that kid. I like him."

"You don't think Dave did anything to protect his car?"

"What do you mean?"

"That kid's got something bad in him now. A spirit, a ghost. Whatever Dave used."

"Jesus. Really?"

"It'll eat him alive by tonight. I'm going back to my hotel room."

"You can do it now?"

"Why wait?"

"Don't you need the full moon or something?"

Neely laughed out loud, got to his feet, and slapped Tony on the shoulder as though he'd just said the funniest thing on earth.

"Sure!" he said. "Let's wait until the full moon!"

He was still chuckling as he went out the back door, into the alley.

Ava wasn't sure how much she seriously wished to know about black magic and sorcery, so she did not make those items a topic of conversation during lunch. But she did provide something of her background, how she'd met Steve, her husband, and how they'd started the restaurant.

And Dave told her a little about himself, although he was guarded. Ava clearly sensed that, but she understood that he likely had good reasons for it, so she let Dave tell her what he wished and did not press him.

By the time they'd finished their lunch, Ava was feeling more comfortable, sufficiently so that she confided to Dave that, if he would help her and act in her behalf simply to do whatever would be necessary, she'd sell the restaurant, whatever Tony wanted to do.

"It's not worth all of this," she said, as they walked back in the direction of the library.

"Are you sure?"

"Yes. I can do better things with my life than waste time with this."

"Do you want me to tell him that?"

"Yes."

He stopped and reached inside the breast pocket of his shirt. The drizzle had let up, and when clouds moved to show the sun, the light was brilliant on pools of water on the sidewalk and in the street.

"Wear this," Dave told her. He handed her the charm he'd taken from his pocket.

"What is it?"

It was like nothing she'd ever seen before, a symbol almost like a hieroglyphic hanging on a silver chain.

"It's a talisman. It's for your protection."

"Seriously?"

"If you're uncomfortable wearing it, then at least keep it in your pocket. It will help."

"Does it make me . . . I don't know. What does it mean?"

"It doesn't mean anything. I made it myself. People have worn these for ten thousand years. Trust me."

"Actually, I do."

"Good."

"Do you have a talisman, too?"

"I protect my home with them. When I'm outside, I rely on myself. That's how it's done. Wearing that will help you. You're not one of us, Ava. I'm speaking frankly. For people like me, I'm a magnet. It can't be helped. The more you get into this, the bigger a shadow you cast, and the easier it is for them to find you. But I have enough of them scared that I'm usually all right."

"You make it sound like you're a criminal."

"Sometimes I feel like a criminal."

"Now I feel much better. Thanks."

When they reached the library, they walked up the hill to the parking lot. As they stood beside her Lexus, Dave told her, "You have my phone number. Call me for whatever reason if you need me, but call me tonight, even if nothing happens, just so we're sure everything's okay."

"I will."

"I'll speak with Tony tonight or tomorrow, whenever I can get hold of him."

"I feel like a tremendous burden has just been lifted. Maybe that's what it was. I put off making a decision, but now that I've done it, I feel a hundred per cent better."

"Good."

"Maybe all I needed to do was decide one way or the other. Thank you."

"Just be sure to phone me tonight."

"I will."

She wondered whether she should shake his hand or what she should do, wondered what a person does to thank someone who's just given you a talisman for good luck. Dave, however, simply nodded and turned toward his car.

But immediately he dropped to the asphalt, groaning. He was on his knees and gasping for air.

"Dave!"

Ava reached for him, getting down on her knees, but he waved her away.

"Don't!" He fell onto his right side. Clearly he was having difficulty breathing, but he warned her, "Don't touch me!"

"Oh, God, what is it? Are you having a heart attack?"

He stared at her, but pain took hold of him, obviously very deep pain pushing through him.

"Is it your *heart*?" Ava looked around to see if anyone else was nearby.

But he wasn't grabbing his heart. Dave had his hands tightened into fists in front of his chest, almost as if he were trying to pull his fists to him while they were being held back by something. He whispered to her, but she couldn't make out what he said.

Ava looked him in the eyes. "What? Speak louder!"

"Tal!"

"*What?*"

"*Talis!*"

"The *talisman?*"

He grunted. Sweat dripped from him, and he clenched his teeth each time pain moved through him.

Ava took the talisman from her pocket and opened the chain to place it around Dave's neck.

He warned her again, "Don't touch me!"

She pulled back. "What should I do?"

"Circle!"

"What circle? Where?"

"Around you! Draw it!"

"Draw a circle around me?"

"*Yes!*"

"With what?"

"*Talisman!*"

What did he mean? Draw it how? Scratch it in the asphalt? What?

She held the talisman in her right hand, pressed it to the asphalt, and scratched a line, looking at Dave the whole time.

"Yes!" he grunted, and exhaled a great breath.

Ava thought he was dying. What good would this do? How could this—?

"Do! It!"

She did the best she could, scratching a line around herself in the asphalt, although she had no idea what kind of circle she was drawing.

She saw his face darken, and his hands. What looked like a shadow was covering his right hand from inside the sleeve of his coat, as if ink there, in the sleeve of his coat, were pouring out to discolor his entire hand.

And his face. It crawled up from beneath his collar, making his face turn purple.

He grunted at her, "*Veni, Paimon, defendere me!*"

"What?"

"Say it!"

"*Wen-ee!* Like that?"

"Paimon!"

"Paimon!"

The black shadow was covering his other hand, so that both of his fists were purple, nearly black.

"*Defendere me!*"

"*Defen-deer-ee me!*"

"*Venite, manes.*"

Someone, a man walking into the parking lot, called to Ava, "Is he okay?"

"No!" she yelled at him, "Call 9-1-1!"

A woman beside the man said, "Oh, dear lord!"

Dave, spitting as he did his best to continue talking, said, "*Venite!*"

Ava yelled, "*Wen! Eye! Tee.*"

"What language is that?" the man called. He had his phone out.

Ava ordered him, "Please, please! Call 9-1-1!"

"Right now!"

Dave grunted, "*Venite manes.*"

"*Wen-eye-tee! May-nees.*"

"*Festinate!*"

"*Fes-tie-nay-tee!*"

"*Audite!*"

"*Odd-eye-tee!*"

"*Mihi!*"

"*Mih! Hih!*! Oh, God, Dave, don't die, don't die."

The sounds of an ambulance came. The siren seemed miles away.

Dave lay back on the asphalt. He whispered, "*Festinate.*"

Ava reached for him, then remembered his warning. "*Festinate.*"

"*Audite.*"

"*Audite.*"

"*Mihi.*"

"*Mihi.*"

His face was no longer purple. And his hands were losing their darkness. Whatever it was, a shadow or blood poisoning or whatever it was, it was going away, his face was unbelievably pale and covered with sweat, but he was no longer purple.

Dave relaxed fully on his back and continued to whisper. "*Venite.*"

Ava whispered, "*Venite.*"

"*Manes.*"

"*Manes.*"

The shadows were gone.

She put the talisman in her pocket again and scooted closer to Dave and touched him.

"*Festinate.*"

"Shh. The ambulance is coming. Dave, the ambulance is coming."

"*Festine,*" he whispered.

The siren was incredibly loud, and Ava was aware of it now. It pulled up just behind Dave, blocking the entrance to the library parking lot, and she heard voices and the crackle of people speaking on radios.

Someone, the man who'd called 9-1-1, touched her shoulder and said something to her.

Ava stood and stepped away from Dave.

The emergency medical techs, two young men, pulled a gurney from the back of the ambulance. One of them said to her, "What happened?"

"He just dropped."

"Do you know him?"

"Yes. No. Yes, I do. He's a friend."

"History of heart problems? Anything?"

"I don't know. He never said."

They lifted him carefully onto the gurney. Dave was barely conscious,

"She reached for him, then remembered his warning."

barely awake.

As the emergency techs moved him inside the ambulance, the woman who'd been standing beside the man in the parking lot said to Ava, "Are you going with him?"

"What?"

"Aren't you going with him?"

"Yes. What? Yes, yes." Ava asked the tech inside the ambulance, "Can I go?"

"Hurry up." He helped her inside and slammed the back doors closed.

The other one ran ahead and got behind the steering wheel and started the engine.

"Right there," the tech told Ava, nodding to a metal bench along one wall.

She sat.

The ambulance started moving, and the siren whined again.

Ava felt light-headed, looking at Dave on the gurney and watching the emergency tech as he slapped the back of Dave's left hand, got a vein, and started an IV line.

She put her hands inside her jacket pockets, and her right hand tightened around the talisman.

She gripped it as though it were the only thing remaining in the world, as though her own life depended on it, hers and Dave's both.

He was alive, she could see that. He was shiny with sweat, but the black shadows or whatever they were had gone, and Ava realized then, as she looked at him, that she had probably saved Dave's life, that she had certainly saved his life, by performing a magic ritual.

She had absolutely no idea how she'd done it, but she'd saved this man's life, this strange man's life, with black magic.

6.

At Northwest Community Hospital, Dave was taken into one of the curtained examination rooms in the emergency department. Ava stayed with him, telling the nurse who came in to start the paperwork that she wasn't related to Dave but was an acquaintance. She didn't even know if he had any family. They'd had lunch not ten minutes before this happened. "He fell to his knees," Ava told the nurse. "He couldn't breathe. He was turning purple."

She had no intention of revealing anything more, not about the shadows she thought she'd seen, and certainly nothing in regard to what she had done, drawing a circle around herself with a magical talisman. Dave was sick. Whatever had happened, the attack or sickness or whatever it was required the attention of doctors to look at his heart and brain or lungs. That's where the problem was, wherever it had come from. Dealing with his health was the most important thing.

Yet she had seen the shadows crawling up him from inside his clothes, and he had begged her to say words she didn't understand, and even with her not understanding, she had been of help. She had saved his life.

Ava watched him, unconscious as he was, breathing, hot, and she could almost feel Dave fighting deep within himself for strength, fighting to stay alive, doing whatever he needed to do not to die. Magic? Was he using magic, deep within himself, to stay alive?

The nurse had gone. She had pulled the curtain almost completely across the examination room entrance. Ava got up and approached Dave, stood close enough to him to hear his breathing. At least his breathing was steady. Occasionally his face would twist into an odd expression, as though he were having a nightmare; then it would relax. He whispered one or two words, but Ava couldn't make them out. Otherwise, he was asleep, or in a coma.

With her right hand, Ava touched Dave's face, then his neck, then his right hand as it rested alongside him. He did not react. She touched his skin where she knew there had been crawling shadows, she'd seen them, and yet there was absolutely no sign of them now.

"I'm a magnet. It can't be helped. The more you get into this, the bigger a shadow you cast, and the easier it is for them to find you."

The curtain was pulled back suddenly, the rings holding it scraping loudly on the rod overhead, and a young doctor came in carrying a clipboard thick with papers.

Ava drew back, taken by surprise, and moved to sit in her chair again.

The young doctor nodded to her but did not smile. He took Ava's place bedside, placed the clipboard on a plastic chair nearby, and took Dave's wrist between his own fingers and thumb, counting the pulse as he looked at his watch. Without looking up, he asked Ava, "No history of anything like this before?"

"No. Not that I know of. I'm just an acquaintance."

"Did he just go down, or was he conscious for a while?"

"He was conscious. He had a hard time breathing, but he was conscious. He talked to me a little bit."

"About what? Any pain? Where was his pain?" The doctor dropped Dave's hand onto the mattress and looked at Ava.

"He didn't— The pain seemed to be all over. He was holding his hands up, like this."

She demonstrated, then wondered if she'd done the right thing. Had Dave done that because of the pain or because of black magic?

The doctor retrieved the clipboard, took out a pen and jotted something down, then said to Ava, "We're going to run some scans. They'll be here in a few minutes. You'll have to get him into a gown. Are you comfortable with that, or should I ask the nurse?"

"Please, ask the nurse."

He went out, pulling the curtain closed behind him.

In a minute, the first nurse returned, drew the partitioning curtain around Dave's bed, and proceeded to undress him and get him into his hospital gown. When she pulled the curtains around again, Dave was lying as he had been only with more of him showing, his chest and arms. The nurse had pulled the bed sheet up to his waist and put his street clothes into a large plastic bag labeled with the hospital's logo.

The nurse told Ava, "They'll be here shortly. Do you need anything? A glass of water?"

"Coffee?"

"Sure. The vending machines are on the other side of the nurses' station."

"Can I ask you something?"

"What?"

"Did he have any marks on him?"

"What kind of marks, honey?"

"I don't know. He was discolored when he fell down. It didn't last long, but he was turning purple."

"No, no marks. I'd say that's a good thing."

"Yes."

The nurse went, and Ava looked at Dave again, then stepped out to get herself vending machine coffee.

So what, she thought, has exactly happened here? Make sense of it, make some sense of it. Strange man shows up and talks to you about your partner making threats and how he's determined to buy out the business. You tell the stranger, "Well, there's some history here, and I am being stubborn."

Okay, be stubborn, Ava thought. Next thing you know, you find out more than you're comfortable with about the strange man, so you talk it over with him in the library, only he shows you books about witchcraft and demonology and all of the Harry Potter stuff. And then, out of the blue, the strange man falls down and turns purple and shadows start crawling up him from under his clothes and he starts talking in Latin or Greek or witchcraft language.

Witches and people casting spells and talismans, and dancing in the moonlight.

"Is this what you think of? Is this what you think it's about?"

"Yes, of course."

And she no idea where God came into this.

"He's right here. And here. We're God."

"I don't find that very comforting."

"I don't find the idea of God very comforting. He feels like a lead weight. Do you think God laughs?"

"I have no idea."

"Have you looked out a window lately?"

"This conversation is way too strange for me."

I'll tell you what else is strange, Ava thought. What had she gotten herself into? What had Tony started?

Because it came back to Tony. It had to. It had absolutely started with him because this was the Tony way, make a mess as fast as you can, make a bunch of demands and act like a spoiled child and cause car accidents and make threats and have everything run into a ditch immediately.

Asshole.

So that now Ava winds up at six o'clock in the evening sitting in the hospital and looking at a plastic bag of clothes that belong to a guy who—

She set her coffee down and took out her cell phone, hit the button for Tony, and waited.

Got the answering machine at his apartment.

Clicked that off and pressed the button for the restaurant, but then clicked that off, too. Would he really be there? And if he were, is this the conversation she wanted to have right now with him at the restaurant?

She pressed the number for his apartment again, waited for his answering machine to come on, but then closed her phone again.

Wait, wait. Do not react. Act, but don't *react*. Be in charge. What are you going to do, ask him why he tried to kill Dave or why he had somebody try to kill Dave? And what if he thinks Dave is dead?

That's true. Tony hired somebody to kill Dave just like he'd originally hired Dave to hurt Ava herself, maybe kill her, but at least warn her. So what does that make Tony now, the godfather of the witchmen who kill people?

But he probably thought Dave was dead. He hired somebody just as weird as Dave to kill Dave, and whoever it was, now they both thought Dave was dead, probably.

Which meant that they'd probably try to kill her, too.

Oh, this is wonderful, Ava thought. This is splendid. Car crashes don't work, so he hires another one of these characters to do it.

"Welcome to my life," she'd told Dave, only now it wasn't just her life but his, too, apparently.

She reached for her phone again to call Tony and tell him, "Look, enough, I will sell the business, is that what you want?"

But then she waited yet again.

Was that all there was to this?

Her life was in danger, but how much good would it help to call Tony and talk to him?

Think about Tony, think about him, Ava thought.

Tony would certainly have done something like this, but then he would be very cool and calm and collected about it afterward. That's the Tony way. Wait. Wait and see. Cause a car accident and then wait and see. Try to kill strange Dave and then wait and see.

Ava took a deep breath. She finished the coffee and looked at the bag of clothes again.

So how was it that she had wound up being the person sitting here looking after this man? Didn't he have any family or friends? Everybody has family and friends.

She left the examination room and walked across the hall to the nurses' station. She asked the young Hispanic woman there, one of the nurses, if Dave had any relatives or other emergency contacts listed.

"Can you give me that information?"

"Let me look." The nurse took a seat in front of a terminal and, after many keystrokes and a bit of a wait, told Ava, "No relatives."

"Really?"

"He never told us if he did."

"He's alone?"

"There's one contact. Interesting. It's one of our doctors."

"That is interesting."

"Dr. Ward, his GP."

Ava wasn't sure what that meant, having one's family doctor listed in the hospital file as the emergency contact rather than family or friends.

Or maybe Dr. Ward was family? Or a friend?

She returned to the examination room, but in a moment the first nurse she'd talked with came in and told Ava, "We have a room for him."

"Oh."

"Did you want to take his things?"

"I guess so. Yes."

Ava picked up the plastic bag and followed the nurse down the hall to an elevator.

While they waited for it, she asked, "Do you know a Dr. Ward?"

"Oh, yes."

"He's Dave's doctor."

"I see."

Ava said nothing more. The elevator arrived, and the nurse pressed the button for the sixth floor.

When the doors opened again, the nurse told her, "Room 623, right down to your left. They may have brought him up already."

"Thank you."

Still uncertain whether she should be doing this, and very uncomfortable with what she had gotten herself into, Ava carried Dave's clothes down the hall and into his room.

It was a private room, one bed, and Dave was in it, all tubed up and unconscious, lying as peacefully as if he were at home asleep, presumably. Or in his coffin, maybe.

A tall, slender black man in a lab coat was standing beside the bed, his back to the window, and he looked up as Ava came in and dropped the bag of Dave's clothes against one wall. He was good-looking and rather young, perhaps in his mid or late forties. His hair was cut short and he had a thin moustache. He smiled at Ava.

"Do you know Dave?" he asked.

"Sort of, I guess," Ava told him. "I was with him when he, when he fell down, when he had his attack."

"Ah."

"Is he going to be okay?"

"I think so. I hope so. He's a fighter, but this hit him hard." The physician looked down at Dave, then again at Ava, and he stepped around the bed, offering his hand to her. "Pardon me," he told her. "I should introduce myself. I'm Larry Ward."

At seven o'clock that evening, as they'd agreed to do earlier in the day, Tony Jasco met with Arthur Neely, coming by the motel where Neely was staying. Neely had told Tony to bring food with him and a bottle of Gatorade or vitamin water. Apparently casting spells was thirsty work.

The motel was out on Northwest Highway in Palatine, an L-shaped building of perhaps nine or ten rooms across from the commuter rail line. Tony parked close to the door of Neely's room. He cradled the Gatorade and a paper bag of drive-thru sandwiches with his left arm as he knocked on the door and waited.

And knocked again.

And waited.

"Neely! Are you all right?"

Nothing. Silence.

"Neely!" He rapped on the door again.

Then heard someone stirring inside, feet shuffling toward the door, and the chain undone and the safety bolt. The door opened, and Tony was looking into Neely's ugly face.

Ugly and tired. The man was truly exhausted.

Neely hung back as Tony came in and deposited the food on the small table by the room's picture window. The drapes had been drawn, and no lights were on, so it was dusk in the motel room. It also smelled as if someone had been burning fruit-scented candles or something all day long.

"Thanks for the food," Neely said, but instead of sitting at the table, he reclined on the bed and put one arm over his face.

Tony took out the sandwiches and grabbed a couple of French fries. He walked across the room to the bathroom area, undid the plastic from a Styrofoam cup, and came back to the table to pour himself some grape-flavored Gatorade. He asked Neely, "How did it go?"

"It worked, I think."

"You *think*?"

"He's dead, or as good as. It's hard to tell."

"What does that mean?"

"It means that he and I are both sufficiently good at this that it's hard for me to pick up on him completely. But my sense is that he's gone."

"Gone, meaning dead?"

"Meaning dead."

Tony chuckled and poured himself some more Gatorade. "You want some of this?"

"Yes."

He filled another cup halfway and walked it over to Neely.

Neely sat up, took the cup, and slurped the drink.

Tony asked him, "Wears you out, huh?"

"It takes years off you."

"Really?"

"There's always a price to pay, Mr. Jasco. It's an eternal truth."

"Okay, then. How come you guys always smell like fruit or vegetables or whatever it is?"

"It's oil. We use oils in our work. We cleanse ourselves with it. We purify our instruments with it. We burn it for the aroma."

"I just wondered."

"Bring me a sandwich."

"Turkey with lettuce and cheese and mayo. Okay?"

"That's fine."

Tony handed it to him, then sat at the table, unwrapped his own sandwich, and started eating. "You're gonna be okay, right?"

"Yes. But give me a day or two to get back to normal."

"Not a problem. That'll give me time to talk to Ava about our business."

"Fine."

"You and me are a good team. I would have never thought it."

"Don't get any ideas."

"I'm just saying. Funny how it works out that you showed up, and I could help you, and you could help me. Very nice coincidence."

"There are no coincidences in this life, Mr. Jasco."

"No?"

"Not in this life or any other. It all ties together."

"Is that like a philosophy or a code or something? Because I never thought about it that way."

"It's not a code. It's the way the universe works."

"Really? The universe?"

"Yes."

"I've never thought of it that way."

Neely sighed. "Of course you haven't."

7.

In the cafeteria at Northwest Community Hospital, Ava and Dr. Ward sat across from each other at a small, round table. Ava knew that she should have something in her stomach, even though she was not very hungry, but she'd eaten nothing since she and Dave had had lunch, so she nibbled on a salad. Dr. Ward had a cup of coffee.

And they discussed Dave.

Cautiously at first, of course, but soon enough, once Ava was honest about what had happened in the library parking lot, Ward was forthright with her.

"So you know what he does?" she asked him.

"Yes. Is that how you met him?"

"Are we speaking frankly here?"

"I certainly hope so."

"Okay, then." She removed the talisman from her jacket pocket and set it on the table between them.

Ward said, "Ah." He placed his hand over it, cupping the charm but not touching it. "It's still warm."

"Is it?" Ava asked him. "It doesn't feel warm to me."

"No?"

"No. Do you practice black magic, too?"

"No, no. He's taught me a few things. It's a matter of being sensitive. You could learn it, too."

"No, thank you."

"Did you contact Dave initially, or did he contact you?"

"He was hired to hurt me, actually. By a business partner of mine. Soon to be former business partner."

"I see."

"Dr. Ward, do you know what happened when Dave had his attack?"

"No. I can imagine, but I didn't see it, obviously."

Ava leaned across the cafeteria table and whispered to him, "He could barely talk, but this is what I used to make the circle. Then he told me to repeat some words, and I did that."

"You likely saved his life."

"I know. Have you ever heard of such a thing?"

"No. And certainly not with Dave. He was being attacked."

"By who?"

"I have no idea. I can only assume that he does."

"My business partner is my thought."

"Why?"

Ava shook her head and poked her fork at the lettuce in her salad. "Because Dave turned him down, is what I'm thinking. He was originally supposed to help him. And now I'm scared." She looked Ward in the eyes. "You're a doctor. How does this work?"

"Sorcery?"

"Is that what you call it?"

He shrugged. "I can't explain it, not entirely. I don't know how it works. I accept it for what it is and observe it. I'm still learning. My theory is that it's actually an evolutionary holdover. Part of a survival instinct from when we weren't as advanced as we are now. But there's more to it than that."

"He showed me pictures in the library of demons and witches."

"Most people still associate it with those things. I'm very impressed that you were able to stay focused and do what he told you."

"Well, that was enough for me."

"Do you think you might be sensitive?"

"No. To do that? No."

"I don't know whether I could have done it," Ward said. "It takes a certain openness. You might be right about your business partner, though, if he's done this to Dave."

"What can I do about it?"

"I'm not sure."

"Find another Dave? How many people are there like him out there?"

"More than you might think, but they hide in plain sight."

"Wonderful."

"They have their own history. I find it fascinating. There's a long history to it."

Ava finished what she could of her salad and closed the plastic container it had come in. "How long have you known him?"

"Years. More than ten years by now, I think, yes."

"How did you meet? Did he try to kill you, too?"

Ward smiled. "No, he saved my life, actually."

"Really?"

"It had nothing to do with sorcery. I was nearly crushed to death. I was in the city running some errands, and I went past a construction site. One of the trucks there, a pickup truck, slipped out of gear, that's the best guess anyone could make, and it rolled backward toward me. It came into the alley I was coming through and nearly pinned me against the side of a building. It would have crushed me and killed me instantly. Dave Ehlert was there at the same moment I was, and he acted immediately. We have different versions of the story. He insists that the truck hit something on the ground that slowed it to a stop, and so he was able to push me out of the way. I say that he stopped the truck in some fashion and then pushed me out of the way. It happened very quickly, but my powers of observation are fairly good, and I know what happened."

"Is that physically possible?"

"Not for most people. Not for anyone, in fact, I don't think. But I believe he did it."

"What happened after that?"

"I landed on the ground, and I had some cuts and bruises. I really think they came from Dave pushing me out of the way, but the foreman on the site insisted that I go to the hospital. Liability, you know. So I did. And Dave actually came by to look in on me."

"This does not sound like the same man my business partner hired to kill me."

"Oh, it's the same man. He's a very complex individual. To explain it would mean taking you into places that you might not be comfortable with. I certainly wasn't comfortable with it when he and I first discussed it."

"Why not? What kind of places?"

"Spiritual places."

Ava sighed. "Maybe that's what he was trying to get at when we were talking in the library. It's not that I'm uncomfortable with it. I just don't know where to begin. I don't understand how what he does fits into anything spiritual."

Ward nodded. "That's a long talk to have sometime, then. I should get back."

"Should I stay with him?"

"Do you want to?"

"I don't know. In a way, I feel responsible. I mean, I'm not, not literally, but I was there, and all of this got started because of me and my partner.

But I didn't even know this man two days ago."

"I'd say that whatever you do will be the right thing. He'll understand, whatever you decide."

"You're talking like he's going to live."

"I believe he will."

"Did the tests they made show anything?"

"No. They'll run more, but there's a limit to the tests you can do, and there's a limit to what tests can show. What he's doing won't show up on any test."

"What do you mean?"

"He's doing whatever he needs to do to get the strength to pull through this. I don't believe he's ever been in this situation before, but I feel he can manage it. He's a remarkable man."

"You're taking this very calmly."

"Maybe it's the training." He stood. "The medical training, I mean. Perhaps we'll be able to talk again."

Ava stood, as well. "I suppose I'd better stay in touch until my partner and I have settled whatever this is that's going on. But it does scare me."

"I'll give you my card. Here." Ward removed his wallet, took out a business card, and handed it to Ava. "Feel welcome to call me. You saved his life, I'm sure of that. That's why I've been as frank with you as I have been. You deserve it."

"I appreciate that."

Ward nodded to her and started off, but Ava called to him, and Ward turned to face her before leaving.

"One more question."

"Surely."

"Are you— You're the only friend he has, aren't you?"

"If people like him have friends—yes, I'm his friend."

Ava did not reply to that. What an odd way to put it. As Ward left, she looked down at his card, an ordinary business card, and then put it into her purse.

Ava lay in bed that night unable to fall asleep, restless, the whole day in her mind. At last she went into the kitchen, put on the water for tea, and sat at the table with a yellow pad and pen, writing down whatever came into her mind—words, nonsense, questions, scenes, names.

The tea kettle whistled. She made herself a cup of chamomile tea and returned to the table.

Who, what, why, when, how— She filled the top page of the pad.

Tony. Dave. When did this start? Car accident. Steve. Talisman. Was it really warm? Witches. Dr. Ward—more than ten yrs. Spiritual—how?

She sipped the tea, yawned, and absently began doodling. She drew the talisman, as well as she remembered it. It was on her dresser; she'd put it there when she'd gotten undressed, but now without looking at it she drew it, and drew it again, and underneath the drawings of it, wrote some of the Latin or Greek words she thought she remembered Dave saying. *Audite. Manes. Festinate. Defendere.* What did any of it mean?

But you saved his life, she thought. She knew it, and she didn't need Dr. Ward to tell her that. So did that mean anything? Was she supposed to be there for some reason to save Dave's life? Did any of it mean anything when you put all of these things together? Did they really add up to anything that makes any sense?

She was too tired to think about it any longer. The tea had worked, or writing things down had. Ava stood, walked to the sink, rinsed out her tea cup, then filled it twice and drank down two cups of water, feeling thirsty for whatever reason. She rolled her head around to relax her shoulders and went out of the kitchen, turning off the light.

In bed, she closed her eyes and breathed steadily to relax, and as she drifted off, at the moment she began to slip away—

A face appeared, and she sat up with her heart running fast inside her. She had to catch her breath; she felt almost as though she were choking.

What on earth was that? It was a hideous face, something truly vicious that she'd seen, a nightmare, plain and simple.

Dear God, was someone trying to use magic against her now, too? Is this how it worked? Is this what it was?

She thought of Dave in the hospital.

"He's doing whatever he needs to do to get the strength to pull through this. He's a remarkable man."

Ava wondered, seriously wondered, if she had picked up on something that Dave himself actually was dreaming. Was that possible? Anything was possible, but was she experiencing it now, too, witchcraft or magic, or was she just so exhausted and twisted in every direction by what had happened today—

Put on the talisman, put it around your neck.

She heard it clearly, as though a part of her were talking to another part of her, herself warning herself.

"Wear this. If you're uncomfortable wearing it, then at least keep it in

your pocket. It will help. I made it myself."

Dear God, was she deeper into this than she knew? Was this dragging her into it, down into someplace where all of these people did magic, doctors and sorcerers and, and *business partners*?

"*He's taught me a few things. It's a matter of being sensitive. You could learn it, too.*"

"*No, thank you.*"

No, thank you.

Her breath was calming now. Ava turned on the light, then in the safety of the bedside lamp, closed her eyes.

No face, no hideous face.

God . . . .

She got out of bed, walked to her bureau, picked up the talisman, looked at it.

She'd done a pretty good job, yes, of drawing it.

She unclasped the chain, put it around her neck, and locked it.

"*Wear this. It will help. I made it myself.*"

Please, she thought, whatever this is, whoever you are, please, please, I need to get some *sleep*, I need to get some rest, I'm scared to death, and I need to *sleep*.

"*He saved my life.*"

"*This does not sound like the same man.*"

"*Oh, it's the same man. He's a very complex individual. To explain it would mean taking you into places that you might not be comfortable with.*"

"*Why not? What kind of places?*"

"*Spiritual places.*"

Spiritual places.

Given everything that had happened during the past couple of days, that's the last place Ava would have thought she'd find herself in, someplace spiritual.

Just let me sleep, she thought, and I'll worry about the spiritual places tomorrow.

She rolled onto one side, wrapped a hand around the talisman for good luck, for strength, and felt herself drifting off again.

No face, this time, no hideous face.

She moved on to a deep sleep.

Neither did Tony Jasco have a relaxed evening. By ten o'clock, he was trying to ignore a powerful headache by putting away the latest in a series of Old Styles, and when his phone rang, the landline in his apartment, the sound of it aggravated his throbbing head with truly remarkable precision, matching ring tone and pain in a duet of exquisite hurt.

Even more hurt came when Tony heard the voice on his answering machine.

He slid down to the other end of the couch and picked up the handset.

"You answering the phone now finally?" said the man on the other end.

"Shit."

"Shit is right. You been avoiding us."

"We will talk. We will meet."

"We talked! We met, asshole! Where's the money? Money, money, money, Tony!"

"I know, I know."

"Where is it?"

"You'll get it."

"Not my question. Where *is* it?"

"It's been slow. I have it. Not now, but in two days."

His caller said to someone else on the other end of the line, "Two days." They both laughed. "No more two days, Tony. How are we going to explain this? What are we gonna do with you?"

"I never welshed before."

"And so we never had to mess with you before. This is not pleasant for us. No, I lie. We enjoy this!" More laughter from him and whoever else was with him.

Tony was feeling the beer and his headache, and now his anger kicked in. He told himself that he had other ammunition now, something more to rely on than his own rather limited negotiating skills. He said into the phone, "I said two days. You will have the money in two days."

"And I told you, no more two days."

"Don't push me."

"Oh, don't push *you*?" He said to the other man with him, "We're pushing him, and he asks us not to do that."

Laughter.

"I been good up to now," Tony said, "and you know that, so I expect you to go along with me for two more days. That's all."

"Tony, that is not all. That is not all. You don't have two more days. This is not how it works. You know the rules."

"Two days!"

"No more, Tony." And he hung up.

Damn it. What now? He could have the money in two days; he could, because in one way or another, whatever he had to do, now he could deal with Ava the way he needed to. No Dave around, that was taken care of, he could get money from Ava now, he knew he could, just give him two stinking days.

So what would they do?

Come here and take it out of him piece by piece?

Highly possible. Only that's not going to happen, Tony thought. I'm not going to have those shitheads coming in here in the middle of the night and doing that. No way, Jose.

God, his head hurt.

He pulled on a jacket, grabbed some of the extra cash he kept hidden in his bedroom, turned the lights out, and left.

Got into his car, remaining alert the whole time to see if the sons of bitches were nearby and keeping an eye on him. He didn't think so, but they could be anywhere.

He got into his Explorer and moved. Drove in circles a few times to see who might be following him, but apparently no one was.

Then he went to find a motel. He briefly considered staying at the place in Palatine where Neely had holed up, but that might not be smart. Better keep your distance from him, too, Tony thought. He headed southeast, into Des Plaines and Park Ridge, to find someplace there to spend the night and figure out what to do next.

8.

Ava awoke with her fingers still gripping the talisman. Images from a deep slumber stayed with her as strong presences, memories standing alongside her bed, fears protruding phantomlike from the wall behind her, hovering, somewhat in this world, somewhat not.

She sat up, letting go of the talisman, and twisted around to look at the wall, actually did it.

No fears protruding from the wall. No memories, no dreams in shapes of any kind.

What on earth had she done to herself while she was supposed to have been sleeping? The same questions as those of last night came to her. Was she deeper into this than she knew? Was this dragging her down into a place where people did magic? Was she herself now performing some sort of magic in her dreams?

Ava groaned and rubbed her throat. The one irrefutable fact for her this morning, whatever else was going on was that she was extremely thirsty. She moved out of her bed and didn't even bother to pull on her robe or her slippers but instead went down the hall into the kitchen, opened the refrigerator, and took the half-gallon carton of orange juice from the shelf on the door.

She squeezed open the pour spout and drank several swallows right from the carton, then carried it to the table, amazed at herself for acting that crudely. But she was sincerely and completely *thirsty*. She retrieved a tumbler from the cupboard, filled it with orange juice, and drank that down. Ava almost gasped because she was out of breath when she finished, and her teeth hurt from the cold juice.

Why so thirsty?

She poured another glassful and forced herself to sip it in as human a fashion as possible while reviewing the tablet of paper she'd left on the table last night.

Tony. Dave. When did this start? Car accident. Steve. Talisman. Was it really warm? Witches. Dr. Ward—more than ten yrs. Spiritual—how?

Spiritual how, indeed.

"I can't explain it. I don't know how it works. I accept it for what it is. I'm still learning."

If Ava had learned anything in this world, it was precisely that: accept the world for what it is. If you're going to be part of the world, if you're going to look after yourself, then act, don't merely react. Be proactive. Broken apart in a car wreck? Get up and start walking. Husband killed? Remember that fact every day when you get out of bed, and keep putting one foot in front of the other. Solve your problems or you become part of the problem yourself. Do something, or something will be done *to* you.

She was in the middle of this, whatever it was. *"I accept it for what it is."* Look at everything that's happened in the past couple of days, Ava reminded herself. How do you put all of that together?

You don't. You can't. You leave them there, the things that have happened, you leave them there, and you do what you need to do and you trust that these things will explain themselves at some point because there's an explanation for everything, there is, there has to be.

She made herself coffee and while it brewed, poured cereal into a bowl.

And had a glass of water because she was still *thirsty*.

She ate the cereal and thought of Dr. Ward and of Dave in the hospital, and Ava knew that, no matter what else she might do today, her first priority was to go to the hospital to see if this strange man was alive or dead.

The pain had been remarkable.

He had experienced much in his life, for in his practice of the arts, Dave had walked with shadows, experienced wonders, and suffered torments, including malevolent hurt from otherworldly flames and swords.

But what had taken him to the ground this time was more than physical pain. The psychic hurt was as deep as life. He had felt as though he were made of fibers, and that each of his fibers was being taken apart gradually, ripped down into threads, and then those threads even more slowly torn into still finer lengths. And how was it possible for him to feel each of those fibers and threads and lengths as they screamed perfectly, each one with a Dave voice? Not physical pain, not nerve pain, but experience more ancient and profound than physical pain. Having his body sawn apart as cuts of meat, rib and rump and round, would have been preferable. Whoever he was, whatever he was, his spirit, or the many lives contained in his one spirit—these had been taken apart as though he had never mattered to begin with.

How else to explain it? He had seen parts of himself floating near him like sparks, loose flames, and those parts of himself had dimmed, their pain had shouted out in darkness as they dimmed, and Dave, the parts of him, had dimmed with them, so that he was disappearing into a hole of pain, spiritual pain of a rich depth, depth that slipped backward in time, depth that went deeper than a single blackness. He had practiced the arts for a very long time, and he was astonished to learn, while he was pulled into many separate fibers, as the parts of him dimmed, as he died, that he could yet be astonished by wonders in this universe.

And meanwhile, with effort he thought beyond him, he had whispered to the woman in the parking lot, to Ava, had whispered for her to scream for him in his behalf: Spirits of the dead, come to help me. *Venite, manes, defendere me.* Hurry! *Festinate!* Paimon, come to help me. *Veni, Paimon, defendere me.* Listen to me, Paimon! *Audi mihi,* Paimon. Paimon, commander of demons and legions of spirits, teacher of arts and philosophy, revealer of mysteries and secret things of Earth and the universe.

Dave seldom called upon the great and powerful elements. He had command of his own universe. He ordered to him his own spirits: he had work done for him by the remains of those he had moved from this world into the next. But not knowing who was attacking him or why, as he lay dying, great strength was needed, and great effort. Therefore, Paimon of Hell, Paimon of legions.

Paimon would demand a price, in time, from Dave for calling upon him. That is the nature of the universe. As above, so below. As with them, so with us. The universe does not give without taking, just as it does not take without giving. Reciprocity, the one true law.

The single time Dave had tried to defeat that law and outwit the universe, he had paid damnably for it, and not with his own life or with his own blood.

And so the pain had subsided. He had seen Ava doing her best for him, seen her looking into his eyes. She appeared to be under water, or perhaps a mile distant, but in fact she was close by and doing her best, and she had saved him, she had pulled his fibers back into him so that the dimming lights did not die but returned to him, and the face he had felt close by in the darkness had gone away.

The face seemed familiar, but he had been unable to recognize it. He had been too full of pain and too heavy, too weighted down with the effort it had taken him to keep his spirit intact, to put the pieces of the face together. But it reminded him of someone, that face, and he trusted that he

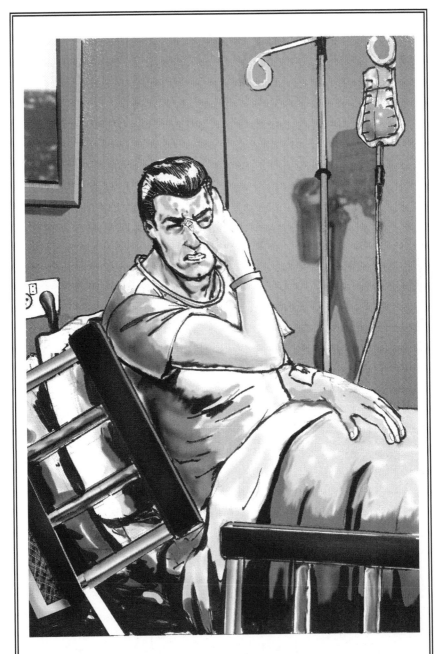

"...their pain shouted out in darkness as they dimmed..."

would remember what to call it, demon's face or man's face, human or not.

And so the pain went away, and he relaxed in darkness so surprisingly warm and comfortable that he assumed he must be in the next world, or in one of many other worlds.

But he was not. He was asleep.

And now he awoke. He thought he was still in the parking lot, and waited for the pain to return because Ava was there, Ava was before him, looking into his eyes, but now with sunlight behind her.

Life.

He was still alive, still here, and the pain and the face were not here.

She said to him, "Can you hear me?"

He nodded. "Yes." It was a whisper.

"I had to come by to make sure you were all right."

He closed his eyes and opened them again.

Ava remained.

He said to her, "Give me some water, please."

A blue plastic pitcher of ice water sat on the overbed tray near the foot of the bed. Ava poured some into a plastic cup. Dave drank it at once, then asked for another cup of water, and a third.

Ava asked him, "What is it about the thirst? I had it, too."

"It happens. It always dehydrates me. It takes the moisture right out of you."

"I drank a half gallon of orange juice."

"One more glass, please."

She poured it and handed it to him. "I met your friend, Dr. Ward."

"I knew he'd be here."

"He was trying to explain some of this to me."

"How far did he get?"

"Far enough to tell me that you saved his life one time."

"That was an accident."

"He said you're a very complex man. I tend to agree. And he said that what you do is spiritual."

"Not what you'd find inside a church is it?"

"Churches aren't spiritual. They have a good business model. People are spiritual. But this is worse than the car wreck. For as long as I live, I will never forget what happened yesterday."

"Welcome to my life, Ms. Beaudine." He smiled.

"It was Tony, wasn't it?"

"Yes. I'm sure of it." He set the cup on the tray and lay back on the pillows.

"What did he do? Do you know?"

"It was him or someone acting for him. I'll find out. They tried to kill me the way I would have killed them. I'm fortunate you were there."

"I have no idea what I did."

"But you did well."

"I don't want to do any of this well. But you have to explain something to me because I had a lot of bad dreams last night."

"What sort of dreams?" He looked at her intently.

"Some kind of a face. And a really scary feeling. When I woke up, I thought I was surrounded by a lot of people, like there were other people there."

"We must have been talking to each other."

"Seriously?"

"Tell me if you remember anything more."

"I will. Is that possible?"

"It's possible."

"It felt very real."

"It was real. Most likely, when you were chanting, you were seeing some of what I saw. You remembered that."

"I don't remember seeing anything."

"Your subconscious does. That was the dream."

"I don't want any more dreams, and if you can help me not to, please tell me now."

"They'll pass."

"Is it because Dr. Ward said I might be sensitive?"

"Yes. I sensed it in you. You have that aspect to you."

"Great. Just great." Ava poured herself a cup of water and swallowed it, and asked Dave, "You want some more?"

"Yes."

She poured it for him. "I'm going to go ahead and sell the restaurant."

"Has he talked to you at all?'

"No. But I don't need this anymore, and I don't want him trying to kill you again or trying to kill me. I've had enough."

Dave was thoughtful for a moment. "When you talk to him, pretend you don't know what happened to me."

"If that's what you want."

"Just— Mum's the word. You don't know yet."

"Okay."

"Whoever did this . . . they'll know soon enough that I'm not dead. But I want to think about how to handle this."

"Okay."

Ward's voice came from the doorway "Still with us, I see."

Ava looked up as he came in.

Dave said to him, "I never left." He fidgeted again, and Ava adjusted the pillows behind him.

Ward picked up the clipboard hanging at the foot of the bed, looked at it, then stood and regarded him. "You've gone through almost twice as much saline as anyone normal would."

"I never claimed to be normal."

"And you aren't. The tests showed nothing."

Ava said to Ward, "How could that be? It was like he was having a heart attack."

"You tell me," Ward replied. "I'd like to catch it on film."

Dave told him, "Keep trying. Not everything that passes through this world belongs in it."

Ward said to Ava, "We've had this conversation more times than I care to count." He did his best to mimic Dave. "'Not everything that passes through this world shows up in this world!'" He asked Dave, "Am I right? All the time."

"All the time."

"I'll be back this afternoon." Ward replaced the clipboard on the bed. "When they bring breakfast, eat."

Dave told him, "I will. I'm hungry."

Ward nodded to Ava. "Make sure he does."

"Okay."

He left, and Ava said to Dave, "I wanted to remember to tell you. Your car. It's still in the library parking lot."

"So it is. I completely forgot."

"Somebody'll complain if it's there too long. You want me to have it towed?"

"No. Thank you. I'll do it, or I'll ask Larry. Dr. Ward."

"Okay."

"Ava, you don't need to stay. I'll be fine."

"I feel safer here than at home. Explain that to me."

He sniffed, a kind of laugh. "They're not going to hurt you, Ava. Whoever this is, he wanted me. He did, or she did."

"Do you have any idea who?"

"Someone like me, only with a worse attitude."

"How many people are there like you?"

"Apparently at least one more than I can account for."

When he drove back to his apartment building at ten that morning, Tony circled it twice to make sure once again that he wasn't walking into anything. He parked on the street rather than in his usual space in the back, in the carport, just in case somebody might be watching and decide to do damage to his transportation. He expected anything.

Except the message that was on his phone, which he played back as soon as he'd locked the apartment door behind him.

"Tony? It's Ava. It's time to end this. I'm willing to talk. Let's put a stop to this. It's not doing you or me any good. It's now . . . quarter of ten. If you get this message, meet me at ten-thirty at the restaurant. If you don't get back in time, call me on my cell and we'll set something else up. But you've got the restaurant if you want it."

Unbelievable. Because of killing the Dave guy? This was good, this was very, very good, yes.

He picked up the phone and pressed the number for her cell phone.

"Ava."

"Did you get my message?"

"Just now. I just walked in. I will be there. If I run late, wait for me."

"I want this done, Tony."

"I understand."

"Bet you do." And she hung up.

Good, good, good.

He ran downstairs and was halfway to Dundee Road before he heard the bad news on the radio at the bottom of the hour.

" . . . officials are still uncertain as to the cause of the fire at *Ava's*, an Arlington Heights restaurant. Firefighters remain on the scene, and police ask that motorists choose an alternate route for—"

They had done it.

They did it.

The idiots, the unbelievable idiots, this is what they had done, they went ahead and did it, even *after he had promised them* that all they had to do was wait—

The unbelievable idiots.

Tony went as fast as he could the rest of the way, but soon enough, he ran into a line of police cruisers blocking the road in front of the restaurant entrance.

He put down the driver's side window and waved a cop over.

"This is my restaurant!"

"Your restaurant?"

"I'm Tony Jasco! I own this restaurant! Who did this?"

"Hold on." The officer spoke into the microphone on his shoulder, turning to look at a couple of other cops standing near the entrance.

They waved to him, and the cop told Tony, "Go on around."

"Who *did* this?"

"Go on around, Mr. Jasco."

He got as close as he could, parking in a corner of the lot next to the employees' cars and Ava's Lexus. Ava and the rest of them were standing together about fifty feet away, by the trash dumpsters, looking at the damage, whatever might be left of the restaurant.

But it was completely gone. The flames were out, or nearly so. Firefighters continued to hose down hot spots, but all that remained were the parts of some walls.

Tony walked toward the hot rubble, not getting very far before a police officer yelled to him to stay back. He stopped where he was. He was vacant, empty in his heart, empty, empty, as he looked at—what? His life or whatever remained of his life? The absolute proof of what a loser he truly was? Proof of how he had been betrayed, tricked, lied to, played royally by these morons who had—

"Tony!"

It was Ava, walking quickly toward him, as angry as he had ever seen her.

"Ava! I didn't know!"

"What the hell have you done?"

"Nothing!"

"Don't you tell me that!"

"Jesus Christ."

"*What have you done, Tony?*"

"*Nothing!*"

But she didn't believe him, and there was no reason why she should. She hovered inches away from him, so close he expected her to lash out at him.

"Shut up, Ava, please, be quiet, give me a minute."

"Give you a minute?"

"Please, please, Ava, please."

He lit a cigarette and smoked it while holding one side of his head with his free hand, trying to think. He asked Ava, "When did it start?"

"Just before they came to open. Eileen got here at five. She told me, Tony."

"Told you what?"

"They were here again yesterday."

"Who?"

"Do not keep lying to me, Tony!"

"Jesus, keep it down!" He saw two police officers looking at them.

Ava waved to Eileen, who came over.

She regarded Tony with airless fury. "They kept coming back, and we didn't have any more excuses to make for you. You're pathetic. These people have families!"

"I tried my best!"

"Tony." Eileen stared at him until he met her look. "What did you think you were doing? Did you think we didn't know?"

Ava asked him, "I had two characters accost me in the parking lot the other day. Was it them?"

He had had enough. He threw his cigarette down and said hotly to Ava, "It's because you wouldn't sell! You made me do it."

"Stop it."

"Where the hell else am I going to get money like that? I kept it going while you were on your back in bed for a year!"

"Who burned down my restaurant, Tony?"

"Shut the hell up!"

Ava stepped toward him and shoved him in the chest with both of hands, forcing him backward. "No! You shut me up, Tony!"

"I only needed two more days!"

One of the police officers nearby walked over. He asked Ava, "We okay?"

She made a face and said to him, "Yeah."

He looked at Tony. "Sir?"

"We're very emotional, Officer."

"Take a break." He looked at Ava again. "Ma'am?"

She nodded to him and stepped toward Eileen, away from Tony.

The officer waited another moment, then walked away.

Ava turned to look at the people who had been her employees for more than ten years. "What do I say to them?" she asked Eileen. "I don't know what to say."

"Honey, you can't tell them much they don't already know."

"Dear God." The anger rose in her again. She turned and looked at Tony. "You have not heard the end of this." She said to Eileen, "Tell them I'm going to do what I can to help tide them over. I can get a little money. They don't deserve this."

"Ava," Eileen told her, "we'll be okay."

"I won't be. Not after this."

She walked hurriedly to her car.

Tony followed and stopped her just as Ava reached for the door.

She faced him, angrier than ever. "Call your lawyer. Because that's the next step in this."

"Ava, please. I'm going to need your help."

"Forget it."

"They still want their money!"

Ava made a face and got into her car, slamming the door. She looked out the window at Tony as she gunned the engine. "You've ruined everything."

"You still have to help me, Ava."

"Steve was right. You're nothing but a piece of shit." She hit the accelerator and turned the wheel sharply as she pulled out, trying to knock him over.

Tony jumped back. "Hey!"

He watched her go. She stopped and talked briefly to one of the cops. The cop nodded and looked back at Tony.

Now what?

But Ava drove on, steering around the fire trucks still in the parking lot, and the cop did nothing.

Tony did nothing, either. Not yet.

Not yet.

But pretty soon, he promised himself . . pretty soon . . . .

9.

That afternoon, when he came by Dave's room, Ward said, "We can't find anything wrong, not that that's a surprise. We're signing you out."

"Thanks."

"You don't look happy."

"Ava just phoned," Dave told him. "The restaurant burned down."

"Really?"

"It wasn't an accident. Apparently some acquaintances of Tony's."

Ward came around to the other side of the bed, stood close to Dave, and kept his voice down as he spoke. "What is it with this woman?"

"I'm not sure."

"But there's something."

Dave nodded. "Everything for a reason. There are no accidents."

"Well, allow us a few."

"But there's a connection. We're supposed to be helping each other, only I'm unclear why at this point."

"Maybe you just like her."

"I do like her."

"You know what I think? I think she's young and pretty and wounded, and we know what that means to you."

Dave eyed him sharply, but then nodded. "Yes. Yes, we do."

"Well, I trust you. For a man with so many bad habits, you still manage to surprise me once in a while."

"I surprise myself."

Ward walked toward the door and left Dave with, "They'll have the papers in an hour or two."

"Thanks."

"Don't thank *me*. I didn't do anything. As usual, you're two steps ahead of me. Three steps."

As he neared his apartment, Tony realized that he had again failed to plan well, plan ahead, and without a doubt was heading into further serious trouble. Why couldn't he catch a break?

He slowed the Explorer as he came into the block where his apartment building was. As the SUV crawled forward, Tony took careful note of every car, truck, and van parked bumper to bumper on both sides of the street. He circled the block, still looking at every vehicle sitting curbside, and finally was satisfied that he didn't recognize any of them. Still, as he pulled into the narrow drive that led to the carport behind his building, he remained vigilant. But apparently he was okay.

For the time being.

At least he could get some things together, fill a suitcase, and high-tail it out of there before the Goon Brothers cornered him.

Still, he should have been more careful, he told himself as he took the stairs to the second floor and picked through his keys to find the one for his apartment. He should have planned ahead. He should have anticipated—

Oh, hell.

He didn't need his key.

The door was unlocked.

Tony didn't care for this at all. Had they been here already? Now he thought he noticed the smell of something like gasoline in the hallway, fuel of some kind. Had they burned down the restaurant and then come here and gotten in and then left to look for him because they couldn't find him?

Hurry up, asshole, Tony told himself.

He eased the door open with the toe of his shoe, looked in, heard nothing, moved one step inside—

And was very powerfully shoved from behind, so strongly that he almost went to his knees.

"Jesus, stop!" Tony yelled.

The door slammed behind him, and he turned to see Manny, the young tattooed Hispanic man with the bad attitude and two gold teeth. Manny stood rigidly, hands behind his back, his powerful arms bent to emphasize his biceps, preventing Tony from even thinking about trying to return to the hallway.

"Stop it," he said again.

From behind him, Ray Sawyer, the young white guy with the bent nose, said, "Tony, Tony, Tony."

Tony turned to face him.

Ray was smiling. He leaned forward with both hands on the back of

Tony's couch and told him, "I been looking for this money you say you got. Can't find it. Lots of other stuff, but no money. You got it shoved up your ass or something? Are we gonna have to cut you open ass-end first to get this freakin' money?"

"I don't have it yet. I told you, two days."

"And I told you, now. My hope was that what with the restaurant, if something happened to your restaurant, you would say, 'Oh, yeah, now I freakin' remember where I put Ray's money,' and you would retrieve it. Maybe between there and coming here it crawled up your ass. Maybe you recall what you done with it. That's something I would do. I would make sure I got the money as soon as possible, so nobody started to cut it out of my ass."

"I will get it."

"But that's just me. I can't speak for you." The smile dropped, and Ray looked past him to Manny and nodded.

Tony turned.

Manny moved toward him.

"Wait!" Tony told him. "Please!"

But Manny moved faster than Tony anticipated. His fist was in Tony's gut before Tony even saw the arm move, and then Manny's other fist was on his mouth, and Tony fell backward, into his sofa.

Where Ray caught him by the hair with both hands and yanked his head back so that Tony, barely able to breathe, gasping powerfully, looked upward and saw Ray's face upside-down.

"Now," Ray said.

Tony nodded, or tried to, and made a squeaking sound.

Ray yanked him up by his hair and pushed him forward.

Tony said, "Ow, ow, ow, *ow!*" and shook his head and rubbed it with both hands as he scooted to the edge of the cushions.

Then he reached for the phone.

Ray said, "You hid the money in the phone? Manny, did I look in the phone? No?"

Tony told him, "This guy can get it."

"Can he get it *now?*"

"Yes."

"Then you may call him."

His hands were shaking, his stomach hurt, his body hurt, and his lip felt as if it were already a dozen sizes too big for his face. Tony took the phone book from the shelf of the end table, found the number of the hotel where Neely was staying, and pressed the keys.

"Room eight?" he said, and waited, and then: "Neely, I need your help. About the money. I need the money." He wasn't speaking well; he was drooling.

On the other end of the phone, Neely said, "Oh. The money."

"You have to help me. This is Tony."

"Of course."

"These two need their money and they need it now and I told them you have it. You have to let me come over *now*."

"All right."

Ray took the phone from Tony's hand and said to Neely, "We're all of us coming. Has Tony made it clear how important this is?"

"Yes."

"And I take it you have the money?"

"I'll be waiting for you."

"Good," Ray said, and there was a note of actual relief in his voice. He reached past Tony and hung up the phone. "Come on."

"Did he say he'd be there?" Tony asked him.

"Yeah. We're all going to go get the money. Let's all go right now. Get up."

Tony did so and stood in front of the couch as Ray came around and told him, "Show Manny your right hand. No, your left. Left hand."

"Why?"

"Just do it, shithead."

Uncertainly, Tony eased his left arm out as though he were offering to shake Manny's hand.

Manny stepped forward from guarding the door, gripped Tony's forearm with his own left hand, and, with his right, took hold of Tony's hand. He very quickly jerked the hand toward him, pulling Tony's wrist apart, and then twisted it away, creating a serious dislocation.

"Jesus Christ!"

"Not the worst we could do," Ray smiled at him. "Not the worst we could do! Just something to keep in mind."

"You broke my wrist!"

"And not your neck," Ray reminded him. "Not your legs. Not your dick. Your freakin' hand, okay?"

"It *hurts*."

Ray said, "We could break something else so that it could take your mind off of your painful wrist. You want Manny to help with that?"

"God, no."

"I mention it, is all."

"I can't move it. It's swelling."

"You'll wanna put some ice on it and get it looked at. After we get the money. Come on. Manny drives. You get to be the navigator."

"Jesus, this *hurts!*" Tony whined.

"Which is exactly the purpose of doing it," Ray affably reminded him.

Tony had no idea what would happen when they reached the motel. He hoped that it would take so long to get there that they'd never reach it, or that they'd get sideswiped by some monster rig, just get creamed all over the highway, over, done with, worry no more. Jesus, how did he manage to foul up everything he touched? No matter what he did, he stepped in shit, and if he was walking on the cleanest sidewalk in the world, he would find the puddle of shit to step in. Even if it wasn't there, he would make it happen. It was his gift, to make shit happen where there had been no shit.

They took the big red Silverado that Tony envied. Put him in the middle between them, Ray driving and, saying not a word, Manny on the other side, sitting with one big tattooed arm hanging out the passenger side window.

God, Tony thought, please, please let us get hit by a falling tree before we get there.

What the hell was he thinking, getting Neely involved in this?

He was thinking that he had nowhere else to turn, he knew no one else, he was dead and buried if he didn't do something, so basically he was stalling for time by phoning Neely and asking for his help.

Still, Neely had played along perfectly. Went along with it as though he had been part of it every step of the way. Never missed a beat.

So what was in it for him? Tony wondered.

Or was Neely just going along with it without having any intention whatsoever of saving Tony from himself?

Who knew if Neely was even going to be there, at his hotel room?

Time to find out. Manny steered the big pickup into the parking lot of the little motel and let it coast to a stop in front of the door to room eight. Turned off the engine and looked over at Ray, who kind of shrugged, opened his door, and got out.

Tony followed as Manny stepped down from his side of the truck.

Ray pushed Tony on the shoulder and told him, "Go on. You first."

Tony nodded and walked up to the hotel room door, with Ray right beside him. As Tony prepared to knock, Ray told Manny, "You wait out here."

"Got it."

Tony knocked on the door.

Waited.

Knocked again.

Tried the door handle.

The door was not locked. Tony turned the knob and stepped in, with Ray immediately behind him.

Same as always. Dark room, drapes drawn, lights off. In the dusk of it, the small room, Tony and Ray both saw Neely sitting in a chair on the other side of the round table that sat in front of the window.

Neely said, "Welcome. Turn on the light."

Tony asked him, "You sure?"

Neely said, "Go ahead."

Tony did.

The brightness caught him and Ray by surprise, the lamps in the room all coming on at once.

As soon as Ray got a good look at Neely, he asked, "Geez, what happened to you?"

"I walked into a wall."

"You are unlucky." Squinting, he stepped in front of Tony. "It smells like shit in here. Give me the money."

Neely said, "Right here." He pushed the chair back and got to his feet, meanwhile lifting into view a baseball bat that he'd been holding in his right hand, hidden by the table.

He brought the bat up and down as quickly as possible, and although Ray started to say something on the order of "Whoa!" or "What!" the heavy end of the bat landed on his left shoulder, immediately breaking the collar bone and pushing nicely into his neck, too. He gasped and choked for air and fell to his knees.

Tony jumped out of the way and hit the wall behind the door.

So that, as Manny came in, hearing the scuffle and pushing the door open hard, it almost hit Tony in the face.

Manny walked into the second swing of the baseball bat. He tried ducking when he recognized what was happening, but the bat was already halfway to him. It caught him perfectly on the left side of his head, perfectly.

Broke his jaw. Crushed his ear. Sent him down to his knees as he emitted a muffled sound, the only thing he could get out.

Neely helped him go down the rest of the way by hitting him on the side of the head again with the baseball bat. Manny dropped and did not move.

Ray, groaning, carefully touching his broken collar bone, began swearing as he got to his knees.

Neely put him down with a direct strike of the bat, also along the left side of the head.

Watching from the wall, Tony was surprised that he didn't see blood or brains or flesh or something flying in all directions from the end of the bat.

Neely looked over at him, then stepped away from the two on the floor and carefully settled the baseball bat into the nearby corner of the room. He suggested to Tony, "Tie them up. They must have some rope in their truck or some tie-downs."

"I can't."

Neely noticed the left hand. "Well," he said.

Tony asked him, "Can you fix it?"

"No, not really. Put some ice on it."

"Shit."

"And get to a doctor."

"There was no reason for them to do it," Tony complained. "I was cooperating. Where did you get the baseball bat?"

"A baseball bat," Neely told him, sitting again at the table, "is a good all-purpose tool. Like a gun. Or a knife. Plus you never know when you might actually have the chance to play a little baseball."

"You're funny."

"No, I'm not. Where did you meet these two again?"

"All I needed was to borrow a little money. Tide me over. Ava's no help. Ray used to come in once a while and I kind of got to know him. I knew who he was, but all I needed was a little money. I didn't think this would happen."

"My friend, this always happens. This is always what happens."

"What do we do now? You really messed them up."

"Wait here."

Neely went outside to his car, opened the trunk lid, rooted around among the things he had stored there, and retrieved a roll of silver duct tape and a can of black spray paint. Then he looked in the bed of Ray's pickup truck and found some tie-downs.

When he came back into the hotel room, he closed the door, wrapped duct tape around the mouths and eyes of both Ray and Manny, and secured their hands and feet with the rubber tie-downs. He finished by binding them both together, back to back, with long stretches of the silver tape.

Neely then pushed furniture out of the way, the bed, a few chairs, whatever could be moved. He placed the two bound, unconscious men in the small space that remained between the furniture and the entrance to the bathroom, then used the aerosol can of black paint to spray a circle around them on the worn old carpet.

"What are you going to do to them?" Tony asked.

"I'm going to kill them. Actually, no. I'm going to do something a little worse than that. Leave now."

Tony nodded.

"Go to the hospital. That wrist isn't improving."

"What do I do after that?"

Neely told him, "These two are not a problem. We have something else to worry about. I'm not sure Dave is dead."

"How do you know?"

"I know. Now go. Take their truck. Here." He leaned over Ray, found the keys to the truck in a pocket of his jeans, and gave them to Tony. "I'll call you tomorrow afternoon. And lose the truck on the way home. Park it someplace and take a cab."

"Okay." More worried than ever, Tony hurried out.

Neely listened to the big Silverado drive away, then took out candles and placed them just so, beginning to prepare his ritual.

An hour later, after Neely himself had left, a young businessman walking past room eight, on his way to get a Coke from the vending machine at the end of the building, detected a horrible smell coming from under the room's locked door, and he noticed a black stain like paint crawling, actually crawling, up the inside of room eight's window—a black stain, all that remained of two men's souls, crawling on the glass.

He ran the rest of the way to the motel office, coughing as he did, and took out his cell phone to call the police.

10.

Late that afternoon, Ava phoned Dave. She was surprised, however, when Dr. Ward answered.

"He's home," Ward told her. "I'm out here with him."

Ava told him about the restaurant's burning down and her suspicion that Tony was responsible for it. More than a suspicion; she was certain of it.

Ward asked her, "Do you know where he is now?"

"No."

"And where are you?"

"Home. Why?"

"Dave's concerned about your safety."

"What does he suggest?"

"Why don't you come out here?"

"Where? Dave's house?"

"Do you know where it is?"

"No."

"Inverness," Ward told her. "I'll give you directions. It's tucked away. You'd go right past it if you didn't know it was here."

Ava told him, "Give me a second," found some paper and a pen, and then took down the address and directions. "Is this all right?" she asked. "Me coming out there?"

"We had a talk. Don't ask me to explain because he keeps things to himself, but he's concerned about you. He feels there's some sort of connection."

"Because of what happened?"

"Yes. And I know that he doesn't think well of your associate."

"No one does. Give me forty-five minutes or an hour to get out there, okay?"

"I'll be here for a while yet. I want to make sure he's well enough to be left on his own."

"*Is* he okay?"

"Yes. He has his own way of coping."

"I can only imagine."

"I'll wait until you get here. Phone if you need to. For any reason."

"Thank you, Doctor."

Relieved, very relieved when she hung up, Ava had to admit that, yes, she surely was uneasy with the fact that Tony was capable of doing anything and that, without a doubt, it would be the easiest thing in the world for him to kill her, or try to. Him or whoever it was who had tried to kill Dave.

What had she told Dave the first time they talked? *"A taxi comes around a corner out of the blue and almost runs me down. My power has gone out a couple of times. I'm waiting for one of the Bowery Boys over there to pull some stunt."*

And what had he said?

"My concern is that you're not safe."

Ava grabbed her keys and hurried out.

It took more than an hour to find the house; she had, in fact, driven past it twice, having backtracked in her attempt to scout it out. Maybe Dave had used some of his sorcery to make sure no one could find it even if it were in plain sight? Finally Ava phoned Ward. He guided her to a gravel driveway nearly impossible to see from the main road. Enclosed tightly on both sides with trees, it looked like no more than a path or a bike trail. And the driveway veered left almost immediately, further disguising it within the shadows and trees so that it was effectively invisible.

Ava could understand why Dave might want such secrecy and reclusiveness, but other elements of the slow drive through the woods provoked in her a further great sense of caution. There were odd wooden shapes sitting atop stakes positioned both close by and much farther into the woods. And oddly shaped—what were they? more talismans?—hung suspended by chains from branches high in the trees. Some of them blinked when they caught the last of the sunlight, watching her and winking at her, these magical items, from their perches in the leaves.

"Do you have a talisman, too?"

"I protect my home with them."

The house itself was easily a quarter mile distant from the road. The crowded trees gave way abruptly to a large gravel area with a very old, stately house on one side and an oversized garage on the other. Ava saw

Dave's Audi, presumably towed there by Ward or by a tow truck, if one could have gotten back here, and next to it a BMW, likely Dr. Ward's, parked near a flagstone walk that led to the enclosed porch. She parked beside the BMW and, when she got out of her car, found herself taking in a good full breath of fresh air, moist air, damp and deep with the scents of earth and trees, pines and nuts and ripe life in every direction. Had she become so unaccustomed to appreciating what was around her every day that what was here seemed new? Or was she alert now because she was anxious? Or was this place incredibly rich with a sense of life because of Dave and his sorcery?

I've crossed a boundary, Ava thought as she took the steps to the tall back door, and realized how peculiar it was for her to think that way. She wondered where the thought had come from.

Or perhaps she didn't.

Ward opened the door just as she approached and held it open for her as Ava stepped inside. They were in a sort of alcove that led immediately into a large old kitchen, all dressed in wood and with a stone floor.

"Welcome," Dr. Ward told her. "Here." He took her coat and led Ava through the kitchen and down a hall into a front room.

On the way, she noticed other rooms off both sides of the hallway, all of them dimly lit, beautifully appointed, many decorated with or completed by antiques, and all of them so quiet that they seemed to be not so much areas to be inhabited or enjoyed but refuges—another peculiar thought. The front room was to the left; to the right she noticed a tall stairway.

The room was spacious. There was a large bay window and, across from it, a tall fireplace. Comfortable chairs and divans were available, and a small wet bar with a wooden counter stood by the fireplace.

Ward had clearly made himself at ease. A glass of whiskey with ice was on a side table under a standing brass lamp, and the Chicago *Tribune* that he'd presumably been reading was folded and resting on the seat of the chair beside the table.

He asked Ava if she'd care for something to drink. "Brandy? Wine?"

"A glass of white wine, yes."

"Liebfraumilch?"

"All right."

He poured her a glass from a bottle on the wet bar and walked it to her. Ava thanked him and sat on a divan cater-corner to the chair Ward had taken.

Each of them sipped, and both of them stayed quiet for a moment

"…was she alert now because she was anxious?"

before Ward said, "I suppose there's no way that this doesn't seem a little uncomfortable or odd."

Ava smiled. "You're right."

"Are you hungry?"

"I am."

"Because I'm going to make myself a sandwich before I go. There are some cold cuts in the refrigerator."

"Then cold cuts it is."

He led her back into the kitchen, took lunch meat and condiments from the large steel refrigerator, and set everything out on a marble-topped island. Ava sat on a bar stool, put slices of ham on a bun, and tore into the sandwich, appreciating the fact that she was sincerely hungry.

She asked Ward, "He's here?"

"Upstairs. He'll be down shortly, I think. You're to be congratulated. Till now, I've been the only person he's let come out here. What happened to your restaurant? It's completely gone?"

"Oh, yes," Ava assured him. "And I'm sure my ex-partner was behind it. This has been going on for more than a year."

"I'm sorry."

"Did Dave say anything to you?"

"No. He'd keep anything like that confidential, any business dealing."

As she ate, Ava gave Ward the background, telling him about the car accident that had killed her husband and broken her leg and about what she presumed were attempts on her life, her certainty that Tony had taken money from loan sharks, either to keep the restaurant running or to cover who knew what other expenses, and now her conviction that he had burned down the restaurant for the insurance money. Either that or the characters he'd taken money from had burned it down to punish him for not paying them back.

Ward surprised her with the comment he made in response to all of this. "It's hard not to fall into the traps of life, isn't it?"

"You're right. It is."

"We have something sad in common. My wife was killed in a car accident about ten years ago."

"I'm sorry."

"It happened just before I met Dave. He may have a point when he says that life takes away with one hand but provides with the other. And it was odd that an accident with the truck almost killed me, too. Life has funny patterns."

"You sound like you've studied philosophy, too."

"You can't live life seriously without becoming a philosopher. And you certainly can't become familiar with a man like Dave and not wonder about what holds everything together."

"Can I ask you something kind of personal? About you and Dave?"

"Ask."

"You're a doctor. And he kills people. I mean . . . he does. Do you— How do I want to say this?"

"How do I reconcile that?"

"Yes."

Ward told her, "I do whatever I can to save lives and not hurt people. Fact. That's what doctors do. But with Dave, I've run into something that's bigger than my professional philosophy. I'm a rational person, and I like to think I behave rationally, but most of us don't behave rationally most of the time, do we?"

"We certainly don't."

"That puts me at a disadvantage. I continue to wrestle with it. I'm not happy about it. I like being rational, but I know it's not sufficient, not the way life digs in and hangs on, not with some of the characters out there and the things they do." He smiled at Ava. "How's that for an answer?"

"It's a good answer."

He noticed that she'd finished her sandwich. "More ham?"

"No. Thanks. That was enough."

"Wine?"

"I'll have another glass of wine."

He fetched the bottle from the front room and half-filled her glass.

Ava sipped and, from her perch, watched the last of the sun go down, heavy with its golds, purples, reds. Brilliant bursts of light slid across the glass of the kitchen windows, and outside, long shadows filled the expansive yard that stretched away to the wood line.

"I like sundown," she told Ward. "Always have. I don't know why."

"It can be peaceful," he told her. "In Hollywood, they call it the golden hour. As the sun goes down, you get a certain kind of light that isn't as harsh as regular daylight."

"The golden hour."

"We can sit outside."

He led her through the alcove by the back door and down a short stairs to another door, which let onto a wide stone patio. The patio was enclosed by a low brick wall. There were comfortable chairs and a few tables. Ava sat in a cushioned sofa; Ward took a metal patio chair and continued enjoying his whiskey.

Ava watched the sunset, closed her eyes, opened them. She glanced at Ward.

He was watching her.

"How does it work?" she asked him.

"Sorcery?"

"Yes. I've had just enough wine that I might be able to understand it if you go slowly. I'm rather intelligent."

"Oh, you're intelligent enough. Do you know the story of the blind men and the elephant?"

"Remind me."

"You have five or six blind men trying to figure out what the elephant is. One of them has the trunk, and he says, 'It's a snake.' Another one has a leg, and he says, 'It's a tree trunk.' Another one has the tail, and says, 'It's a rope.' And so on."

"None of them appreciates the whole thing. They only understand a part of it."

"Correct. And that's where we are with things like this. When you start medical school, you're told that half of what you're going to learn is not true, only we don't know which half. So you continue to learn for the rest of your life. That's what I try to do."

"Seems like you're pretty good at it."

"It's like looking at the sunset. On the one hand, it's just wavelengths striking our retinas. It can be explained in a material way, and that's all it is. But that's like saying that poetry is nothing more than the letters of the words. My father used to say that the greatest book ever written was in the dictionary; all you had to figure out was how to arrange the words in the right way."

Ava chuckled. "He was right."

"Yes, he was. It's how to arrange them; that's what it comes down to. And we're the ones who arrange them. We're the ones who have to figure out how all the parts of the elephant go together so that we aren't blind anymore and can see what we have."

"And it's right in front of us all along."

"Correct."

"And if we figure it out," Ava said, "then we're the ones who see how beautiful the sunset is even though we know it's just atoms or—what were they?"

"Wavelengths."

"Wavelengths. And the wine is just wavelengths?"

"Wavelengths and atoms."

"Then that explains why it's so refreshing." Ava finished and set the wine glass on one of the tables. "This is good," she said.

"It's very dry," Ward told her.

The sun was nearly gone, and the woods were dark, the lawn all of shadows, and the only light on the patio was that coming from deep within the house, finding its way to them through the kitchen window. They were very nearly shadows themselves, no more than voices in the dark. They might have been the blind men in the story.

"What I think it is," Ward said quietly, "is that it takes place on a very small scale, not a big one. People think in terms of spirituality and what they automatically do—we all do it—is to look up at the sky. That's where heaven is. That's where the gods are. We automatically think in those terms. But what the mystics have proved and sorcerers, too, these seekers, is that it's not outside us. It's inside us. You know, they have this saying, 'As above, so below.' It makes you think that they're talking about heaven above, the skies above, and we're small, we're below, down here. You practice magic and you're the one who's below heaven. I don't think that's true."

"So what is it?" Ava asked him.

"I think that the phrase was deliberately said that way or mistranslated to put people off the track. They said it that way to discourage people. There have been a lot of imposters and fakers, and there have been a lot of people who weren't very clever who were fooled, or who needed to be fooled, and this has been going on for thousands of years. The people who really knew what they were doing, it's as though they were giving a child busy work and telling the child to go over there and color while the grown-ups have a serious discussion. And it worked; the ruse worked. All of us now think that sorcery and magic are foolish. Astrology—foolish. And that's what the magicians want us to think. They don't want us to take it seriously. They want to be left alone, and if all of us accepted these things as fact, they'd have no peace. It's a very ancient spiritual tradition to give the mob just enough to keep them interested so that they do what they're told and leave you alone. Only the initiated are given the truth. Only the ones who are worthy of knowing the truth are burdened with it. There's still a little of that attitude in medicine. In most of the disciplines, I'm sure."

"But whoever it is who tried to kill Dave—he's not worthy."

"Of course not. And in every spiritual tradition there are renegades and outlaws and liars who managed to master the skills and understand the truth, and then they bastardized it. But that doesn't change the fact that there's a fundamental truth, a few people are able to access it, and some of those people master it. Dave is one of them. And this other man, too, presumably."

"So what is it?"

"It's small. It's smaller than the drop of water on the side of your glass. Everything we can see, and I mean the whole universe when you look up at the sky, everything—let's say it fits into the drop of water. So think how small we are."

"Incredibly small."

"'As above, so below.' What's above us isn't the sky; it's us. We're the big ones; we're the universe. Everything on this level, where we are now, this is the above. And the below is inside us. That's where the universe is for spirits and demons and angels, whatever they are. They're inside us."

"So when Dave does whatever he does, what is that?"

"He's enlarging something that's inside us to our size. He's calling it out from within himself. It's within all of us. People think that it's like calling up a spirit from another dimension or from the sky, like in a movie. Maybe it *is* another dimension, but it's inside us, or inside the world we're in."

"But when I was close to him," Ava said, "when he was having his attack . . . I know what I saw, or what it looked like I saw. It was like I was having a nightmare. They're in me?"

"Maybe. And in me, too. Or perhaps in Dave, and because you were so close to him, you were seeing what he saw."

"That's the impression I got from him. We even had kind of the same dream."

Ward told her, "If I had the answer, I'd tell it to you. But at least I've learned to accept this for what it is. I don't dismiss it, and I don't pretend it's not there. Dave doesn't have a lot of patience with people who act superior to these things. Lots of people are very smug when it comes to these matters."

"And you're not. That's not a question. I'm not insinuating anything," Ava said. "I must be feeling the wine."

"I'm learning from him. I like that."

"But you don't know any magic yourself?"

Ward shook his head. "I'm here to make sure he stays healthy. He needs to stay healthy."

"And he's not?"

Ward was silent for a moment. "I'm wondering whether to let him tell you, or whether I should."

"Tell me what? I don't think you have to tell me anything."

"But I think he wants to. You saved his life, is why. He sees something important in that. The way he sees things, people's lives keep intersecting and intersecting, and it can go on that way for a long time. He sees a purpose in it. And he's obligated, I suppose, because of what you've done for him."

"So is he sick? You said he needs to stay healthy."

"Not sick. Old. Older than he looks."

"Really?"

"He's at least a hundred years old."

"Are you serious?"

"More than a hundred. But physically he's no older than forty. I've drawn his blood. I've run tests. Listen."

A noise caught them both, a moan, a low sound, something vocal, that Ava thought must be coming from the woods but then realized was above them, and issuing from deep within the house.

"What is that?" she asked.

"Shh." Ward waved at her.

The low sound went silent.

Ward said, "I haven't heard a voice like that in a long time."

"What was it?"

"I think he's just released a spirit. That's what he calls it. Releasing a spirit."

"It sounded like someone was dying."

"No. He's freed something. To keep everything in balance . . . there's a tradeoff. I suspect that he's gotten his health back, but to do it, he set a soul free."

"A soul?"

"It's part of what happens," Ward told her. "When he kills someone, he owns that person's soul, and he can do whatever he wants with it."

11.

They sat quietly for several long minutes, Ward saying nothing more and Ava asking him nothing. She listened for more of the voice to come, but it did not. She looked at the woods and, shifting in her seat, realized that she had had enough wine to make her light headed.

Then she and Ward heard footsteps in the kitchen, and the sound of the refrigerator door opening.

"Well," Ward said, getting out of his chair. "Here he is, back among us."

Ava followed him into kitchen, walking a bit uncertainly.

Dave, in jeans and a loose sweatshirt that he seemed to have pulled on hastily, was standing at the island, downing glass after glass of apple juice. The refrigerator door was open behind him, surrounding him with a nimbus and putting the front of him in shadow so that, when he looked up and spoke, Ava thought he was a dark cloud with a voice.

"What time is it?" he asked them.

"About half past eight," Ward replied.

"And it's still Friday?"

"Yes," Ava said.

Dave turned, closed the refrigerator door, and walked to the kitchen entrance, where he turned on the ceiling lights, fluorescent and bright. Ava and Ward both winced and blinked, but the brightness did not seem to affect Dave.

Ward stepped to the island and placed his whiskey glass there. "I've filled her in on a few things."

Dave looked at Ava.

"Like how old you are," she said to him.

He nodded.

Ward asked, "Are you okay?"

"Yes."

"Come sit. You want a shot of B$_{12}$?"

"No. Just more fluids." He finished the glass he had on the island, then said to Ava, "Your restaurant is gone?"

"Yes."

Ward said, "Bring the juice, but come sit. I have to be going pretty soon. I have an early start tomorrow."

They went into the sitting room, Dave taking the chair Ward had been in and Ava moving to the divan cater-corner to it. Ward carried the bottle of apple juice to the wet bar, poured Dave another glass and walked it to him, then sat in a lounge chair in a corner, between Dave and Ava.

Ava reached just inside her blouse to pull out the pendant she was wearing. "I still have this," she told Dave.

"Good. Hold onto it." He looked at Ward. "I know who this is, finally."

"Who? Is that the voice we heard?"

"Yes." He asked Ava, "You understand?"

"Dr. Ward explained."

"That was the soul of a man I killed a very long time ago, and he served me well. I don't like having to go on without him; he was wise. But he told me what I needed to know." He said to Ward, "His name is Neely. Arthur Neely. I never knew about him before now, and I'd almost forgotten about his brother. His brother was named Carl."

"What happened?"

"They lived in Arizona. Carl hurt several important people."

"He was a sorcerer?" Ward asked.

"Yes. A few of them actually tried to help guide him, but he thought he was very clever, and you can't have people running around who don't know what they're doing. So they hired me." Dave said to Ava, "This was the late nineties."

She nodded.

"I tried reaching Carl, but he's weak and doesn't show up very often. Arthur, the brother, blames me, and he wants me to answer for it."

"This is who's helping Tony?" Ava asked.

"Yes."

"Is he strong? He must be," Ward said.

"I'd like to know how he tracked me down. I have my suspicions, but I'm not certain. I know what I'd do." Dave went quiet and sipped his apple juice.

Ava's cell phone rang. She'd left it in her purse beside the chair and after a few bars of some light jazz, she found it, took it out, and flipped it open.

As she did, she told Dave and Ward, "Tony."

Dr. Ward frowned.

Ava said into the phone, "Slow down! You're all over the place. Take a breath." And then, "Never mind where I am. Where are you? Oh, really? Oh, really? Well, you deserve it. Stop it! Just tell me—" She looked at Dave and rolled her eyes as she listened to Tony barking on the other end of the call. After a minute of that, Ava said to him, "Where was this? Where? Did you call the police? Tony, did you call the police? All right, stop. No, tomorrow afternoon. Then tomorrow evening. You better make up your mind before I hang up. Fine. I understand. Fine." She closed the phone.

Dave and Ward looked at her, waiting.

"He's scared to death," Ava told them. "He just got out of the emergency room. Those two characters he owed money to—they're dead. The ones with the truck. They broke one of his hands, but then Tony and—what was his name?"

"Arthur Neely," Dave told her.

"Him and Neely killed them, or Arthur Neely by himself."

"Where?" Dave asked her.

"A motel in Palatine. I can call him back and find out which one."

"It can wait. We can find it. What else did he say?"

"He's scared of Neely. Really scared. He has to meet him tomorrow afternoon, and he thinks Neely wants to arrange things in some way so that he can really kill you, and he wants Tony to help him. He says that Arthur Neely knows you're not dead."

"That was inevitable," Dave told her. "He'd sense it, sooner or later. Is that all he said?"

"Yes. He's backed himself into a corner, and he knows it."

Ward stood and stretched, pushing his arms out in front of him. "You could have waited," he told Dave. "If you'd waited, you would have found out anyway that this was the man you want. I think you're pushing too hard, too soon. "

Dave shrugged. "I learned some other things."

Ward yawned. "I have to go."

Dave nodded but did not stand. He looked out a window, deep in thought.

"Ava," Ward said.

She stood and walked with him into the kitchen and then out the back door, following him down the steps into the gravel parking area.

"Are you going back tonight, too?" Ward asked her.

"Yes. What time is it?"

He held out his wrist and looked at his watch. "Nearly ten."

"Then I should be going, too."

"Make some coffee."

"I will."

"You still have my card?"

"Yes."

"Use it and call me if you need to."

"I promise I will. Thank you for everything you said tonight."

"Not at all."

"I mean it. I appreciate it."

Ward was silent for a moment, as though hesitating, and then he spoke frankly to Ava. "Don't be afraid," he told her. "Don't be afraid of Dave. I'm sincere about that."

"Okay."

"You can't be—" He paused briefly, then said, "When I was a boy, there was a man at my mother's church who must have been close to eighty. Maybe older than that. I thought he was the oldest man on earth. His grandfather had been born a slave. What this old man knew about life, what he'd been through, what he knew going back to his grandfather and farther back than that— Despite all of that, he was at ease with life, and I realized, years later, that he could only be that way because he'd experienced just about everything you can. At some point, life doesn't have any more surprises for you. I used to listen to that old man, and you'd have thought I was listening to life itself talking. I'm telling you this because Dave reminds me of that old man."

"Does he?"

"With him, you're listening to life itself. That's why I'm telling you not to be afraid."

"Thank you."

Ward yawned and said, "I am now going to listen to some good jazz and drive carefully and then get myself some much-needed sleep." He went to his car.

Ava walked back inside and returned to the front room. Dave hadn't moved. He remained slumped in the same posture, staring out the window.

She told him, "He's a very good person, isn't he?"

"The best." Dave looked at her. "Cool head, warm heart. Like the Buddha. I depend on him. He keeps me sane."

"I should get going, too."

"Sit for a bit."

Ava moved to the divan.

"When you meet Tony tomorrow," Dave told her, "I'll go with you."

"Whatever you say."

He fell quiet again.

Ava opened the silence by asking him, "How do you think Arthur Neely learned so much magic? He must really want to hurt you."

"He probably didn't know enough to understand what he was getting involved in until it was too late. Like me."

"Really?"

"Whatever we do, if we practice it enough, that's what we become, and no matter what it is that gets you there, we all finally reach the same place, anyone who's disciplined enough. I've met monks who have more in common with intelligent criminals and statesmen than they do with other priests. You reach a point where you see how everything is more alike than different. True of Neely, too, apparently."

"But Dr. Ward—" She deliberately stopped herself.

"He doesn't kill people. But he's seen behind the curtain. It's very tantalizing."

"So what's behind the curtain?"

He looked at her now. "A world full of wonder," Dave explained. "Our world. Who we are. We're all living a big lie, Ava, but that's what we're taught. The big lie is this: We persist in thinking that we can improve on what we've been given, and so we persist in doing damage to what nourishes us. A woman I knew said that it's as if we keep eating pieces of our own heart. We're slowly devouring our hearts, and we think that by doing that, we're nourishing ourselves, but actually, we're killing ourselves. The world is our heart. Do you know what the word *maya* means?"

"No."

"Well, you've heard the term, being in a state of grace."

"Yes."

"Every culture has the same story. We used to live in a perfect world, and we lived in harmony with that world, and then we lost it. We fell. Human beings are the fallen. We're cast out of Eden, or we're trying to reach a state of grace. There was a golden age, and we fell from that. Plato called it the dimension of perfect forms. *Maya* is the knowledge that this world is an illusion, and beyond it is something perfect."

"So what does it mean?"

"The golden age is inside us. The perfect world is the world just as it is, when we're open to it and not distracted. We know that when we're children. It's the sense of wonder. It's a state of awareness. You know that everything is exactly as it should be, and you're taking part in something that's a wonder simply because it *is*, because it exists. That's what we experience when we perform sorcery. That's what all of us have lost."

Ava said, "It sounds like what my roommates used to try to do in college when they meditated."

"They were on the right track. Once you've experienced the wonder, you realize how dirty and small we are, and what a mess we've made of the world. We're devouring our own heart. And we keep doing it because we think we're smarter than the world. We're very clever. And we're killing it and killing ourselves." He asked her, "Why do you have a bird on the business card for your restaurant?"

"I don't know. I like birds. They're free. They can fly above it all. They can fly above it all and not get caught up in everything." She smiled. "Maybe they have a sense of wonder."

"See? You sense it, too. We all do. We remember when there was a sense that life's perfect."

Ava asked him, "I want an honest answer to this. Am I going to stay safe, or should I be prepared for something really bad?"

"I don't know."

"Would you tell me if you did know?"

"Yes. Yes, I would."

"I have another question. How are you and I connected? That's the word Dr. Ward used. That's what you said. We're connected."

Dave leaned forward, pressing his hands together. "You saved my life. That wasn't supposed to happen."

"Why not? Wasn't I supposed to be there?"

Dave told her, "I've already pushed things further than I have any right to. I should be dead by now. But here I am, and because of that, I'm knocking things off balance. The fact that you're even here talking to me is because I'm interfering with your life. So you've wound up being involved in part of my life simply because I've lived long enough for us to meet. Did Ward tell you about my daughter?"

"No. You have a daughter?"

He looked out the window. "My wife died a long time ago, and my daughter had an accident when she was eighteen. Her name is Miranda. I've been trying to correct that mistake ever since."

"I'm sorry. Is she in pain?"

"She's dead, Ava. Her body's dead. Her soul is trapped. I made a mistake, and now my daughter is trapped. She's not part of this world, but she's not in the next one yet, either. She's not dead, and she's not alive. She's caught . . . ." He held his hands in front of him, palms facing each other, fingers spread, as though describing or molding the space between them. "She's here," he said. "She died in 1931."

"Dear God."

"That's why I'm staying alive, and why Larry helps me. I need to try to save her. It's as simple as that. I'm a father. I love my child. I've used the arts to twist a lot of things out of shape, and I've stayed alive long enough for you and me to meet and for you to save my life. So whether you're paying me back for something or whether I owe you, that's what's happened. I have my own little corner of the universe here, and I've knocked it completely out of synch with everything else. Now you're part of it, too."

He had been born in 1886, Dave told her, in rural Ohio, and likely would have been just another of humanity's anonymous lives, here and gone, except that he was bright, he very early fell in love with books, and he was dissatisfied with the brief education typical of the time for farm children. When he turned fifteen, he ran away and never returned home. He made his way from town to town, working hard to earn money, until he arrived in New York City and settled there in 1905, when he was nineteen.

He worked as a laborer for a while in a stable because nearly everything in the city was still horse drawn at that time, but he found himself attracted to the theater. He acted in some small plays, none very successful, and wrote a few, as well, and for a time performed in very early silent movies, when they were one reel long, no longer than ten minutes, and were filmed on rooftops in midtown Manhattan or in the woods in New Jersey. Here he met his wife, Evelyn, an actress; they married in 1911 and their daughter, Miranda, was born in 1912. He continued to try to write but eventually found work in a bookstore, and by the mid teens had become partner with the owner. When the owner died in the influenza epidemic of 1918, Dave took over the store. And he would have continued to live a normal life in this fashion were it not for the Great War, or more specifically, what followed the Great War, the great period of spiritual exploration and the occult underground of the 1920s.

The scale of death and destruction of World War I, the enormity of lives lost, the sheer scale of the devastation, was profound. Everything that anyone had felt secure with before 1914 had been turned upside-down; by the millions, people sought answers for their anguish. Americans and Europeans turned to spiritual exploration, and by doing that, they opened doors to wonder that had been closed since before the Age of Enlightenment. It was very much a precursor of the same sentiment that happened with the youth movement in the 1960s, Dave told Ava, except that in the 1920s, particularly in Europe, the need was driven more by morbid hunger than by narcissism and self-indulgence.

There had been an underground of interest in the occult in the late nineteenth century, and sorcerers had secretly set up lodges in London, Berlin, Dublin, New York, and a few other major cities. The magicians of the Golden Dawn and other leagues had been involved in what were essentially temper tantrums and altercations, but these were nothing compared with what occurred during and after the Great War, when sorcery was used for the first time in the modern era as it had not been since the Middle Ages. This new generation of sorcerers caused a great deal of trouble, much of it misunderstood or misattributed at the time. For example, there was a French gendarme who became too interested in the after-midnight frolics of certain sorcerers and witches; he suddenly died of a heart attack one night in his sleep. Well, how could it be proved that he died as a result of sorcery? Couldn't it merely have been his own bad luck or ill health? Or what of the businessman from Philadelphia, traveling by ocean liner back from London, who decided that he could fly like an American bald eagle and leaped overboard one night to drown at sea? Did he act in this fashion because he had been manipulated by a sorcerer whom he had double-crossed by business trickery? Or was it more likely that he had had an excess of port and, drunk and happy, tipped over the side? This is how sorcery works. And in the 1920s, for the first time in a very long time, in small ways and large, sorcerers began to regain their art and exert their influence on their fellow human beings.

Dave himself had become interested in the arts during book-buying trips to London and Paris in the 1920s. On his return, he had joined a secret league in 1923. His wife, too, in the very modern spirit of the times, joined the sorcerous group. Much of the activities seemed to be an excuse for sexual experimentation among the members, who considered themselves very sophisticated, but there were also real experiments into the mysteries, the great arts, and Dave soon learned that he was adept at these things.

But open warfare occurred between a league of sorcerers in Berlin and those in London and New York. It was very much anticipatory, Dave explained, of what would happen under the Nazis. During the 1920s, practitioners of the dark arts in Berlin, Hamburg, and Vienna targeted enemies in England and America. Without going into detail, Dave made it clear to Ava that his wife had been killed during these first sorcerous wars, and that he himself murdered several men and women by means of the arts. This underground warfare of shadows, dreams, demons, secret energies, and spiritual forces reached a climax during the worldwide depression of the 1930s. Dave, in trying to protect his daughter, Miranda, from dark forces, had inadvertently harmed her. This was the source of his misery: he had misworked a ritual, and now Miranda existed between two worlds, unalive but also not dead, her spirit in suspension, untouched by enemies but unable to grow and move on.

The secret sorcerous wars of the early twentieth century continued. During World War II, occultists and practitioners of the arts in England, France, and America conducted their own parallel war, a shadow war, against the magicians of the Third Reich. Dave became adept at taking souls, and each that he took he kept under his control, so that eventually he had at his command more than a hundred spirit lives who would answer him as he wished. They saw for him where his own eyes could not see; they listened for him when his ears could not hear; and they killed for him when he so ordered, so that death came unattached to anything in this world—this sad, damaged, poisoned, modern world, as lost as a blind giant crashing through a forest, this angry and ambitious modern world.

He had moved from New York to live in many places and settled into a life, or a series of lives, whereby he assumed a name, settled someplace, and let it be known that he could be of assistance to anyone who wished to make use of his peculiar skills. Many sorcerers, after the devastation of World War II, gave up the arts willingly, wounded and chastened by what they had undergone. Others, their hurts still open and painful, continued the fight around the world, but their numbers decreased as time moved on. Dave had worked for a time as a publisher and editor in Pittsburgh, then served as a police detective in Akron, Ohio, and finally had come to Chicago and settled himself at this house.

The Arthur Neelys of the world, he told Ava, were to be expected, now. Given his experience in fighting the sorcerers of the Third Reich, no doubt he should have been more aware when he and Ava were at the library. But the Arthur Neelys are always out there.

His long life had taught him many things, but this above all else: that believing part of the world to be good and part of it evil was a pretense and, even worse, a willful lie. In this world to which we have caused so much damage, surely many of us concocted this deception as a means of making sense of what seemed senseless. Still, this is no excuse. To say that good and evil exist separately is to say that part of a person is good and part of that person evil, and so he or she should be cut in half. Then the evil part could be discarded so that the good part can get on with a blameless life. How likely is that to happen?

"Life is about staying alive," Dave told Ava. "It's not about good and evil. This is true for everything that exists. Believe me—everything. Here or anywhere else."

The evening was turning late, Ava had had several glasses of wine, and her day had been exhausting. She was very tired. Still, when he was done, she had one more question for Dave:

"How does it work? What does it feel like? Your art."

And Dave told her, "It's the freshest air you've ever breathed. It's the sweetest water you've ever drunk. It's the warmest sunlight. You feel so alive, you realize the life you've been living is like you've been buried alive. You've been living underwater, and now you can breathe. There's nothing between you and the air and the water and the sun. You've heard people say that we're spirits in a material world? We're spirits having a physical experience?"

"Yes."

"It's true."

"Is my husband okay?"

Dave told her, "Probably."

"Can I talk to him? Seriously. I mean it."

"No. I'd advise you not to. Don't try it."

Ava nodded and leaned forward. She told Dave, "I'm asking because… I'd give anything to have him back, even for an hour. I want Steve back. I just want to hold him one last time. I never had the chance to hold him one last time."

He watched her.

She said, "I'm sorry. I'm very tired."

He stood. "Don't try driving back. I have a room here where Larry stays sometimes. Sleep there."

"I will if you insist. I'm beat."

"It's upstairs."

He led the way. The room had its own bathroom, everything was private, so Ava bade Dave goodnight and, as soon as he closed the door, undressed and got under the covers. Immediately she felt as though she were sinking into a cool bath or relaxing on a pleasant stretch of beach or in a meadow.

She held onto her talisman and fell asleep that way, and had no nightmares. But she dreamed, not only of the restaurant burning but also of Steve. He returned to her in her dream, distinctly and clearly, and she spoke with him so effortlessly, she was so pleased to see him again after all this time, that she abruptly awoke, sat up in bed to get closer to him, and understood then that it was three in the morning and that she was in Dave's house, and alone.

Ava lay there for several minutes, still partly in her dream, not wholly awake and not wishing to be.

She thought she heard something, did not, and then received an impossible thought that she could not dismiss.

Still not fully awake, still wanting to talk with Steve, still seeing his face, she got out of bed, pulled on her blouse and pants, and left her room. She went down the hall to where she surmised Dave's room was. She pushed open the door.

It was a large room and not wholly dark. Light came in through a large window.

She heard Dave stir, and she went to his bed and quickly slid under the covers beside him.

He said something, as alert as though he were awake, but Ava whispered to him, sincerely, "Please, hold me. Nothing else. I just want to be held for a while." He put his arms around her, and she relaxed there and slept.

12.

hen she awoke, Ava was alone. The clock on the nightstand on the other side of the bed showed that it was nearly ten in the morning. Could that be? Had she really been so tired? Was it because of the wine? Or had Dave done something to her so that she would sleep soundly and long?

She did feel refreshed, she realized—but chilly. Although she had her blouse and pants on, she wondered if she should wrap herself in a blanket or whether Dave had a heavy robe in his closet. She felt the coolness of the morning as she crossed the polished wooden floor to the closet. The doors opened outward, and Ava was surprised to find so few clothes there. A sufficient number of shirts and dress pants and suits, yes, but not much more.

There were a few dressing gowns, and Ava took one of these, a silk one. It was big on her; it covered her nearly down to her ankles, and she had to roll up the sleeves.

The bedroom was large, as sizable as the living room in her own home, and nearly as complete, with bookcases along one wall, an entertainment center with a big-screen television, a standing lamp and comfortable chair in one corner, and a private bathroom. It was nearly an apartment in itself. A single large window overlooked the back yard, the wide lawn and the trees, and the only thing unusual about it, Ava noticed, were the charms tacked to each of the four corners of the window frame. More talismans.

She walked to Dave's mirrored bureau, drawn there by the many items decorating it. Framed photographs, primarily, but also an art deco cigarette lighter, surely from the 1930s and still in remarkably good condition, and two glass figurines no more than eight inches high, elongated sylphs or nymphs, clearly from the same period or earlier. And there were four children's wooden blocks, their letters painted in bold colors, but with the paint worn now and chipped away in places. Old. Well used and old.

In the antique frames were photographs of what must be Dave and his wife and his daughter. In the first, probably Dave's wedding photo, he and the woman were dressed very elegantly, looking as though they had stepped out of a silent movie or an ad in old magazine. When had he said he'd gotten married? 1911? In another beautiful frame, the border all done in silver ivy and leaves, was a family photograph, Dave and his wife and the daughter, surely no more than three years old. A third photo was of Miranda herself, perhaps at age fifteen or sixteen. She and her mother shared striking good looks. No wonder the wife had been an actress; she had the eyes and face and figure for it, the beauty and, clearly, the commanding presence.

The fourth and last photograph was from a later period and was of an attractive blond woman, German or Scandinavian. The quality of the photograph was different from that of the others; surely photography had changed from 1911 to the 1930s to whenever this picture had been made. The 1940s?

"Her name was Astrid," Dave said behind Ava.

She put down the frame and turned to face him. "I hope you don't mind."

"No."

"She's quite lovely. Were you married to her, too?"

"No. We were on opposite sides during the war. She was a Nazi."

"But she meant something to you."

"Yes. She was gifted. She's the only person who ever frightened me."

"Really?"

"It's true."

"Not even this Neely character?"

"Not yet. We'll see."

Ava picked up what she presumed was his wedding photo. "Your wife?"

"Yes. That's Evelyn."

"She's very beautiful. Your daughter, too. Is that her?"

"Yes."

She set down the frame and told Dave, "I have pictures like this all over my house. Of Steve and me. It never goes away, does it?"

"No."

"Even for someone like you?"

"No."

"Sometimes I think if I concentrate hard enough, I could walk into one of our photos and stay with him in there. Like the photograph is real, and I'm not."

"Do you want some breakfast?"

"'Her name was Astrid,' Dave said…"

"Yes. And a shower."

"Right through there."

"I won't be long."

"Take your time. I can fix whatever you'd like when you come downstairs."

Dave left, and Ava removed the robe, looking all the while at the framed photographs, and thinking all of the while of her husband.

The first thing to do, Dave told Ava over toast and coffee, was to get to the motel where the two smart guys with the pickup truck had been killed. He'd already been online; the news accounts told him which motel it was.

"I'd like to come with you," Ava said.

"You might be safer here."

"Why is that?"

"You'll be better protected here."

"But don't I have this?" She dangled the talisman. "I'm more interested than ever. That's understandable."

"It is."

"What do you think is there? Something this man left behind?"

"Yes. Everything we do leaves something behind. We all leave a trail."

"Do we?"

"Even if it's just an echo. It's inevitable."

"Is that why you stay here when you can?" Ava asked him. "Because otherwise people could find you, like outside the library?"

"That's exactly why. I left something behind, or Neely's good enough to have found me some other way. It's possible. Anytime I do something, I'm vulnerable for a moment."

"Even when you practice magic?"

"It's all part of the balance, Ava. It's all part of the give and take. If you want to participate, you're going to be vulnerable."

"Just like everything else in life."

"Yes. Just like everything else."

"People don't want to die thinking that they don't have the answers,"

Dave said. "That's where it starts. If we die without knowing what all of this means, then what's the point? Life has no meaning. No one wants to be that alone. We're all born in the middle of something, and we don't want to die without knowing the ending. But there are a lot of gaps to be filled."

"So we create religion," Ava said. "Or anything else that fills that need."

"Correct. And then those of us who are paying attention, we spend the rest of our lives trying to get past that. To get to the truth, we have to unlearn what we've been taught."

They were in Dave's Audi, driving with the top down. It was a little after noon, and the morning was unusually warm. Dave was taking his time getting to the motel, not hurrying.

He wanted to draw Ava out.

He asked her, "Isn't that why you're here? Why you wanted to come along?"

She considered it. "I don't know. Maybe."

"I think that whatever your life had been, when the accident happened and your husband died, you got shocked. This is what happens. It's as though you were sleepwalking, and it shocked you awake."

"That's a good way to put it."

"A lot of people have described it that way."

"But that's what happened. You're exactly right."

"And now, more shocks. Tony. Me. Neely. What have you walked into?"

"That's exactly how it feels."

"We fall back on habits," Dave said. "I've noticed it in myself. We get a shock, we're thrown off balance, and then we try to fit in whatever happened with what we're comfortable with, even though everything's changed. But the more we try to do that, the less sense it makes. Something happened. We can't go back to doing what we're told. We're seeing life for what it is."

"But even then," Ava told him, "people need to have habits. That's not a bad thing. Maybe whatever gives you a little comfort is a good thing."

"I agree. And I have great respect for our capacity for denial. People walk around with tunnel vision until the end of their days. But sometimes the shock is too great. It's hard to stay in denial and fall into habits after that."

She looked at him. "So is that you or me?"

"Both of us, probably. Maybe it's what brought us together."

Ava told him, "I have to tell you something. That picture of your daughter—I saw her in my dream."

"When?"

"In my nightmare. The night after you had your attack by the library?"

"Are you sure it was Miranda?"

"Maybe it wasn't. But I saw a lot of ugly things and in the middle of it all, very quickly, I saw the face of a beautiful young woman. It didn't belong there, but there she was. Although I have to tell you that I hate this feeling that there are things inside me and I can't control them."

"But it seemed to be Miranda?"

"When I saw her picture in your room, I knew it was her. It's the first thing I thought of. And there's something else."

"What?"

"Remember when I told you about the woman who read cards for me? She said that my marriage would be happy, but that my husband would die young. I would struggle after that, but I'd meet someone who would show me the truth."

"What else did she say?"

"I should have written it all down, but I didn't want to. I didn't want to think about not having Steve around. It felt like bad luck."

"Well, she saw this coming," Dave told her. "I've met a lot of people with that gift."

"Don't you have it?"

"No. I'm blind, like everyone else."

"Whatever's going on," Ava said, "you can see why I feel the way I do."

She closed her eyes and enjoyed the breeze, the open car, then looked at the trees and big houses zipping by. Horses grazing behind fences, way out in a field. Trees. She asked Dave, "What do you actually think you'll find at this motel?"

"Whatever's left of them. I want to get inside the room, so when we get there, I'd like you to wait in the car. Although I'm debating asking you to talk to whoever's in the office, just to keep them out of the way."

"I can do that."

"Good. They probably haven't had it cleaned up yet."

"I know this sounds weird, but do you know how he killed them?"

"No. But there are only so many ways that make sense."

"How many ways have you used?"

He looked at her. Ava wasn't being sarcastic; she was sincere. "All of them," Dave told her. "Name one, I've used it."

"Against the Nazis?"

"Against everyone."

"So what was it like to kill Nazis? They were the bad guys, right?"

"They die like anyone does."

"Do you have their souls now, too?"

"Yes.

Ava said, "I've been carrying this around since the accident, but—I really want to know what happens to us."

"After we die?"

"Yes."

"Ava, I'm sure your husband is fine."

"But do we like . . . hang around for a while? Or watch what people are doing who are still alive?"

Dave told her, "Mostly we rest. Most of us have to put up with so much crap while we're here that we take a nice, long rest."

"Unless they ran into you."

"True. I don't give them any rest."

"Do we feel any pain after we're dead?"

"We do if we caused pain on earth."

"Really? Then you're going to feel pain, aren't you, if you die?"

"Lots of it," he told her. "Lots of it. I have a lot to look forward to. We're here."

They'd come down Northwest Highway through Barrington and into Palatine, with its strip malls on both sides of the road, the auto tune-up shops and the insurance storefronts. At the south end of the village, just before the intersection with Route 53, they saw the motel on their left, opposite the Metra train tracks and a road leading south into a series of industrial parks. Dave made the turn and drove slowly past the office at this end of the L-shaped building. Through the office window, he saw no one at the counter.

Good.

He parked in the corner of the L, turned off the car, and got out.

Ava asked him, "What do you want me to do?"

"Wait here. No. Stand by the door. If someone comes by, pretend you're trying to look inside."

"I won't have to pretend."

She stepped out and joined him at the motel room door. Lengths of yellow plastic tape—Police Line Do Not Cross—were hanging on either side of the door frame; probably some kids had come by and torn the tape, trying to get into the room.

Dave removed a thin wire or metal rod from inside his jacket pocket and a credit card, it looked like, and began working at the lock and bolt.

Ava said, "I'm surprised they don't have electronic key cards."

"A place this small, it's not worth the investment."

"Did you notice the window? It's all black."

"I know."

"Did the police do that? To keep people from looking in?"

"No. There." He'd worked the lock free. "That's what's left of the Doofus Brothers in there."

"What do you mean?"

He replaced the pin and card inside his jacket pocket. "When we die," Dave told Ava, "we're free. Call it your spirit or your soul."

"That black stuff is what's left of their souls?"

"Yes."

"Is that what I saw on you when you were on the sidewalk?"

"Yes. I was dying."

"And that happens when we die?"

"It does if you're killed by a sorcerer."

"And *you* kill people that way?"

"Listen." He pushed the door open and looked inside the room.

"I don't hear anything," Ava said. "Dear God, it smells horrible!"

He opened the door farther and stepped inside. "If someone comes, tell them you think your brother was killed here."

"All right."

He closed the door, and Ava heard nothing more from inside the room. The terrible odor lingered, and she wondered what it was—burned flesh? day-old blood? what sorcery smells like? *what souls smell like?*—even while she tried to keep from imagining what must be in there.

She stepped to the window and touched her fingers to the glass, trying to establish what the black material was like, right there on the other side. It resembled black shoe polish or some kind of dried film, like something that had spilled on the inside of an oven and gotten baked there onto the enamel.

That's what happens to our *souls?*

"Help you?"

She looked up and saw a tall, elderly man walking toward her down the sidewalk in front the motel room doors. He didn't seem angry to find her there.

"No. Thank you. I was just looking."

"That room's locked. Somebody got killed in there."

"That's what I heard."

"Did you need a room?" He looked from Ava to the Audi behind her, then back at her.

She told him, "No, not really. I'm sorry if I seemed flustered."

"What can I do for you? Come down to the office."

"No, I'll be all right." Ava didn't feel panic, exactly, but she was unnerved by having to explain herself at this moment, when on the other side of the window, right there on the inside of the glass that had that black material on it—

The door opened behind her, and Dave stepped out. He asked, "Ava?" He saw the old man.

Who told him, "You can't go in there. The police were in there. I'm waiting for the crew to come clean it."

Dave told him, very politely, "I know. I just wanted to check before they get here."

"Oh?"

"Ava, are you ready?"

"Yes."

He touched her arm to steer her back to the car and offered his hand to the old man. "Mr. Dwight?"

Somewhat uncertainly, the old man put out his hand. "My name's Brinkley."

"Brinkley. Sorry. Dwight was the man I spoke with yesterday. Thanks for your time."

"Can I ask your name?"

"No need," Dave told him, and smiled.

Brinkley watched as Dave got into the Audi, started it up, and backed out, then nodded and grinned in a most friendly fashion as he drove out to the highway.

"Very smooth," Ava told him. "I was flustered. I don't know what got into me."

"Well, we got what we came for."

"Did we?"

He pulled onto Northwest Highway, shifted gears, and tapped the left side of his jacket. "We did."

"Dare I ask?"

"The usual," he said. "But if I'm lucky, there's something left of Neely in here, too."

"So now what do you do?"

"I do a little mumbo-jumbo," Dave told her. "I do some old-fashioned mumbo-jumbo like mama used to do."

13.

She wanted to know. She wanted to know first hand.

"Do we feel any pain after we're dead?"

"We do if we caused pain on earth."

She wanted to know, and she told Dave that as they drove back to Inverness.

She wanted to be there when he did whatever he was going to do with whatever was left of those men in the motel room.

It wasn't morbid curiosity, Ava told Dave. It wasn't some attempt to conquer her fear. And it certainly didn't mean that she wanted to learn how to do what he did, perform a ritual, and practice the arts. She wanted no part of that.

But she wanted to know—the truth of it.

She wanted to know that such things could be done on earth.

She wanted to know that what she had been through, the accident, Steve dying, dealing with Tony, the restaurant, what had happened to Dave, all of it, as trivial as it might be to anyone else, or as mundane or ordinary, not at all unusual—

She wanted to know that it fit in somewhere, that she was part of something, that she hadn't been the victim of some joke, that her life wasn't a joke, that she wasn't something ridiculous, that people aren't simply . . .

Ridiculous.

"Actually, that's one of the more profound philosophical dilemmas," Dave told her when they returned to his house.

"It doesn't feel particularly profound."

"You want to know that whatever you are, the sense of you, that you belong."

"I don't want to be forgotten," Ava told him. "And if I can see Steve, or talk to him. Is that possible?"

"It's possible. Is that your wedding ring?" He looked at her left hand.

"Can we use it?"

He told her they could but warned Ava, "Don't get sentimental. The spiritual world is no place for that."

"Really?"

"It's as hard as a rock."

She watched him, sipped some of her wine, and wondered whether he was thinking then of Miranda. What must it mean to have done such a thing to his own daughter? What was it even like, how she was now, and for him to have lived for so long with this guilt, this knowledge—this fear for her?

She asked him, "Why are you really letting me do this? I know I drive a hard bargain, but why?"

"Because I believe you when you say you saw Miranda in your dream."

"I'm not lying. It was her."

"I understand. Whatever it signifies, I want you inside the circle with me when I do this."

"So what exactly do we do? One of the women at the restaurant claims she's a witch, but I never took her seriously."

"Did she light candles to attract love and money?"

"Yes, she did."

"We won't be doing that," Dave told her. "Once we're inside the circle, you don't move. You stay put; whatever happens."

"Okay."

"You'll endanger us both if you don't."

"All right."

"You'll hear them talk. We might see something; we might not. I want to find out about Neely, but these men were weak in life, so I'm not sure how much I can learn."

"But we'll be safe inside the circle?"

"Safer than any place else on earth."

"As long as I don't move."

"Correct."

He let her into the attic, the one place no one else ever was allowed to visit, not even Larry Ward. But that's how important it was to him that she might be in contact with Miranda, might know something he didn't know. Anything. Miranda was more important to him than anything else and anyone else. Whatever it meant, his daughter appearing to Ava in a dream, Ava should be here with him.

A light switch was at the top of the stairs. Dave turned it on and went in first.

There was one ceiling fixture. It glowed directly above them as they came in, and it gave out just enough light that Ava could see generally, no details, but sufficiently.

The room smelled sweet. It was the oils and the scents of all of the candles he must have burned.

The attic was not as vacant as Ava might have thought. It was large, in fact, with a tall ceiling, and all of it covered in solid wood. At the far end of the room were an old wooden desk and chair, filing cabinets, and a bookcase that contained not only books but also scrolls, of all things, actual scrolls.

Ava did not ask to look at them.

In the middle of the room was a large circle painted on the floor, and a table inside it, and across from it, attached to the attic wall, a tall mirror, very old, at least six feet tall, in an extremely ornate metal frame.

At this end, as they came through the door, was an altar. There was no other word for it. It was large and draped in dark cloth. On the far side of it was a tall chifforobe. From some of the drawers, Dave took metal bowls, candles, boxes of incense, jars of oil, wooden matches, and a knife, a long, decorative knife, as well as a small envelope, a coin envelope.

He carried these to the wooden table that stood in the middle of the large circle. The circle was of blue paint and at least eight feet in diameter, and with a row candles set just inside it.

Dave returned to the chifforobe and began undoing his shirt.

"Where do you want me?" Ava asked him.

"Beside me. At the table. Face east."

"Which way is east?"

He nodded. "That way." East was the wall with the mirror on it.

She walked into the circle and asked him, "You have to take your shirt off?"

"I don't have to, but I prefer it. I'll be naked, Ava."

"Oh."

"It's easier that way."

"Do you want me to be naked, too?"

"Not necessary."

"Okay."

He removed his shoes and socks and then his pants and hung them on the closet side of the chifforobe.

"I mean, I can do that if it's necessary. I don't care."

"Whatever you'd like to do."

"Okay." But she decided not to.

Naked, he walked to the table, set out three candles, and lit them, then walked back toward the door, reached for the switch, and turned off the light.

As he came back toward Ava, she watched him, then looked away and smiled.

Not bad for a hundred. Maybe one hundred is the new thirty . . . .

Dave struck another long wooden match and, crouching, proceeded to light the twelve candles around the edge of the circle. Then he joined Ava at the table.

"Breathe in and out slowly and calmly," he told her.

"Okay."

She did, and he guided her until she felt herself relaxing.

He lit a number of candles on the table and the incense in one of the bowls. The smoke lifted, very sweet, and Ava noticed that it didn't annoy her. It was pleasant.

Dave poured oil into his hands and rubbed the oil over his chest, belly, arms, and shoulders, and up and down his legs and buttocks and the small of his back. He dripped a bit more of the oil over his shoulders, then wiped the last of it across his neck and over his face.

"What is that?" Ava whispered to him. It seemed proper, for whatever reason, to keep her voice low.

"It's a mixture of my own."

It was earthy, it reminded her of trees and of soil, perhaps of wild berries, anything earthy and ripe and wild.

He picked up the long knife, holding it in both hands, and told her, "I'm going to speak Latin."

"Why Latin?"

"For me, Latin is best. We call this up from inside us, Ava. The cadences work for me. It comes from within. It will help me if you keep quiet."

"I promise."

"I'm going to draw the circle now. Once I'm finished, you don't leave until we're finished. If you're uncomfortable, you should go now."

"I prefer to stay."

He marched slowly around the inside of the circle and moved the sword up and down and in a circular motion as he said, "*Impero manes venire mihi*," repeating it several times, and, "*Suscitate*." I order the spirits of the dead to come to me. Awaken. "*Suscitate, manes. Suscitate. Servate me.*" Awaken. Serve me.

He placed the knife on the table, faced east and, with his back to Ava, held out his open right hand. "Let me have your ring."

"My wedding ring?"

"Let me have it. I felt warmth."

Ava removed it—it came off easily, she'd lost so much weight recently—and pressed it into Dave's hand.

He set it on the table in front of him and moved his hands over it, back and forth in some kind of pattern, and repeated, "*Suscita. Suscita.*" Awaken. Awaken.

In front of him, just beyond the perimeter of his circle, above the candles, as dim as it was, movement occurred. In the mirror, the reflected candle flames, and the lights on the floor as well as those on the table, grew brighter. The reflections intensified.

Ava whispered, "Dave—"

"Shh!" And in a whisper of his own, he ordered her, "Close your eyes. I'll tell you when to open them."

She did.

But she could sense the light strengthening in the mirror, growing brighter.

"*Suscita. Suscita . . . .*"

She kept her eyes closed.

"*Suscita . . . .*"

But she heard a knocking sound—

"*Suscita,* Steven."

A knocking sound, tap tap tap, which Steve and she had always done, their little signal. He would tap, and she would tap in answer. From a room, in a hallway, on a window. I'm outside in the garden, tap tap tap. I'm here, tap tap tap. And though her eyes were closed, Ava could tell that the light was bright, almost harsh, and she couldn't resist, she opened her eyes just as Dave said, "Now."

She screamed.

"*Steve!*"

And nearly fell to her knees. Reached out for the table and held onto the edge of it as Dave caught her arms to hold her up.

He was in the mirror. Not all of him. The top of him. His legs were somewhere in the darkness at the bottom of the mirror, and he seemed to be walking. Could he still walk?

"Steve!"

He saw her and smiled, then turned his head to one side.

Ava looked at Dave. "This is a *trick*! This is some hocus pocus *trick*!"

"It's not a trick."

"This is *sick*."

"*Look at him!*"

It was Steve, it was Steve, it was him, and he saw her. Now he had his legs, and behind him—what? Trees? What kind of trees were those? Were they even trees?

Steve lifted his right hand and tapped it against the air, and the knocking sound came as though he were striking wood.

"Does he recognize me?"

"Ask him."

"Steve!" Her face was wet, the tears were coming and coming, Ava wiped her eyes, dear God, it was *him*, and he was looking at her, she reached toward him—

Dave pushed her arm down. "Stay inside."

"Is that him?"

"It's him."

"Am I dreaming? Is it real?"

"It's real. To him, we look like that."

"It's like a dream."

"Yes."

Ava asked Steve in the mirror, "Are you in pain?"

He shook his head no. He said something to her.

"I can't hear you!"

He spoke again, and she heard only part of what he said, "*I wish*," but heard it in a different way, not with her ears but with some other part of her, heard it with her whole body.

"*I wish*."

What did it mean?

"Steve, I can't hear you," Ava told him, and she sobbed. She asked Dave again, "Is it really him?"

"Yes. Doesn't it feel like him?"

"It *does*. I *feel* him. We're *both here*." What had she said to Dave? "*I don't want to be forgotten*." And to the mirror: "Steve, I am so sorry this happened!"

He smiled at her again, looked off to his right, then again at Ava. He said to her, once more in the voice that resonated throughout her body, in her muscles, deeply inside her, so that she knew as well as heard—

"*I wish we could have, too.*"

And that was sufficient.

She couldn't see any longer; her vision was blurred, she was doing nothing but crying. She had to sit, sit.

Dave helped her to the wooden floor. She crouched there, then fell onto her left hip and wiped her face.

"It was him, it was him, it's real."

She looked at the mirror again, could see the bottom part of it under the table, but it was dark once more, with the candle flames reflected in it, small and bright.

"Why couldn't he stay?"

"How long would you have wanted him to stay?"

"I don't know."

"He has no sense of time. He doesn't have a clock."

"It's too—" Ava looked up at Dave. "It wasn't a trick?"

"No."

"That's what we did. We tapped like that. Like when he came past the kitchen or if he was at the computer and I was, I was doing laundry. It meant we loved each other." She told Dave, "It was too easy."

"Was it really?"

She let her head drop and cried openly. "It was too easy," she said, sobbing, getting air into her, crying. "He shouldn't have died so fast. He shouldn't have died."

Dave let her cry.

Then, "I felt something as I drew the circle," he told her. "I thought it must be him. Ava, I have to continue."

"I know." But she didn't move.

"Stay there," Dave told her. "Don't move outside the circle."

"I can't because of the candles."

"Just stay there."

She did, and wondered if she should, in fact, crawl under the table and sit there, but she didn't.

She sat where she was, aware that Dave was doing more, but thinking of Steve and what she had seen.

Was it him?

It had been him.

I don't want to be forgotten, she thought. I don't want to be alone.

And what had Steve said to her?

"*I wish we could have, too.*"

Everything between them was in that sentence. Everything. The two of them.

Ava watched as Dave tore open the coin envelope and dropped whatever was in it into a brass bowl. Hair, no doubt, or blood, or skin, maybe. He sprinkled in incense, then dropped a match into the bowl.

Whatever was in it came up in an orange-green flame.

"*Venite, viri irati.*" Come, you angry men.

Again the lights in the mirror blossomed, enlarging as though providing an opening, and first one, then another something came from within the mirror, white blots of brightness from far back in its depths, from around its edges, and enlarged into faces, then into bodies with arms and hands and legs.

They screamed, the faces, low the way men bring out their hurt, hard, low.

"Tell me," Dave ordered them.

The white guy with the bent nose—he said nothing. All he could do was scream. Although he was a ghost or spirit or no more than a phantom of light, his face darkened as he let out his agony, and blood poured from his eyes and nose and mouth.

"Stop!" he howled. "Stop it!"

Then he turned around and around, spinning slowly, holding up his phantomy hands and wiping his hands over his face.

His hands caught fire, and his face, and he shrieked and ran backward in the darkness, disappearing. His screams still came from far away, from far back in the depths of the mirror, whatever was there.

Ava whispered, "Dear God."

The other one, the Hispanic man, all tattoos, didn't scream but kept his mouth tightly clenched as his head moved from side to side. His head jerked back and forth, left then right, again and again. It was though he suffered from a neurologic disorder so that his head did as it wished, separate from him, left and right, back and forth.

"Tell me!" Dave ordered him. "Or are you as stupid as your friend?"

"What did he do to us?" the Hispanic man asked Dave. "*Está comiendo mi alma!*" It's eating my soul! "*Ayúdame! Ayúdame!*" Help me!

"Give me something," Dave demanded. "Where is he?"

"Look!" said the Hispanic man, staring at Dave. He came closer, reaching with his hands, trying to come through the mirror. "*Mírame!*" Look at me!

But then he was covered in a shadow, and he screamed and drew back.

His face filled with blood, too.

"Afraid!" he said loudly, and moved away, beyond the left frame of the mirror.

"Did he torture them?" Ava asked.

Dave didn't reply. He gestured again over the burning incense and waved his hands over the candles.

The candle lights in the mirror moved, sliding away to the right, and greater darkness was within the mirror. It looked as though the darkness in the mirror were moving to the left, as though Ava and Dave were on a train or a car, looking out the window.

The movement stopped. They saw the Hispanic man, a white blur, very far away within the mirror. He screamed from that distance, in a small voice that carried. "*Ayúdame! Ayúdame!*" Then the darkness took him. He whooped from the deep distance.

Dave made a gesture of finality. The mirror quieted. The reflected candle flames settled.

Ava stood and looked at him.

He was sweating, covered with oil and sweating. He was gasping, said he was very thirsty, and she felt thirsty now, too. Why? It was the same as after her dream, but what was it about being within this circle and looking into the mirror that made her so dry? What was it taking from her?

"Father."

Dave groaned.

Ava looked.

Another white space in the mirror, a white form, horizontal this time, floating, it seemed, or relaxing, a young girl, Miranda, looking at them and smiling, nude and as ghostly perfect as glass or frost, reclining on her stomach as though she were lying on a beach or floating elegantly under water.

"Father."

And Dave, dry mouthed, unable to say her name clearly, spoke as well as he could, "Miranda."

"She is a help, Father," Miranda said, and, floating, looked at Ava and smiled at her. "You are to help him."

"How?" Ava leaned forward on the table. "How?"

"Because of who you are. Because he has answered your fears."

"How will I help him?"

"No fear," Miranda told her, and looked at her father. "There should be no fear."

Dave yelled at her, "I need more than this! Please!"

"No fear," she repeated. And then, "I am tired."

She went into the darkness, or the darkness took her back into itself. The mirror settled again.

Ava, dry, thirsty, looked at Dave. "What did she mean?"

"I'm not sure. She's not strong enough to tell me everything I need to know."

"What did she mean, no fear, that there should be no fear?"

"You don't need to be afraid any more."

She thought of Steve.

And of her own fears. I don't want to be forgotten. I don't want to be alone.

And of Miranda.

You are to help him. Because of who you are. There should be no fear.

14.

eely phoned at three that afternoon and told Tony to meet him at the motel he'd moved to. This one was in Rolling Meadows.

Tony could tell the guy was still very tired. Doing this shit really did take a lot out of him. But Tony complained about having to meet him at another motel room. "Can't we, like, meet someplace where it doesn't smell so bad?"

"Just get here as soon as you can," Neely ordered him. "I'm going to finish this. And get me more Gatorade."

"Right, right."

Bastard, Tony thought. But what could he do? You have gotten yourself boxed in real good this time, Tony my friend, my very dumb friend.

On the way over, he took a long detour and went by the motel in Palatine where Neely had killed the two guys. The pull was irresistible.

But there was nothing to see. Tony coasted into the parking lot and stopped in front of room eight, and while the engine idled, he looked at the door and the window. The door was X'd with two long strips of yellow tape, the kind used at crime scenes, and the window had been blacked out with shoe polish or paint. Nothing. Not even a bad smell, at least that Tony could tell from where he was sitting.

Farther down the lot, an old man came out of the office. He carried a big, beat-up red toolbox and headed away from Tony, went around the corner toward the front of the building by the highway.

Time to go, Tony told himself. No sense drawing attention to yourself.

He looked again at the door and window and couldn't imagine what had gone on in there.

Or maybe he could.

He bought two bottles of Gatorade on the way to Neely's hotel and burned up a couple of Camels, as nervous as he was.

But Neely told him to be at ease.

"You have nothing to worry about," the sorcerer told him as he closed the motel room door behind Tony.

Neely reached for one of the bottles of Gatorade, opened it, and began gulping it down. He sat on the edge of the bed. "How's that wrist?"

"Hurts like hell. I can't use it for shit."

"Well, you don't need it for this."

"For what?"

"Your partner at the restaurant. She can get to Dave, meaning that I can get to Dave. You get to help. That's it."

"That's it, what?"

"You tell her I want something of Dave's. Anything. Spit, snot, anything."

"You tried that before," Tony reminded him.

"And *she* bungled it!" Neely said loudly.

Tony, sitting at the table by the window, pulled back in his chair. This was the first time he'd seen Neely angry.

Then the sorcerer smiled, if you could call it a smile. "Find out what she did. I'd like to know. It wouldn't have to be much." He looked at Tony. "You find out when you see her."

"All right, all right."

"And tell her to stay out of the way this time."

"Why can't you leave it alone?"

"What?"

"I screwed up. Now I lost my restaurant. What do I do now? Maybe I should just walk away. I ain't made for this. Maybe I should just leave it alone."

"You aren't me."

"No, I'm not."

"You're afraid."

"I *am* afraid."

"Well, let's not leave it alone, okay, Tony?"

Neely set the bottle of Gatorade on the nightstand and got up from the bed. As he approached Tony, he slipped his right hand into his pants pocket. Just that fast, Neely pulled out a pocket knife, flipped it open with a snap of his wrist, and sliced Tony on his left cheek.

"Jesus, Neely!"

Neely pulled a handkerchief from his back pants pocket and handed it to Tony. "Wipe the blood and give me the handkerchief."

"Why?" Tony asked him. "I haven't done anything to you!"

"And now you won't."

"...pulled out a pocket knife...and sliced Tony..."

Tony wiped the side of his face and returned the stained handkerchief to Neely. "So now you're gonna kill me like you killed Ray and Manny."

"But they're at peace now. No more worries and cares."

"Bastard."

"I have no reason to kill you, Tony. All I want is Dave. Help me, or get out of the way. Now go talk to your friend."

Tony didn't move.

"Now."

"Go to hell!"

"Do whatever you want in your spare time," Neely smiled. "Right now, I just want Dave Ehlert. So get him for me."

It had been him. Steve. Really him. Really there, and talking to her in his own voice. Still . . . alive.

"*I wish we could have, too.*"

And everything in her that Ava had brought to that moment, seeing him—

I don't want to be forgotten. I don't want to be alone.

Dave poured her another glass of grape juice, and Ava drank it half down before moving her eyes from the window, from the darkening back yard, still looking at Steve, to see Dave across the kitchen table. He'd taken a shower and was in a heavy robe, now.

Ava told him, "I was thinking about what you said, how you described it, like a golden age, or people looking for something perfect. Like a state of grace."

"Is that what it seemed like to you?"

"Kind of. Not when I was looking at him or feeling him, but right now, thinking about it— Yes. It's as if we were together again but in this really extraordinary way."

"You weren't burdened by being on earth," Dave told her. "That weighs us down."

"Is that it?"

He nodded.

"I told you I'd do anything to be with him once more, just for a little bit, but now that seems . . . I don't know. He was . . . happy."

"Maybe he was happy that he saw you."

"He could see me, couldn't he?"

"Certainly."

"He said, 'I wish we could have, too,' and I think I know what he meant."

"What?"

"It's like he was reading my mind. I wish we could have had more time together, or I wish the accident hadn't happened. Something like that."

Dave watched her.

"What about your daughter?" Ava asked him.

"What about her?"

"I mean, what *she* said. About me helping you. Did it help to have me there?"

"I think it did."

"What did I do?"

"Let me ask you this. Did you feel anything when you saw Miranda?"

"I sensed that—this'll sound really weird—but I sensed that she felt like she and I had something in common. I think she understood my loss."

Ava saw Dave swallow and take in a breath, as we do when we're holding in deep emotions. He cleared his throat.

She said, "I think that's what it was."

"You and she have something in common."

"I guess so. I think so. That was the feeling."

"That makes perfect sense to me." Dave sipped from his glass of juice.

Ava's cell phone came on with the light jazz. Her purse was on the table; she took out the phone, looked at it, and told Dave, "It's Tony."

"Tell him to meet you in the park. The same one where he and I met."

"I'm not up to this. I'm not."

"I'll arrange something. Just tell him."

She opened the phone. "Tony? Yes. Calm down. I know. Calm down." She listened, frowned at Dave, then told Tony where she would meet him, in North School Park in Arlington Heights in one hour. Yes, she knew that that's where he'd first met Dave. That's where she wanted to meet him. "Yes. Yes. Tony, please. Not anymore, Tony, not you and me. No. I understand. I know. I understand. I can tell him that."

When she'd hung up, Dave asked her, "Well?"

"He's really scared."

"As he should be."

"Neely wants him to get me to give him something of yours. He's supposed to give it to Neely so that Neely can try to kill you again with it."

"They never learn."

"But Tony doesn't want to do it. He's afraid. Neely cut him with a knife or something and took some of his blood. Now Tony wants you to help him before Neely kills him."

"Of course he does. This has happened a thousand times before."

"Dave, I'm not up to this. I'm still shaking."

"You're not going to meet him."

"Then what do I tell him? Why did you have me tell him that?"

He stood. "I'm going to meet him."

"Oh, no. You're going to kill him."

"I want you to stay here. Don't leave. Tell me that you'll stay here until this evening."

"I promise. I'm in no shape to go anywhere."

"That's all I ask. Get some rest."

"I just want to go have a good cry."

"Then do it. I'll be back in a couple of hours. Don't leave."

"Uh-huh."

He went to put some clothes on.

Cool, late in the afternoon, strong with autumn, the leaves and skies of autumn, trees turning bare, the world going inward, winter coming.

Tony, on his usual park bench, didn't realize that Dave had walked up behind him and was standing there until he felt a hand on his right shoulder.

"Tony."

He turned around quickly and looked up. "Ava's supposed to be here. *Not you.*"

Dave walked around to the front of the bench and saw the small pile of cigarette butts at Tony's feet. He crouched and retrieved three of them, and said as he stood, "These come in very handy."

"Don't, man." Tony started to get up.

Dave pushed him back down, hand on his chest, and looked him in the eyes. "You're in trouble from every direction, Tony."

"I know that. I need help."

"How'd you hurt your hand?"

"Ray and Manny did it."

"What happened to your face?"

"Neely, that asshole. Which is why I need your *help*, Dave, right now."

"You are a sorry little man."

"*Help me.*"

"Here's my dilemma. Do I kill you, or do I let Neely kill you?"

Tony watched Dave's face. There was a long moment. A breeze came. From behind, birds chirped. Farther away, children yelled at each other, and Tony heard the sounds of their footsteps. It didn't matter in the least. Life didn't matter in the least.

Dave asked him, "What would be interesting to know is how he convinced you to help him. Why would you even open that door?"

"To hurt you. Because you double-crossed me."

"You make a deal with the devil, with one devil, to hurt another devil. And that helps you how, Tony? Didn't it ever occur to you that Neely came to you so that he could use you? You didn't need him. All you had to do was walk away from me and from Ava. He saw you for what you are. You're an angry, frightened man, and he used your anger and your fear against you. He could play you however he wanted to in case he needed to. And now he doesn't need you. If he ever did. You were a little bit of extra insurance. He was just being careful, putting you between him and me to see what I was going to do. And here you are, between him and me."

Dave stepped away, and Tony got to his feet. "Please," he said. "I don't deserve this."

Dave turned his back on him.

"You lousy mother!" Tony called after him. "I know how to stop you! I'll figure it out! You will *not*—!"

He ran.

Caught up with Dave and grabbed him by his jacket and turned him around.

Dave let him.

"Not like he killed Ray and Manny. Come on, Dave."

"Get out of here."

"You know what I can do?"

"Nothing. Go away."

And what *could* he do? Tony stared at him, and Dave wasn't moving. He couldn't get past him, couldn't get through, what could he do? Run the other way? Run for what?

But he did run, angrily, ran past his park bench and toward the street, to his car.

And Dave knew exactly what Tony would try to do.

It was dusk when Dave returned home. No lights on in the house, as usual, not even with Ava in there somewhere.

And she was still there. He sensed her presence in his house, all of her loneliness.

"She felt like she and I had something in common. I think she understood my loss."

This woman and his daughter. He had not considered that when he first sensed something about Ava, when he first talked to her over coffee. What is it about her? Ward had asked him, and David hadn't known.

But of course it was loss and loneliness. Stronger than fear or rage, of course it was loss and loneliness.

He moved quietly in the darkness, not sure where she was but wanting to let her rest, until he heard movement coming from the front room, light sounds, and stepped carefully to look in on her.

Ava was on one of the couches. She had showered, her hair was still damp, and she was in one of his big heavyweight robes. She was lying with her back toward him, and the sounds he heard were muffled sobs. He couldn't tell if she were awake or if she were sorrowful in her sleep.

Dave backed away quietly, moved through his house, and went up the stairs to his attic, unbuttoning his shirt as he went.

Ava. This was all Ava's fault. He had to see Ava. He could get to Ava, kidnap her if he had to, and stop this shit, make it stop.

Tony drove as fast as he could to Ava's house.

And found no one there. Two Chicago *Tribunes* rolled up in plastic by the front door. No lights on. Nothing.

If she wasn't home, where was she?

In a motel somewhere?

Not at the restaurant. That was burned down. But with one of the women who worked there? With, what's her name, what was her name, the hostess, Eileen, what was her last name? Eileen Something Something. Damn it!

Tony didn't know what to do. Go back to Neely? Maybe that was best. Go back to Neely and explain that Dave was going to kill him and ask Neely for help, for some idea of what to do.

God damn it, he thought, as he pulled onto Route 53 and hit the accelerator. He had been right there, right next to Dave, had stood this close to him, he could have scratched him or done anything, gotten anything from him, and Neely could have used that, he wouldn't have to wait for Ava to get to Dave, Dave had been *right there in front of him*, and so why hadn't Tony done anything? He could have reached out, scratched him, stabbed him with a pencil—

No.

He couldn't have.

That was the point. Dave might as well have been daring Tony to make a move like that.

And the thought had never even crossed Tony's mind.

The guy was too powerful. The sense of him, or how he controlled the situation when you were sitting this close to him. You couldn't get past that, at least Tony couldn't. He might've tried, but the thought had never even occurred to him, and that was the point. Dave blocked it out of your head before you even had time to think of it. He had that kind of power.

God damn it, Tony thought, this is not my fault!

He slowed down as the rush hour traffic began to back up. Going north on 53 even this late in the afternoon, it could clog up. He was just getting close to Euclid when he started to feel cold. The turnoff for Northwest Highway was only a couple more miles, but suddenly Tony felt like he was coming down with the flu, he was shivering like crazy.

He was freezing cold, but he was also sweating. He felt his legs going numb, as if they were in ice or in freezing water. He could no longer feel his right foot on the accelerator. The car seemed to be slowing down. He pressed on the accelerator but felt nothing.

Drivers behind him began honking their horns.

He steered into the right hand lane so that he could take the exit for Euclid Avenue heading west. That would get him to Neely's motel just as easily as taking Northwest Highway.

But it was becoming very dark. Tony reached to turn on his headlights and realized that they were already on. More drivers honked behind him.

Was he going blind? Was Dave getting at him this fast? Was it possible? Was he *dying*?

He wiped his face and saw that his hand was black, as black as if he had dipped it into fresh oil.

"*Jesus Christ!*"

He pulled off to the right as well as he could. He wasn't quite at the exit for Euclid Avenue when he sensed the Explorer slowing down and rolling still in the gravel on the shoulder, then tilting to one side as it settled into the grass just beyond.

"*Help me!*"

He was almost blind. He reached for the rearview mirror and tried to see his face. There was no face, only a head covered in black paint.

He couldn't breathe, and now his chest was cold, and he couldn't breathe, he couldn't feel his chest, he began to cry, he was in such utter terror, and he rocked from side to side, side to side, faster and faster, trapped, and tried to hit his head against the driver's side window.

It was all black now, too.

Tony pushed his face up against it, it was icy cold, but he thought that maybe it would help him breathe. He fumbled for the button that would open the window, and he found it, and the window went down slowly. Tony felt his head falling into the open air as the window went down, and he was trying as hard as he could to see, *to see*, and to breathe, but the air felt so *cold*. He thought he heard someone scream.

The scream came from a middle-aged woman who had been in one of the cars behind Tony's. When she saw the Explorer move off the road as though the driver were no longer in control, she'd feared the worst, that the driver had had a heart attack. She'd parked on the shoulder and gotten out, was careful about the traffic whizzing by, but walked up to the Explorer to see whether she could help.

She had expected to see an elderly man leaning unconscious over the steering wheel.

What she found was a dark husk sitting with its head out the open driver's side window. The head looked more like a charred piece of wood than anything human, and then it dropped from its shoulders and bounced on the grass.

She screamed.

15.

adjacent to his quiet room, where Dave kept the portrait of Miranda, was a smaller room that held mementos from early in his career, some of them innocent and of only personal interest, others grisly and more intimate, such as the finger bones of one of his enemies, and someone else's pocket watch, partially melted into an odd shape and touched with blood, and a book of sorcery bound in human skin—not an unusual procedure for the seventeenth century.

Dave had stopped taking such trophies decades ago, but he continued to maintain his files. Six tall, wooden cabinets held notes, letters, newspaper clippings, magazine tear sheets, and photographs going back more than a century. In the top drawer of the sixth filing cabinet, he located a large manila envelope from 1998 with "Neely" written on the front in the symbols of Dave's personal secret code. The envelope contained only a few items, which told him that killing Carl Neely had not been a matter of great consequence. There were newspaper clippings, several photographs of Neely taken clandestinely, a page ripped from the Phoenix phone directory, and a torn sheet of notebook paper. Most of the writing on the sheet of notebook paper was done in Dave's code—runes and geometric shapes and signs from ancient alphabets. The remaining lines listed the names of places associated with Neely, their street addresses, and times jotted down next to them—clearly referring to when Dave was tracking Neely in anticipation of the kill.

The newspaper clipping, however, mentioned that a second person had been hurt in the fire that destroyed Carl Neely's house: "Also burned was Arthur Neely, 32, the victim's brother, who was taken to Phoenix Memorial Hospital."

Carl Neely had become involved with a minor group in the Phoenix area; in the mid 1990s, he had killed a man he'd met in a bar who had also claimed to be adept in the arts. Over the next few years, Neely had traveled the Southwest and Midwest, studying with perhaps half a dozen scholars and adepts, improving his skills. For reasons that could only be surmised, he had killed one of his tutors, an old man named Fosey, a respected magician in Oklahoma. This was sufficient to bring Neely to the attention of Fosey's longtime associates, and Dave had been hired by a master in Dallas to neutralize Carl Neely.

Dave had not recalled, however, anyone else present at the killing, certainly not Neely's brother. He remembered tracking Carl Neely for about a week and establishing that he regularly returned to a very nice home in Scottsdale, where he apparently lived alone. The house and its grounds were not well protected, and Dave had been able to confront Neely there without any problem. But they had been alone.

No matter. Arthur must have been nearby and likely entered the burning house after Dave had left. And he had surely gone on, after his accident, to gain training from people who had taught him well.

Time to find out more. Dave returned the envelope to its drawer and closed the file cabinet. Then he went upstairs into his attic. A thorough ritual was not necessary; he was not performing a sending, he was not demanding the spirits he had killed to perform acts of revenge, and he was not calling upon the demons inside him or requesting anything in particular from the population of demons and spirits beyond.

He wished only to communicate with Carl Neely.

How many souls had he taken? He had begun keeping count very early. We carry our personalities with us when we pass, and so the insane fool in life becomes an insane foolish spirit. The angry woman remains angry; the wise seek more wisdom; the malicious try to perfect their evil ways.

Carl Neely. Which was he? The seventieth? The ninetieth? Best to try to find him by what Neely remembered from when he was on earth.

Dave pulled a chair in front of the large mirror in the middle of his room. He retrieved a tablet of paper and a pen from his work table, sat, and began writing words and symbols while he chanted a slow phrase.

He wrote the word Phoenix several times, and then drew a picture of the bird, the fiery phoenix. Our brains and our spirits read the world literally; Carl Neely might have only vague remembrance of walking the streets of downtown Phoenix, Arizona, but an image of a flaming bird might awaken him or pull him closer to Dave.

He wrote down Arthur's name, and continued to chant.

He wrote down the street addresses Carl Neely had frequented. He wrote down the names of the people Neely had killed. He drew a picture of the front of Neely's house in Scottsdale, as well as Dave remembered it.

And gradually, as he chanted, the mirror took on light. Shapes whispered far away within it, and flashes erupted silently—spirits, the men and women he had killed, being pulled toward him, attracted by his chant, his thoughts, the words he had drawn, the pictures.

A woman, large and old, whom Dave did not recognize—here and gone in a burst of light. The very sad face of a beautiful young woman, truly beautiful, red haired and green eyed, looking at Dave and then turning, looking behind her, facing Dave again and shaking her head no.

She floated on, and was followed by a man in his thirties, dark haired, tanned, with a snarling grin, egotistical—

"Carl?" Dave asked him.

The head simply stared.

Dave ordered him, "Go into your brother's dreams. Warn him—"

But Carl Neely looked above Dave, then beyond him, and smiled as well as he could, and then began to weep. He made sounds, nonsense sounds. He moved upward, so that Dave could see the light of him stretch away, toward the top of the mirror, and then he screamed. Dave heard the scream in his mind, and the cry was sufficiently disturbing that the glass in the old mirror quivered.

Useless. That's why he had never attracted this dead man until now. Carl Neely was dead in body and spirit both. Insane, or thoroughly emptied of whatever had motivated him on earth. He wasn't going to visit his brother or anyone else in dreams. All he was going to do was float, making sounds and smiling, for as long as the material universe and its spiritual echoes dragged on . . . .

Dave came down from the attic and went into his quiet room. He picked up the phone near his comfortable chair and pressed Larry Ward's number.

Ward came on immediately; no voicemail. "Make it fast, please," he told Dave. "I'm behind schedule."

"Do me a favor."

"If I can, sure."

"Arthur Neely was admitted to Phoenix Memorial Hospital in April of 1998. Badly burned."

"Interesting."

"Whatever you can find out about that, I'd like to know it."

"I'll call Tim O'Neil. He's still at Phoenix Memorial. Got to go."

"Thanks, Larry."

It might mean nothing, information from the hospital, or it might prove to be useful. Anything at this point could assist in deciding the next step.

Dave went downstairs to the front room and saw that Ava was still asleep on the leather couch. Wake her up, or let her sleep?

Dave quietly returned upstairs.

And in his quiet room, he made another phone call, this time to Dallas. "Bill? Dave Ehlert. Yes, I know. I need to jog your memory. Tell me what you can find out about a character named Arthur Neely. I visited his brother in Phoenix in 1998. That's right. No, he's been interfering with my life. Anything you can find out. Who trained him. Where he's been. Mention my name if you need to. Thanks. I appreciate it."

Time to find another way to neutralize Carl's ambitious little brother.

By ten that night, Neely understood what had happened.

In his motel room, he had created a makeshift window by aligning candles in front of the bureau mirror across from his bed. It was difficult for him—he had difficulty concentrating. This had happened to him previously, and it was happening more frequently now, although Neely wasn't sure why. But sufficient light was pulled from the candle flames that he saw, deep within the mirror, Tony's corpse leaning out of the Explorer, then breaking apart, the head, an arm, a portion of shoulder, as an annoying woman screamed.

So.

He had prepared himself for disappointment, but not for defeat. And he would not allow this disappointment to pull him into defeat.

He owed that to his brother.

Kill him for me, Carl had said, just before he died.

Neely had promised that he would.

And he had promised himself that he would do it in the only way that mattered.

A bullet would have stopped Dave and put him in the ground, but use of the arts not only would kill him, it would also undo all of the other things he'd ever accomplished.

Such as freeing Carl. Dave had him now; he was holding Carl's soul and could do with it what he wished. Not good. Not right.

Sometimes at night, in the months and years after his brother's death,

Neely woke up hearing Carl beside him, in the room with him, or standing at the foot of the bed, telling him, Kill him for me. On windy days, or in the rain, or as he sat alone in open fields learning to master the skills he had chosen, the arts of personal sorcery, of shadowy self-defense, silent murder, and of attaining visions of wonder—all through those years, he had heard his brother alongside him, telling him, Here's what to do. Kill him for me.

Kill him for me.

Promise me.

They had been raised in Phoenix, Arizona, where their parents, both of them accountants, had moved in the eighties to take advantage of the Sun Valley's population growth and business opportunities. They made a good life for themselves, and when the elder Neelys died within a month of each other, Carl and Arthur inherited a tidy sum and a nice home in Scottsdale.

The brothers were two very different kinds of men. Arthur, younger by six years, was quiet, a loner, content with his job as an auto mechanic in a small garage and, ironically, the more mature, careful with a dollar, slow to make decisions, very private, self-absorbed and intense. It was he who looked after his older brother, Carl, who, with his gift of gab and ambition to have nice things, did very well for himself in a series of sales jobs; by the early 1990s, he was pulling down large commissions representing a software development company. By then he was in his late thirties, juggled women the way he did his credit card balances, and was living comfortably in his parents' house; he'd bought out Arthur's interest, which benefited them both. Carl liked the big house, and Arthur had invested the money he'd made from the sale.

For a while after their parents died, the brothers stayed in touch, but as time passed and their lives moved into separate paths, one slow and one fast, they saw less of each other. Carl spent more and more time away from home, and the Scottsdale house sat vacant for long stretches. Eventually, nearly two years went by without Arthur's having heard anything from Carl. He was therefore very surprised when Carl phoned him one night in 1995 and asked to be picked up at a location far outside the city—in the desert, in fact. Arthur was annoyed but, at one in the morning on a very warm spring night, drove way the hell out there to find his brother standing alone in the parking lot of a saloon, hands in his pants pockets, staring straight up at a bright full moon.

When Arthur asked him where his car was, Carl had told him, "Out in the desert," and then, laughing, volunteered that he had just killed a man.

Arthur had told him, "You're drunk. Now get in the car."

But as they drove farther into the desert to retrieve Carl's car, Arthur noticed that his brother smelled funny and had something on his face and hands that looked like charcoal.

Arthur asked him, "What the hell have you been up to?"

"Give it another mile and I'll show you."

They could have been anywhere. There was nothing but scrub and saguaro cactus in every direction, and the bright moon, when Carl told Arthur, "Right there. There."

Carl slowed down, pulled off the road and into the desert, and parked with his headlights aimed at what remained of somebody's son or brother.

"He pushed me too far," Carl explained.

"What the *hell* have you done?"

"I just wanted to know if I could do it, and I did."

Arthur got out of his car and walked toward the body, then put a hand to his mouth as though he were going to be sick, came back and got behind the wheel again. "Where'd you put the rest of the body?"

"Nowhere. That's what happens."

"That's how *what* happens?"

"That's how he died, Art."

"Jesus Christ, he's half burned up."

"Not to worry," Carl told him.

"Not to *worry*?"

"Not to worry at all."

"Damn it, where's your car?"

"Down there." Carl nodded, then got out and started walking farther down the road.

Drunk as he was, Carl made it back home in his expensive little import, and Arthur had followed him back to the house, thinking all the while about what he should do. Was it possible that Carl really *had* killed the man in the desert? Perhaps he only thought he had. But why? Was he that drunk? Or high? Had he gotten into it with one of the regulars at that excellent night spot, and had the two of them taken it out into the desert and had Carl somehow actually, yes, committed murder?

He didn't ask Carl that question when they got back to their parents' house. Arthur didn't want to know, not that night, not immediately. He was scared.

As it turned out, Carl avoided him for the next several weeks, not answering his phone or even coming to the door the couple of times Arthur came by. For several nights after their middle-of-the-night adventure in the desert, Arthur watched for an announcement of the murder on the ten o'clock news, but there was nothing on television or in the *Arizona Republic*. After a week of this, he drove back out to the desert to see whether the body was still there.

It was not.

Coyotes had gotten to it, surely.

When the two of them got together again in a few months, Arthur tried to mention the incident, but Carl wouldn't even let him finish the question. He apologized for being so drunk that night and explained that it wasn't he who had killed whoever it was out there, it had been some guy in the bar. Still, Carl had wanted to see the body. Who wouldn't want to see a dead body?

But it had indeed been Carl who had killed whoever it was out there in the desert. A year passed, and toward the following winter, in early November 1998, Carl phoned Arthur, and he was no longer so happy-go-lucky.

"I need your help, Art. I need your help right now."

"What is it?"

"Come over here immediately. But if you think somebody's following you or if there's somebody else here when you get here—Art, just freaking run like hell."

When he reached the house at ten that evening, Arthur found his brother sitting in an easy chair in the living room with his latest glass of Scotch in his left hand and one of their father's firearms, a .38 revolver, in his right. The lights were turned off throughout the house, and Carl told his brother not to turn one on.

As Arthur seated himself in the couch opposite the easy chair, Carl asked him, "Here's my question. Think about this, now. What would you do if you could do anything? What would *you do* if you could do anything?"

"I don't know."

"I do. I know," Carl told him. "You'd do exactly what you *are* doing, only you'd do it bigger. You'd do it faster. But you'd do exactly what you're doing because we're no better than that. We're no better than that."

He explained that he was drinking as much Scotch as he could so that he'd be relaxed enough to explain to Arthur what had happened to him over the past few years and why he was going away tonight, leaving the state. The gun was in case somebody showed up while he was doing the explaining, and it wasn't for him; it was for Arthur's protection.

"Bullets might help," Carl told him. "Probably not, but maybe."

And then he explained.

He had become, his brother realized, something of a philosopher since their middle-of-the-night adventure in the desert.

All of us yearn for things, Carl told Arthur, but when life gives us what we want, we're surprised by the completeness of what has been provided. We get more than we had anticipated, but still, having gotten what we wished for, we come to tire of it and resent it. We blame life for playing tricks on us, but the fault is wholly ours because, really, all we've asked for is to be more of who we are. That's how we trick ourselves.

"I certainly have," Carl explained, and told his brother that for the past several years, he had very seriously been practicing black magic. "No," he said, "I mean it. Follow me on this.

"I met some people while I was driving around, and they were into this, and so I tried things with them, you know, like at a party, and I liked it, so I wanted to know more, and they guided me, they were a big help, they helped me make sense of things because I'd been confused without knowing it, and I discovered the truth.

"The truth, Art. No shit.

"We've lost ourselves," Carl explained. "It's modern life. It's poisoning us. We fall into habits, we're robots; we might as well be sleepwalking. The truth is right in front of us, hiding in plain sight, a wonder so obvious that we keep looking past it. But when you readjust your vision—call it whatever you want, it's who we are. Magic, sorcery. We can access it just like people have been doing for thousands of years. We're animals. What we do is we release the animal in us, all of our instincts, all of our potential and our souls, who we really are.

"It's the truth," Carl rambled on, "and the truth is beyond good and evil. There is no wrong. There is no murder. There is no death. There are simply spirits involved with each other, us and everything else, it might as well be forever, and some of it is in this world, some of it is beyond this world, and some of it—it's inside us. Everything is. The world, everything."

This was his state of mind the night he'd killed the man in the desert.

"He challenged me," Carl explained. "And I did what I had to do. It feels incredible.

"Only now, I'm the guy some other people want to kill. I've been practicing, and I killed an old guy, and now they're after me. You piss off the wrong people, it's like anything else. People who do this, we live in the spaces between other people's lives, like in the cracks in the wall, and we have our own little groups, like in high school. Really. This is how far advanced we are. We're still in the fourth grade. There are rivalries. Sometimes they kill each other for fun, you know, for practice. Only, only, if you kill someone, they're yours, Art. You own their soul. You can use them.

"But I killed the wrong guy," Carl continued. "And now they want to kill me. They hired a guy, he's famous, and I know he's close. You know how you kill a sorcerer? You get another sorcerer. It takes a thief. Now, I can try to fight him, or I can keep running, so I'm going to keep running. Art. Art? You don't believe me."

It took him a long time to say that, yes, he did believe him, only he didn't know how much of it to believe. "Go to the police," Arthur told him. "Or hire someone yourself. Can you do that? Or get a bodyguard or a lawyer or something?"

Carl had laughed. Laughed and then promised that he would. "When I get out of here," he told Arthur, "all right, I will. I'll hire a bodyguard!"

But he wanted his brother to know everything, so he had written down the facts, and he had some books, he wanted Arthur to have these, and if something did indeed happen to him, there were people Arthur should talk to who would help protect him. A notebook of his, some books, some files, and an address book were in the box on the coffee table.

Arthur wasn't sure what to say.

Carl told him, "Don't say anything. Just take this stuff and go, Art. Really. Get out of here. And if anybody tries to follow you or you think they are, you get right back here. And take this gun."

"No."

"Take the damn gun."

"*No!*"

All the next day at the garage, Arthur wondered what to do. Go to the police himself? Talk to the people on the list Carl had given him, get their advice? Convince Carl to see a therapist? He tried phoning him on his lunch hour and when he clocked out and again when he got home.

No answer.

He drove over there, to their parents' house, saw Carl's car in the driveway, and rang the doorbell. Waited, and rang it again. Knocked on the door. Called Carl's name.

And heard Carl answer him, but sounding as though he were a million miles away.

Arthur unlocked the front door and walked in. The lights all were off, as they had been last night, and Carl was still in the living room, although no longer in the easy chair.

He was sitting cross-legged inside two circles of black paint drawn right on the carpet.

And he warned Arthur, "Don't come any closer!"

"Carl, what is this?"

"He came here, Art. He was here. Right after you left. He trapped me."

"Come on. We're going to the hospital."

"*Don't come any closer!*"

Arthur didn't. He stayed where he was.

"If you do," Carl warned him, "if you cross the line, if *I* cross the line, I die, or we both die. This is how it works. I had to protect myself, and so I drew the circle around myself. That's what we do. But then he put another one here. If I try to get out, his spirits kill me."

"You've been in there all day?"

"Yes."

"Carl, this is sick."

"*Stay away!*" And he started to cry. "I have really messed up, Art. He wants me to starve to death, or try to, try to get out of here. And I *can't!*"

Arthur sat on the couch. "Let me think. I can phone for an ambulance. Or paramedics. Someone must know what to do."

"Promise me something."

"What?"

"Kill him for me."

"The guy who did this?"

"Kill him for me. Do everything you can, please. Learn how."

"Who is he?"

"Dave Ehlert. His name is Dave Ehlert."

"Where does he live?"

"I don't know."

"Well, how do I find him?"

"Talk to the people I talked to. Some of them might be pissed off, but some of them will help you. Art, I'm scared. This creep, he's going to have my whole soul. It's worse than being dead."

"Let me call the police."

"No!"

"Let me call the paramedics. Please, Carl."

"Listen to me. Are you listening?"

"Say whatever you need to say."

"I have to try to do this. He did it one time, this Dave guy. He's a legend. He did it and some Nazi he knew did it. This guy is really *old*, Art, I am not kidding. This dude is ancient and he knows what he's doing. *Promise me.*"

"I promise."

"Learn for me. Learn to do what I never did. Find Dave Ehlert and kill him."

"I will."

"Swear it."

"Carl, I swear."

"Promise me you'll be careful."

"I will."

"This shit can eat you alive. Promise me you'll be careful."

"I *promise!*"

"Okay. Okay." He was sweating terribly, and he was plainly frightened. "Now, please, okay? Go."

"I'll go lie down in the other room."

"Leave, Art!"

"I am *tired*, Carl! Let me go lie down for a while."

And he did. Went into his old bedroom, which Carl had turned into a computer room, and stretched out on the leather couch there, pulled up a pillow, and stared at a patch of moonlight striking the wall across from him.

Call the police? he wondered. Call 9-1-1?

He nodded off and, after what seemed like only a minute, awoke to the sound of his brother screaming and to a horrible smell and wild light, light coming down the hall from the living room.

Fire.

Out of the room. Down the hall.

"*Carl!*"

The living room—

Carl was there, on fire, on his back, one arm, his right arm, lifted toward the ceiling, and he was already dead, he had to be dead, but he whispered, "Arrrrrt," as the arm fell and the hand broke free, a lump.

The carpet was on fire, the drapes, everything. The fire moved fast, green fire, the flames were *green*, but Arthur went to Carl, he couldn't leave him there, he dropped to his knees and went to him.

"…he listened to the sirens in the distance."

The green fire roared. It took Carl, what was left of him, ate him, and it shattered the glass in the living room window, took out the ceiling, and with great force blew Arthur across the room, back toward the hallway, where he screamed, grabbing the left side of his face, slapping at his left arm and leg and foot, which were on fire, glowing, and burning *green*.

He lay there for a long time, it seemed, aware that he was still burning, or at least it felt that way, and he listened to the sirens in the distance.

What would you do if you could do anything?

He closed his eyes and opened them, didn't see much, and imagined that he was dead or asleep. Dead, probably.

"Promise me."

"I promise."

"Learn for me. Kill him. Swear it."

"Carl, I swear."

They found him, the fire fighters, and took him out into the crisp night, got him to the hospital, and he stayed there long enough to remember everything and long enough until he was thinking clearly, and then he left. Escaped. Just went in the middle of the night one night.

Got back to his apartment, took whatever he felt he needed, Carl's notes and books, clothes and money and car keys, and some Gatorade for the thirst that had bothered him for more than a week, and started driving.

"You know how you kill a sorcerer? You get another sorcerer."

He would start with the first name on his brother's list, and whatever he needed to do, he would do it.

"He's going to have my soul. It's worse than being dead."

No matter how long it took.

"Learn for me. Kill him. Swear it."

"Carl, I swear."

I swear.

16.

It was nine at night when Dave came downstairs again to look in on Ava.

She was up. Sitting at the kitchen table and sipping a glass of grape juice, and with an empty carton of yogurt and a teaspoon in front of her.

She turned and looked at him as Dave came in, tried to smile, then shook her head and wiped her left hand through her hair and scratched back and forth.

"'Joy is a partnership,'" Dave said. "'Grief weeps alone.'" He walked to the sink and looked out the window at the back yard.

Ava asked him, "Who said that?"

He turned and faced her, pressing his hands backward against the counter. "Lines from a poet from when I was a boy. Completely forgotten, now. Frederic Lawrence Knowles. Poets used to have names like that."

"Well, he's right about grief being alone." Ava sipped some of the grape juice. "And I feel like I'm living completely without a clock. I'm floating. Have been for a year. I was sound asleep in there."

"Well, don't apologize."

"Did you do what you were going to do?"

"Yes."

"I don't want to know any more about it. Okay?"

"Okay."

"I should go home. Is it safe for me to go home?"

"I think so. But wait until morning, at least."

"I feel like I've been living here for a month."

"Life without a clock will do that."

Ava breathed a little laugh. "Nothing fazes you."

"Not true. I can get very fazed. You were there."

"And what do you do about that, now?"

"It's in motion."

"Is that how you say it? It's 'in motion'?"

"Phone calls are made. People who know people talk to other people. It's all very mysterious."

Ava didn't reply to that. She picked up her empty yogurt cup and the spoon and her tumbler and walked them to the sink and rinsed them out.

"Is it possible," she asked Dave, "that Steve knows I'm here and could find me here?"

"Yes."

"I don't know what to think anymore. I'm floating. But he was here."

"Did you see him?"

She shook her head. "But when I was sleeping on the couch, I heard him knocking, like he always did, and he said something, only I couldn't tell what. But I sat up, or I woke up, and I heard the knock again, and I thought I saw someone standing in the corner of the room. It was dark, I mean, the room, and whoever it was standing there was dark, but he smiled at me. It's like I could see the smile inside my head, and I knew he was smiling. Is that what it's like?"

"Sounds to me as though he wants to see you again pretty badly."

"Really?" The hope in her voice seemed desperate.

Before Dave could answer, his phone rang. He walked to the wall and took down the handset. "Yes," he said. "No, I phoned him earlier. Whatever you can tell me."

He turned his back to Ava, preoccupied with the call, and she looked into the hallway, then walked past him, leaving the kitchen to head upstairs. Dave was right: best to stay here until morning and get a fresh start.

But she turned, then, and walked into the front room and looked at the couch where she'd been sleeping. She looked at the corner where she'd seen—Steve?

"Sounds to me as though he wants to see you again pretty badly."

And what had she told Dave when they were in the attic and impossible things were happening, Steve appearing and ghosts and Dave's own daughter trying to float into the room?

"It's like he was reading my mind. I wish we could have had more time together, or I wish the accident hadn't happened."

She wanted to hear the knocking again, Steve tapping to let her know he was still here, right now, but Ava didn't hear it, so she went back down the hall and past the kitchen, where Dave was talking into the phone and writing notes, and walked upstairs to the guest room.

Before getting any sleep, Dave tried again to track down Neely by means other than contacting his lost brother, but he had no success. Either the man was extremely good at what he did, which Dave was beginning to doubt, or he was out of his mind, slipping away, as Dave had explained to Ava. Neely was probably losing track himself of who or where he was half the time. Pretty soon there'd be nothing there. Like his brother.

He got six hours of sleep before his phone rang. He'd expected it to be Bill Radovich in New York, but it was John Fortune. Dave had an uneasy relationship with John Fortune, as he had with Bill. Sometimes partners in crime, sometimes competitors, none of them had gone so far as to intrude on each other's domains. Occasionally, when strength meets strength, caution rules. This was the understanding between them, and so far it had been as successful as a powerful oath. Dave considered that the nearest thing in the mundane world to the life he led was the gangs of criminals that had risen to dominance after the fall of the Berlin Wall. Bullies. Sharks. Wolves. Predators. That's all they were, Dave himself and the others like him. An accident or a misstep by any of them, and domains would be contested, territories rearranged—and a soul new to death would be freed to suffer under one or another of them.

John Fortune lived outside Pittsburgh. He was perhaps in his sixties by now, a large, courtly man of ability and insight. Dave had met him after the war. Since then, Fortune had become involved in assisting sorcerers and mystics so damaged by their work in the arts, or so harmed by errors they had committed, that all that remained for them was to suffer and die. Yet Fortune was no humanitarian. His intention was to retrieve some of what these broken people had attained and use such knowledge to his advantage. He had claimed, in some instances, to have done so. Perhaps he had.

He greeted Dave with "*Salut!*" John Fortune was no more French than Dave, but he had picked up this annoying habit somewhere and persisted in it. "And good morning," he said brightly.

"Good *early* morning," Dave told him.

"I have not met this man Neely personally, David. Let me make that clear."

"Thank you."

"Heard of him. He's a smart-aleck little prick."

"No need to get personal."

Fortune laughed. "But I want to be sure that you and I stay on each other's good side."

"Always the best consideration for us both. So what about him?"

"I have bits and pieces, that's all. But for whatever good it does you, here it is."

Fortune told Dave that, so far as he could tell, Arthur Neely had traveled the Southwest and the Midwest for nearly ten years after Carl's death. He'd spent a lot of time with a husband and wife in Nebraska named the Oakleys. They were dead now, whether by natural causes or not, Fortune did not know. But they had begun his instruction, and Fortune was of the impression that they had also had something to do with the education of Carl Neely. At the very least, they had taught both of the brothers to regard the world not as an object or a stage but as a living partner, surely the fundamental awareness required in awakening to the sorcerous potentials within us and surrounding us. And because the Oakleys lived humbly on what remained of an old farmstead, Neely, during his residence with them, would have learned to be in harmony with the natural patterns of the earth and the seasons, our birthright, and gained strength and insight from that while shedding the artificial conditioning of the mundane world.

Meditation, visualization, divining, speaking with the dead—these would have been taught to him as well as the mechanical aspects of the craft, talismanic magic and sympathetic magic, the use of incantatory language and syllables and focusing of the will. He would have entered states in which he confronted the shadow aspects of himself, and he would have greeted these demons within himself, understanding that he could use them as he wished, for it is we who have brought them into our world, these demons and bright souls and guardians, all of the things named by the thousands throughout history. We have created them from within ourselves and loosed them upon time and the universe. These things live alongside us now and attempt to use us as we use them. Demons regard themselves as people. To them, we are the demons.

Fortune was uncertain when Neely had moved on; the informants he had spoken with overnight did not know. But Neely next was known to have spent time with a man named Lawrence Leopold in southern Ohio. Leopold taught him sufficiently well that Arthur was able to perform his first kill under this man's guidance. The victim was an elderly magician against whom Leopold held an old hate. So fairly early, then, Neely had taken blood, and a soul, no doubt after practicing on dogs, cats, rabbits—anything available. He would have become intoxicated with the sense of power that comes from using sorcery as a weapon, simply from taking life in so personal and elemental a way. And without doubt he would have learned much more about death. We think of death as darkness, but for the dead, death is a land of light. The dead are warm; we are cold. Our life, for them, is a burden, weighty and strange and slow, and gladly done with.

Fortune told Dave that Leopold, too, was now dead; it was possible, although not certain, that Neely himself had killed him.

In any event, no one could account for the next three years or so of Neely's life. In fact, one of the individuals with whom Fortune had spoken was surprised to hear that Arthur Neely was still alive and active; he thought the apprentice magician had been done in years earlier.

But no. When he resurfaced, it was in Manhattan in 2006, where Neely was employed by a powerful businessman named MacLeod. Dave had heard of MacLeod; he hired young sorcerers as bodyguards, hit men, and all-purpose enforcers. It was possible that Neely might have gained a little polish, working for the cosmopolitan MacLeod; certainly Neely would have done some traveling, domestically and internationally, on errands for his powerful new boss.

Neely's acquaintance with MacLeod led directly to the magician's relationship with a woman in Pittsburgh named Nicole Prentiss. She had mastered many skills herself; she had, in fact, also been employed by MacLeod for some time. Whatever job or appointment had brought them together, it was known that Neely and Prentiss carried on a romance. This was not as unusual as it might seem; a living monstrosity like Neely would have been very agreeable to Nicole's singular taste in lovers.

"And here's the last little bit I can impart to you, David," Fortune told him.

"You've already been a great deal of help."

"By the time he was with Nicole, your Arthur Neely said that you were his hero. He wants to be like you."

"That's different."

"And I can point you in the direction of something very valuable. Nicole is in a facility near here."

"One of yours?"

"Yes."

"Is she in bad shape?"

"The truth? She gave up the arts two years ago, or so she says. We've employed her as a kind of matron for the cases we have out here."

"Would she be willing to talk with me?"

"I've already taken it upon myself to ask her, and she says she will."

"Good."

"She told me that she thought you'd be dead already."

"Because of Neely?"

"She's aware of what he was trying to do. Apparently she holds his abilities in high regard."

"Then I would indeed like to talk with her. What do you know about their relationship?"

"Not a great deal. More serious on her end than for him. Typical male. But they were together for a number of years, and *she* left *him*, not the other way around."

"And how soon after that did she decide to give up the arts?"

"Very soon after that. We're talking a couple of years since then, as I said."

"Sounds like cause and effect to me. Something happened to break them up."

"Indeed."

"Well, whatever she can tell me, I'd like to hear it. I'm certainly willing to fly out there."

"I'll have Nelson contact you."

"Who's Nelson?"

"Cameron Nelson is the young man who handles things for me."

"Fine."

"Consider staying for a meal if you're coming all that way. We have some excellent dining."

"All right."

"I recommend the Bigelow Grille or the veal at Bravo Franco."

"Thanks. I'll consider it."

"I merely suggest them, David. I'm here to help, as I said. I'm not setting a trap for you. I have no interest in pissing you off."

"Thank you, John."

"I'll have Nelson phone you with the particulars. He can set things up for you and meet you at the airport."

"I'll leave immediately. What else should I know about Nicole? Anything?"

"I don't think so. She's a strong personality, but I believe she's changed from the days when she knew Neely. She's sincerely doing her best to take care of our charges at the home."

"Then let's say that she is."

"Nelson will be calling you soon. As I said, I'm being extremely helpful because I intend to remain on your good side. This goes in the ledger."

"Understood."

"But if you want to make a financial donation to assist with those of us who have suffered in the search for personal enlightenment, contributions are always welcome."

"John, if I thought it meant anything to you, I'd say that I admire your salesmanship."

"Compliments are also welcome, day or night. You'll be hearing from Nelson inside the hour."

Only a moment after Dave hung up, the phone rang again.

It was Larry Ward. "I don't have much," he told Dave. "This Arthur Neely character was in bed for a week at Phoenix Memorial, and then he just up and walked out in the middle of the night."

"He sounds like a man who would do that."

"As I said, not much help."

"I just got off the phone with John Fortune in Pittsburgh."

"You've mentioned the name."

"There's a connection there that I'm going to follow up on. I'm flying down this morning. Arthur Neely has worked very hard to get where he is."

"I can only imagine."

"I'll probably be back this evening, but I may get something to eat."

"Try the veal at Bravo Franco; its downtown. It's excellent."

Dave chuckled. "You're the second person to recommend it."

"Really? Anything more I can do?"

"I don't know. Keep an eye on Ava if she'd like that."

"Happy to. Have a safe flight."

Dave went upstairs and, in his bedroom, went online to order his round-trip ticket to Pittsburgh. He took a quick shower, then headed downstairs to make himself breakfast.

In the kitchen, he heard the water running upstairs. Ava, showering. He added two eggs to the skillet and set out an extra plate and coffee cup.

Cameron Nelson phoned just as Dave was putting out the scrambled eggs. Nelson indeed sounded young—twenties, thirties.

"Mr. Ehlert?"

"Yes."

"*Salut*, as our friend would say."

"*Salut*, Mr. Nelson. I've booked a flight to arrive around two this afternoon."

"Fine. I understand we'll be going to the facility Mr. Fortune has set up."

"I need to talk to Nicole Prentiss."

"I hear she's waiting to talk to you, too."

"Do you know her?"

"Only somewhat. But I admire her. She has a calming effect on our clients."

"That's interesting."

"Some of us . . . She seems to have come around full circle. Which is an interesting visual for those of us who've undertaken the search. But she's returned wiser and softer."

"We all come back to where we started, Mr. Nelson."

"That seems to be the nature of the path. I'll pick you up at the airport whenever you say."

"Let me give you a call just before I land."

"Fine."

When he returned the handset to the wall, Dave saw Ava standing in the entrance to the kitchen, watching him with a sad expression.

"Scrambled eggs," he told her.

"Thanks."

She took a seat and told him, "I need some fresh clothes and, no offense, some fresh air."

"No offense."

"You know what it is?"

"What is it?" He sat across from her.

Ava lifted her coffee cup and held it in both hands as she sipped, then told him, "I don't want to know about this. That's what I've decided. I liked it when Steve was alive and we were both so dumb that we thought we could own a restaurant and that that was enough. Isn't that what life is for?"

"Yes," Dave agreed. "That's exactly what life is for."

"So if he's on the other side or whatever you call it, and I can hear him and he can see me, I'm okay with that. I can live with that. I don't know how long I want to live with that, but I can. And whatever Tony was doing and this Neely character that wants to kill you . . . . I'm really trying here, Dave. Does any of this make sense?"

"Of course."

"I don't want you to patronize me."

"I'm not patronizing you."

"It's like finding out what disease looks like," Ava said. "Doctors have to know, but I don't. I want to be happily ignorant. Is that wrong?"

"Not really."

"I wanted to live happily ever after with my husband, and that's gone now, but I can manage to deal with that as long as I know he's safe and as long as I can get through each day. That's all I want. I still have this." She pulled out the talisman he had given her. "Can I keep it?"

"Absolutely."

"So I'm more or less safe."

"You're safe."

"And I can go back to whatever kind of life I had before Tony almost destroyed it."

"Yes. You can."

She let out a strong sigh, a strong breath. "I owe you a lot, and I'm very grateful, but now I want to do whatever I need to do to get back on the clock."

Dave smiled.

"I want to go to my own home," Ava told him, "and sleep in my own bed, and then call my insurance agent and see what I can do about the restaurant. If I can give a little money to the people who worked there, I want to do that."

"Good for you."

"Good for something, anyway. Then I can think about next steps. I might move back to Ohio."

"Is that where you're from?"

"Originally, yes. I still have some cousins there, fourteen times removed."

"I was born in a little town near Washingtonville."

"Really? Down by Cincinnati. I was born in Youngstown."

"Kind of a rough place."

"Parts of it." Ava asked him then, "How soon do you have to leave?"

"I have a few minutes yet. Remember, if you need anything, call Larry Ward."

"I will if I have to." She finished her eggs and went to the coffeemaker to pour another cup. "It's nothing personal, but if we don't see each other for a while, I'm okay with that, too."

He let out a genuine laugh. "We can let it go."

"It's too bad because I like you, and you're a very decent man."

"Let's not carried away."

"No, you are. I think you are. You're a decent man. But the world's a bad place for decent people."

"Yes," he said. "It is."

17.

"**A**rthur Neely said that you were his hero. He wants to be like you."

Dave was not flattered by the sentiment. On the flight to Pittsburgh, he turned it over in his mind and decided that what Neely was doing, or trying to do, was to imitate the man he meant to kill in order to *know* the man he meant to kill. To defeat your enemy, become your enemy. And it had taken Neely far enough to enable him to have nearly put Dave down for good.

Was Neely sufficiently intelligent or talented or intuitive to anticipate that Dave would be unguarded at such a moment? Hard to say. Maybe he'd simply taken a chance and gotten lucky—taken a chance by putting other people in harm's way, Tony Jasco and whoever it was who'd broken into Dave's car.

Give credit where credit is due, though, Dave thought. Neely had gotten that far.

But now what? Even if Neely had been sufficiently sober or sane to accomplish that, whatever he was doing now had taken him off the map.

"*They were together for a number of years, and* she *left* him, *not the other way around.*"

"*And how soon after that did she decide to give up the art?*"

"*Very soon after that.*"

"*Sounds like cause and effect to me. Something happened to break them up.*"

So here was this young man who's seen his brother killed and decides he's going to take revenge. Studies the arts for ten years. Puts himself through changes he never would have thought possible, and it starts to make him unbalanced. He meets Nicole, and they're perfect misfits together, and what does that lead to?

Nicole respects what Neely has accomplished and thinks he's even good enough to kill Dave. But then she leaves him, and right after that, she walks away from the life that has been very good for her, but she doesn't turn her back on it completely. She decides to help people who've seriously compromised their souls.

So if I were Arthur Neely, Dave thought, what could I have done to push her away? If I were that driven, and I was starting to get lost in the pull of it, the way that opening yourself to the hidden world pulls you in—yet I felt close to Nicole—then what did I do that ended the relationship?

Couples break up for two reasons: you're not giving me what I need, or you're doing something to hurt me. Whether you're young or old, whether it's sex or money or power or love or lust that lit the fires, whether you speak English or French or German or Sorcery—none of that matters. Either you're not giving me what I need, or you're doing something to hurt me. Honest people come together for trust and companionship, and if you jeopardize one or both of those, then why be involved at all?

After that, it's specifics. There's a world full of needs and wants and desires and kinks and hopes and fears, enough to take anyone in any direction, and pretty far in that direction, too. But it always comes down to those two things.

Neely and Nicole had been together for some time, so presumably they were satisfying each other's needs and wants and desires and kinks. Fortune considered Nicole to be a strong person, but still—what else could it possibly have been?

Neely had hurt her, or threatened to hurt her.

So what had he threatened her with?

"You were his hero. He wants to be like you."

Be like me, Dave thought.

That certainly opened the door to any number of possibilities.

Home. She was home again after—how many days had it been? Two? Ava felt as if she'd been out of the country, her sense of time and place all turned around.

Of course, she reminded herself, she might as well have actually been out of the country, this one or any of them, given what she'd been through.

And home felt like another country, now, too. That had been apparent when she pulled into the driveway, noticing details that typically never stood out, tics that gave the place its personality and that blended into each other. A paint smudge on the brick. One of the flagstones on the walkway leading to the front porch lifting up. Rust around the mailbox. The way it happens when we've been away for a while from what we're used to and see it fresh on our return.

But she was in charge of her life again, at least, Ava told herself as she got out of the Lexus. She unlocked the front door and took the two days' worth of mail out of the mailbox, stepped inside and marveled at how small her place was. She noticed the fragrance of it, too, the candles she kept around and the fresh flowers she replenished twice a week on the table in the dining room.

Ave walked into the kitchen and dropped the mail onto the table. The kitchen was small, too, but the phone on the wall was the same size, and the red light on it for voice messages was blinking. She walked to the phone, pressed the button to replay the messages, and meanwhile got herself a glass of orange juice.

The first message was from Larry Ward, letting her know that if she wished to get together, give him a buzz. The second was from her insurance agent, regarding the fire that had burned down the restaurant. Two blank ones—sales calls, obviously. And one from Eileen from the restaurant, checking to see how Ava was doing. Dear Eileen.

She sat and, as she finished the orange juice, went through the mail, making one stack for bills and anything else that looked important and a second stack for fliers, ads, and other junk mail. The junk pile made a quick trip into the wastebasket under the sink. Then she dialed her insurance agent's office. He was unavailable, but Ava told his assistant to please let him know that she'd called. She'd been away for a couple of days, but if they needed anything from her about the restaurant, let her know.

Then she started going through the bills but, after opening the first three or four, gave it up. The bills could wait. She was tired. She looked through the kitchen entrance into the hallway but fell into a stare, with no idea of what she was looking at.

"*So I'm more or less safe.*"

"*You're safe.*"

"*And I can go back to whatever kind of life I had before Tony almost destroyed it.*"

"*Yes.*"

Well, no, I can't, Ava realized. No, I can't, because whatever you call life, that's not it anymore, whatever kind of life I had.

She was tired.

And sad. Close to self-pity, which is never a good thing, but sad in some profounder sense, sad that people like Tony ever existed, that they destroyed their own lives along with everyone else's, and sad that people like Dave had to do whatever it was that they did, mumbo-jumbo, deep sorcery, whatever he chose to call it, and sad that people she cared about, the people at the restaurant and her customers, had to suffer, and generally sad because life is sad. Life's not happy; we can play and we can be happy, but life itself is not happy, not at all, not at all. It ends but it doesn't end and it *should* end, it should, because it's so—

Sad.

"If I can see Steve, or talk to him— Is that possible?"

"Don't get sentimental. The spiritual world is no place for that."

"Really?"

"It's as hard as a rock."

So what good was that if the spiritual world is as hard as a rock and the so-called real world is no place for decent people? Doesn't leave a lot of room for the rest of us air-breathers and walking wounded, does it?

Ava stood and went into the bedroom and closed the blinds, took off her shoes and blouse and skirt and lay down on the bed in her underwear. She knew she should take a shower and relax, take a shower and have a glass of wine, but instead she lay there, closed her eyes, and told herself it was all right, whatever she thought of, whatever came through her head or her heart now, it was all right.

She was tired.

She threw out her right arm, letting it fall onto Steve's side of the bed. How many nights now had she slept here without him? This was the new normal life.

She tapped the mattress. Soft taps. Not real taps, but maybe Steve would hear and from wherever he was, he would tap, too.

Ava began crying before she realized she was going to do it, and the sobs took her whole, pushing hard as if they were her soul escaping and leaving her airless. It was complete again after such a long time, the aloneness after such a long time, with Steve remembered in a thousand different ways but all at once, and as he'd looked in the mirror, alive, half there but alive and knocking, tap tap tap, knocking—

"Don't get sentimental. The spiritual world is no place for that."

"Really?"

"It's as hard as a rock."

Is it really?

When she awoke, Ava wasn't surprised to see that she'd slept for more than an hour and that it was quarter after four in the afternoon. She showered and got into fresh clothes, and because her stomach was empty and growling and her head knotted with tension, she went back into the kitchen to make some food. She put a dinner into the microwave but didn't want to wait even the three minutes for that to be ready, so she opened a can of applesauce and ate that to settle her stomach while the microwave counted down.

And once she finished the hot dinner, she made herself a cup of tea and reached for the phone again. She played back the message from Larry Ward. Somewhere she had his card, no doubt in her purse, but she wrote his number down again as he dictated it in his message, and then Ava phoned him.

It was his cell phone, and she left a message.

"I didn't think I'd need to do this, I really didn't. This is Ava. Larry, Dr. Ward, if you could return my call, I know you offered to talk to me if I felt I needed it, and I think I do. I would really appreciate it."

She left her number, wondering if he'd even get back to her today, and then called her attorney and left another message.

"Lana? Ava Beaudine. I'm sure I'm up to date on this, but I want to double check. It's about the power of attorney I have on file. I want to make sure everything's valid. I know I named you, and I don't really anticipate anything, but you might have heard that the restaurant burned down, and it worries me. We can talk about it if you want to. Call me when you have a minute."

She hung up and sipped her tea.

"I don't really anticipate anything."

But of course she did.

He was lying on the bed in his motel room, Arthur Neely, thinking about the night he had died, or nearly died, with his face on fire and half of his body on fire. Green fire. And Carl lying there with one arm raised, Carl looking up at him with his eyes gone, with most of him gone.

"Promise me something."

"What?"

"Kill him for me. Do everything you can, please. Learn how. Art, I'm scared. This creep, he's going to have my whole soul. It's worse than being

dead."

Worse than being dead.

Many things were worse than being dead; Neely was now convinced of that. He had thought, the night of the green fire, that he himself must be dead, but he hadn't been dead at all. He had been in a far worse situation. He was being reborn, reawakened to life, all on fire and reawakening to life, beginning the journey of a lifetime.

He had slept in cold fields in the snow, practicing, imagining himself still on fire, preparing himself for what he would do, for things far worse than being dead.

He had killed people, quite a few of them, and liked it, taking them apart with sorcery.

He had inserted his own eyes and heart and breath into living animals and gone jumping and running with them, eaten raw flesh with them, eaten warm struggling animals smaller than he, and it was more or less the same as taking people apart, body and soul, with sorcery.

And then he had begun to lose himself.

Neely wasn't sure how. He was still debating that, the how of it, the why and what of it, how he had begun to lose himself. Had he pushed himself too far, too fast? Was he incapable of doing what he wished to do, as though it were a matter of mere talent or aptitude? Some days his concentration had fallen off, but that was to be expected. Other days, he had gotten so drunk on the power of it and the feeling of love or unity or unitiveness or the whatever of it, the seduction of it, that he had wandered in many interesting places, inside himself, inside mirrors and bowls of water, through smoke and shadows—

Losing himself.

"*Listen to me. Are you listening?*"

"*Say whatever you need to say.*"

"*I have to try to do this. He did it one time, this Dave guy. He's a legend. He did it and some Nazi he knew did it. This guy is ancient, Art, I am not kidding. He knows what he's doing.* Promise me."

"*I promise.*"

"*Learn for me. Learn to do what I never did. Find Dave Ehlert and kill him.*"

Learn for me.

Done things he was sure Carl had never learned to do.

And here he was now, lying in a motel room, tired, still on fire, losing himself and not knowing why.

Why.

Neely sat up and looked at the clock radio on the nightstand by the bed. A little after four in the afternoon.

He had killed Dave once.

He could do it again.

He wasn't losing himself. Other people were getting in the way, but he wasn't losing himself. Tony Jasco. That woman partner of his. Who knew who else?

He was tired, is what had happened.

He had been pushing himself for a long time, now, months, almost a year, closing in on Dave Ehlert, pushing himself. No one could put that much on himself and not pay a price. He needed to relax. He needed to recharge his batteries.

That was it. He needed to recharge his batteries. Prove to himself that he still had it, that Dave couldn't outfox him, that he could do whatever he wanted.

What would you do if you could do anything?

Just what I'm doing, Neely thought. Just what I'm doing right now, Carl. Pushing myself for all I'm worth, doing it for you, doing it for myself, pushing too hard, but doing just what I'm doing now.

"It's worse than being dead."

I'll tell you what's worse than being dead, Neely thought. What I'm going to do next to that evil shithead, that's what's worse.

He needed to recharge his batteries, that was all. Prove himself to himself.

Neely removed clothes and walked into the bathroom. Turned on the shower.

Relax, he told himself. Take a warm shower. Then take a drive. He relaxed during long drives. Take a drive. See where it leads you. Practice. You need to practice and recharge your batteries.

That's all you need.

That's all you need.

18.

The Greater Pittsburgh International Airport is north of the city, in rural Moon Township. This proved to be a time saver because the facility where Nicole Prentiss lived was northwest of the airport, even farther out, nearly at the Ohio-Pennsylvania state line.

As Dave had surmised, Cameron Nelson was young, certainly no older than thirty, tall, lean, and with the studious air of a scholar. He admitted as much to Dave as they left the airport and drove north on Highway 60, climbing up and up, into the low green Allegheny Mountains.

"I taught philosophy for a couple of years," he said.

"Is that your degree?"

"Yes. I'd still like to go back for my PhD, but for the time being, I'm happy working for Mr. Fortune."

And that was all of the personal information Nelson provided. For the remainder of the drive, he and Dave were largely quiet, other than for Nelson's occasional comments on the weather—usually overcast because of the mountains—and an indication of where they were going—a remote location, at least in the sense that it was well out of the way and deep in woods that still would be familiar to a Seneca Indian or James Fenimore Cooper.

Dave stayed alert during the drive, although he did not specifically anticipate danger, not from Nelson and not from John Fortune. There was no logical reason for them to be a threat to him; Dave did not seriously consider that Neely and these two men could be partners in any fashion. Neely was a loner, and an unbalanced one.

Still, Dave typically tried to remain on guard and aware of his surroundings whenever he was away from home. In his house, on his grounds, he could protect himself; in the open, he was fair game, as Neely's taking him by surprise had clearly demonstrated.

Before reaching the turnpike, Nelson exited Route 60 and drove west on Route 51, heading toward Ohio and rural Columbiana County. But before he crossed the state line, he took a series of unpaved country roads that led them well away from the gas stations and family-style restaurants on 51.

The land out here was flat and gray and brown. Broad fields of scrub and tall, wild grass moved alongside them, and where the fields of tall grass ended, the land was held by ancient woods of maple and oak, sycamore and elm, birch and pine. Occasionally deer looked out from the trees. As Nelson turned his lightweight Mazda down a risky, narrow gravel road, a V of Canada geese, flying south, honked high above.

Life, leaving.

The narrow gravel road, hardly wide enough for a single vehicle, continued for three or four miles, with the woods close on both sides and growing heavier and darker the farther back they went. That was the impression, that they were leaving something behind, life or light, and moving through whatever it was that kept all of this land, memories or climate or history. A light rain began, a drizzle, and the trees bordering them turned so dense and dark that, for a few minutes, Nelson turned on his headlights, as though it were evening.

Then the trees pulled back, the skies lightened, and Nelson turned off the headlights. He made a right into something like a driveway that banked upward and ended at a chain link fence. The fence surrounded an old brick farmhouse, its ancient barn, and a few acres of grounds.

Nelson honked his horn, and almost immediately a middle-aged man in jeans, jean jacket, and baseball cap came out of the front door of the farmhouse, moved quickly down the wooden steps of the porch, and jogged the hundred yards or so of gravel drive between the fence and the chain link gate.

He lifted his right arm and called "Mr. Nelson!" before taking a key from his jacket pocket and opening the large lock on a thick chain that held the gate closed. He pulled the gate open, backing up behind it as he did, and Nelson goosed the Mazda forward, parking it just short of the porch as the gatekeeper put his lock and chain back in place.

As Nelson got out from behind the wheel, he told Dave, "This is Baxter."

The middle-aged man, somewhat out of breath, approached them and, as he heard his name, nodded to Dave and said to him, "Sir."

"This is Mr. Ehlert," Nelson told Baxter.

"I was told to expect you. I have tea and refreshments if you like."

"Actually," Dave replied, and turned to look at Nelson, "I'd like to see her as soon as possible."

Nelson said to Baxter, "Nicole."

"Right, right." Baxter nodded. "She was out in the barn a little earlier."

He stepped around the car to lead the three of them across a stretch of damp, uncut grass.

As they walked, Dave saw another building behind the farmhouse, long and low, essentially a motel of twelve rooms.

"Some live in the house," Nelson told him. "Or they have a room there in the back. But some of these people want to live outdoors, so we do what we can. They have the barn. They can camp under the trees. A couple live in holes."

When they'd first approached the gate, Dave had seen two or three figures walking or standing in the yard; now he saw a dozen of them, men and women both, of various ages and sizes and races, some more or less in command of themselves, the remainder clearly lost.

As he walked alongside Nelson, following Baxter, his eyes met those of an old woman whose face was the sole part of her protruding from under several layers of blankets and shawls. She watched the men and called to Dave, "*Est-ce-que je vous connais*? Do I know you?"

"*Peut-être, Madame,*" he replied, not slowing down. Perhaps.

And perhaps he did; from the war.

She kept her eyes on him. "*Peut-être,*" she muttered. "*Peut-être. Alors . . . .alors*"

Standing under an apple tree near the barn was a young man in his twenties, blond hair wet from the drizzle and hanging down his back. He stared directly in front of himself, facing away from Dave and the others. He repeated a single motion, lifting his right hand as though preparing to catch a busy insect, reaching out quickly, then pulling back and examining his fingers. Lifting, reaching, pulling back, examining, continually.

Just outside the wide entrance to the barn stood a woman, young, perhaps in her thirties, but with white hair, and naked. Despite the chill air, she was shiny, covered with sweat, and she kept her eyes on the ground as she turned slowly around, using the long stick in her hands to trace a circle in the gravel. "Come," she said. "Come. *Venite.*" Turning and turning.

Nelson led Dave into the barn.

It was not what he had expected; the spacious interior was domestic. Cubicles lined the four walls, each with its own bed, nightstand, and standalone metal locker. Above the cubicles were lofts, which served for storage. Private toilet and bath facilities were accessible in each of the four corners of the barn. The floor was concrete, and clean. In the wide central area were couches, chairs, and tables. The entire building had been reinforced with steel and concrete; beams and blocks remained visible in places.

Remarkable, how Fortune had refurbished the entire structure into, essentially, a communal dormitory. The rural exterior was a ruse; from a distance, to outsiders, the farmhouse and barn appeared to be innocent, rustic buildings.

Nelson led Dave toward the central area; Baxter followed. They passed perhaps a dozen souls. A few had been restrained, tied to their mattresses or chained to metal stakes driven through the floor into the earth, as one would keep an animal. Held in place by collars or leather belts, the chained rested on blankets, all of them apparently asleep, although they moaned from deep within themselves. Farther back in the barn, Dave saw the physically injured. Most of them had suffered burns, although one old African-American man was missing a left foot and most of his right leg. A young red-headed woman lying on a cot stared at the tall angled ceiling and whispered to herself, but otherwise did not move. She weighed no more than sixty pounds, surely. Whatever she had done to herself, it was taking her from within, and she was very near death now, no more than bones with skin pulled over them, bones and skin whispering and staring at a ceiling.

Nicole was crouched in the central area, talking in a low voice to an elderly white man sitting in a well-worn wingback chair. He did not acknowledge her, simply stared—at her, at something. As Dave and Nelson approached her, Nicole rose and faced them.

In her early forties, she was slender, almost boyish in build except for the full bosom. Her auburn hair was long, falling to her shoulders. She was lightly freckled and had serious gray eyes. Despite the beginnings of fine lines around the eyes and mouth, Nicole looked ten years younger than she was. She wore jeans and old tennis shoes and a tee shirt: *Pittsburgh Steelers Super Bowl XLIII 2008 Champions*.

She extended her right hand, and Dave noticed a tattoo on the inside of the wrist: the sigil of a demon. A quick glance, and he saw the same sign on the inside of her left wrist.

The demons and angels we create within ourselves and give to the universe . . . .

She said, "Mr. Ehlert," with a bit of West Virginia twang in her voice.

"Nicole." He took her hand.

She held his grip firmly, met his gaze, then raised both forearms for him to see clearly. "Sathay," she told him.

"Harmony and beauty," Dave remarked.

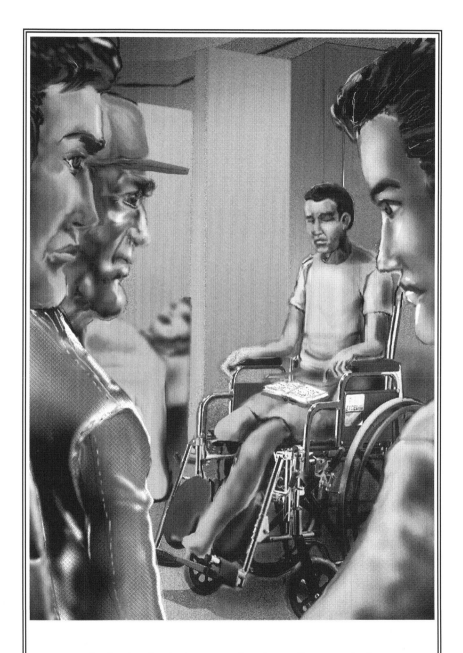

"...farther back Dave saw the physically injured..."

Intriguingly, Nicole pressed her wrists together, the sigils touching, and bowed shortly to him. "Magus."

It was a dramatic gesture, and a profound one. He hadn't expected it. In the old days, sorcerers greeted each other in this way out of deep respect— and as a sign that neither would take unfair advantage of the other.

Without hesitation, Dave returned the compliment, crossing his forearms and bending toward her.

Nicole smiled at Nelson. "I like your new friend," she said, and, before Nelson could reply to that, asked Dave, "Shall we walk?"

"Whatever you like."

She nodded to her right. Dave moved alongside her as Nicole led the way to a side door across the barn. The door was open, and damp air came in, but the drizzle had stopped.

"Well, he didn't kill you, after all," Nicole said.

"He came close."

"He's one pissed-off guy right now, I can tell you."

"Have you spoken with him?"

"No. I want nothing more to do with him, and he's aware of that. I'm going by how well I know him."

"And you know him well."

"I know him well. I got closer than I intended to."

"How's that?"

They had come to the door, and Nicole led the way outside. There were plastic lawn chairs under an awning. The chairs were dry. Nicole sat in one; Dave took another beside her.

A hundred yards away from them, a young man in his twenties was sitting on the lowest branch of an apple tree. He was wet from the rain, and he was watching them. He waved to Nicole and yelled something that could not be understood in any language. Gibberish.

Nicole returned the wave. "Chuck!"

He laughed and spoke more gibberish.

"I can't read him," Nicole explained to Dave.

"Have you gotten through to anyone here?"

"A few of them. At least now they remember to use the toilet. It depends on what they did to themselves." She said, "It's the easiest thing in the world to hurt yourself with this, isn't it?"

"Yes."

"Well, we get what we deserve, most of us."

"Are you happy here? Working for John Fortune?"

She kept her eyes on Chuck, crouched on the limb of the tree. "I owe him a lot. Maybe I can help him. But mainly it's for me. For what I did. Keep the balance a little bit." Then, in a quieter voice, as though admitting something even more private, Nicole told Dave, "I've agreed to this because I think you should kill him. I'll feel better if he's gone."

"All right."

"What finally happened is that I let myself get too vulnerable. I thought I knew better, but he's . . . persuasive. He really creates a mood."

"Go on."

"I permitted myself that luxury. That's the only way to put it. You're his big hero. You know that, right?"

"Yes."

"He did his research on you, as much as he could. There are a lot of stories. We know about your wife and your daughter."

"No, you don't. Not everything. Let's be clear about that."

"Fair enough. But you're here for the truth, right?"

"Absolutely."

"Well, the way Arthur sees it, you're what you are because you killed the people you loved. He thinks it helps you."

"It doesn't. And that's not what I did."

"I'm telling you what *he* thinks. That's what I was looking at. He kills me, he gets to be you, only bigger and badder. I didn't take him seriously, not at first, but he woke me up. He was this close with the knife one night, and I'm still trying to remember how I got away from him. I took a good look at myself after that. But I always was attracted to the bad boys."

Nicole turned her arms so that she could look at the sigils on her wrists. "These go back a long time. I want to remember what attracted me in the first place."

"The sense of wonder," Dave said.

Nicole looked up again at Chuck in the apple tree. He was still watching her.

"I liked the vulnerability, I admit it," Nicole said. "You're . . . so awake and aware. Total innocence. Here we are, and there's everything, and we're it, we're everything. How much more awake and alive can you be?"

Dave didn't answer her.

"You want to believe that there's something out there, and it's not out there at all, is it?"

"No."

"It's not about us. We don't live our lives for ourselves."

"I'm impressed," Dave told Nicole.

"Are you patronizing me? Because I don't need that."

"Not at all. It took me a long time to achieve that particular star of illumination."

"It's because of my grandma. She had the gift and she saw it in me, and that's where it started. She told me to be careful with it, but she was sure telling that to the wrong girl! I'm glad I did it, though. I'm glad I had the experience. And I can see why people like Arthur get so lost in it. Do you remember the first person you killed?"

"Yes."

"I was high for a week afterward. You put yourself completely out there, and you feel it in a way that's indescribable. I still can't put it into words. You're taking all of them, taking everything they are, going back however far they go. All of them."

Dave told her, "It's the only way to know the truth."

Nicole looked him in the eyes, his deep eyes, all of him in there. "I can't do it anymore, Mr. Ehlert. I'm not judging you or anyone else. I'm not qualified to judge you. But I've been turned around. You start out, you think you know everything, and you wind up here. You meet the Arthur Neelys and you wind up going back to what your grandma said. At least I did."

She stood and reached into her right jeans pocket. It was a tight fit, but she retrieved a small plastic baggie and handed it to Dave.

The baggie contained a lock of dark brown hair. "His?"

"Yes," Nicole told him. "I took it when he didn't know."

"Thank you." Dave placed the baggie in the inside breast pocket of his suit coat. "Can you tell me anything else about him? Do you want to?"

"If I could, I would. If I knew where he was, I'd tell you."

"I was hoping for that."

"But I can't go back to the arts."

"I'm not asking you to. It wouldn't help, anyway."

"He's too far gone."

"I can't trace him at all."

"He was already that way before I left him. It was making him sick. But, believe me, I know him. He leaves no stone unturned and no unfinished business. If he thinks it'll help, he'll try to find me and kill me yet."

"You're protected here. By Fortune?"

"Yes. And being around these people. But it's not Mr. Fortune's fight, is what he says."

"He's right. You're basically in a vacuum here. Good thinking."

"Only I'll feel better if you can kill him."

"So will I, Nicole."

"Call me Nicky. I'm Nicky."

"All right, Nicky." Dave stood and crossed his arms again, wrist to wrist, and bowed once more. "Thank you."

Nicole bowed again, as well. "Just kill him for me."

"For you and the rest of us."

She walked him back into the barn.

The old man who had been sitting in the wingback chair was on his feet now. He shuffled toward Nicole as she walked toward him.

She told Dave, "This man . . . I heard he killed four in one night, very old magicians. But somebody finally got to him. Maybe they found a way to come back and get to him."

"Maybe." Dave looked at the old man, his vacant eyes, his broken posture, and thought of the many others he had seen that way, or worse. Dead inside, eating themselves alive, or simply lost.

It calls to you and it pulls you in.

Nicole again gave Dave her hand. "Mr. Ehlert."

"Nicky." He held her hand, nodded to her, smiled slightly, then joined Nelson and Baxter, who were standing by the open front of the barn.

The sun had come out, raising a mist. The three walked slowly across the grass, returning in the direction of the car.

Nelson asked Dave, "Was she of help?"

"Of great help."

"Good. I'm sure Mr. Fortune will be pleased to hear it."

"Tell Mr. Fortune that he can call upon me as needed."

"I will. I'm sure he'll be *extremely* pleased to hear that."

As they passed her once more, the old woman in the lawn kept her eyes on Dave, but she said nothing. And as Dave and Nelson got into the Mazda, Baxter walked to the metal gate and unlocked it. He waved to Nelson as the car moved onto the driveway.

Dave asked Nelson, "And what is Mr. Baxter's reason for being here?"

"He owes Mr. Fortune a favor, so he works here to help out."

"Mr. Fortune keeps his favors and his debts well in balance, doesn't he?"

"He does, Mr. Ehlert. It's a good way to be in this world."

In the mirror outside the passenger side window, as they drove away, Dave looked at Fortune's odd little farmhouse and compound. He wondered whether John Fortune had had any *good* fortune in discovering what some of these people held within themselves.

And what was he himself searching for? In the medieval texts, it was always power or treasure or knowledge, asking the spirits for gold and silver or the ability to command armies and nations, whatever people considered to be important on earth in the sixteenth century. Is that what John Fortune considered to be important for himself in the twenty-first?

Then again, maybe he had learned the simple folly of such ambition, of treasure and power, of hoarding the things of this world. Maybe he simply wanted to know everything he could and sought to feed his own curiosity—insatiable, endless, wholly human curiosity.

In any event, when Nelson dropped him off at the airport, Dave rented a car and drove downtown. Pittsburgh is one of the more complicated American cities in which to drive—its highways and roads form something more like a maze than a means of local travel—but Dave had managed it previously during other trips to the city. Besides, he was hungry, in the mood for a good meal, and feeling more relaxed than he had been when he'd arrived this afternoon.

As promised, the veal was superb.

19.

Ward returned her phone call early that evening and apologized for taking some few hours to do it.

"I should be apologizing to you," Ava told him, "bothering you this way."

"Don't ever say that. I told you to call. What can I do?"

She told him how sad she was feeling but how she'd been trying to fight it since coming back home that morning. "Is this normal?" she asked Ward.

"I think you're just getting readjusted."

"I've been thinking about it all afternoon. I tried calling Eileen. From the restaurant. But she's not answering. What I really want is talk to someone. Maybe I need a therapist."

"Maybe you just need a good listener."

"I want to get started in a new direction. Pick myself up like I did after the accident and just get started. Maybe move back to Ohio. I think I need to do that. I feel kind of silly, now, calling you about this."

"Where are you now?"

"Home."

"I know you're near the hospital. Can you come by?"

"Is there someone there I can talk to?"

"Let's you and me talk first. I'm about done here. Have you eaten?"

"No."

"Well, come by and we'll eat in the cafeteria again."

"Would you want to come here?"

"I could."

"As long as it's not out of your way."

"No, I can do that."

"I guess I'm just tired and need to stick close to home."

"Give me your address."

Ava did, and then said to Ward, "This isn't normal for me. This is really different for me."

"I'm sure it is. Give me twenty minutes. Half an hour."

"I'll fix you something. What can I have ready for you?"

"A sandwich. Anything on a roll."

"I'll see what I have."

He liked her small kitchen and, as he ate deli ham on a bun, with extra mustard and a pickle and a can of diet Coke, Ward told Ava that it reminded him of being back in college with his wife, eating simple food because you're so driven to do other things at that moment in your life that all you ever do is grab something on the run.

"Did your wife study medicine, too?"

"No, no." Ward swallowed some Coke. "Lawyer."

"Did you have any children?"

"Both in college now. Out of town. My son's studying engineering. Evan. Karri wants to be a designer." He finished the sandwich and the Coke, sat back and took in a long breath. "Thank you. That hit the spot."

"After all you've done, hey, I'm happy to return the favor." Ava smiled, but it was not a full smile.

"So we're feeling down."

"Doctor, yes, we are. And I want to fight it."

"'Thought breaks the heart.'"

"Who said that?"

"It's an African proverb."

"It sure is true."

"I think you're asking too much of yourself. After everything that's happened? This is more than anybody needs."

"Should I talk to someone?"

"Sure. I can recommend some people. Is that what this is?"

"I can't get Steve out of my mind. It doesn't make me—" She wanted to be honest and express what she felt in the best way she could. "When I saw him, and when I heard him— Have you ever experienced that with Dave, seeing someone like that?"

"No."

"If there's something better after this, or even anything after this— It wasn't a trick."

"No. I know that. Does it give you any comfort that you saw your husband, or knowing that you'll see him again?"

"I don't know. That's what everybody says. I just took it for granted. But

Steve was still dead. I guess we kind of put it out of our mind, or try to, until you really have to deal with it again. Am I right?"

"You're absolutely right. Look at it this way. If none of this had happened, what would you be doing now?"

Ava thoughtfully pushed her lips out. "Sooner or later, I'd have let Tony have the restaurant. And then I'd start making plans to move back home."

"And that's what you'd like to do now?"

"I guess so. The weird thing is that now I know Steve's okay. That's what's really different. I didn't even know that I was worried about it until it happened, seeing him again. Is that natural?"

"Sure."

"Maybe it was from spending too much time in Dave's house. Does it get to you, being in his house?"

"It's a very different environment."

"Did he do it on purpose, create an environment?"

"I don't know. I don't know if he can help it," Ward admitted. "It's a reflection of him."

"Did you know that he's naked when he does a ritual?"

"Oh, yes."

Ava smiled. "I thought they wore big robes or something, like in a movie."

"I asked him why one time. It's very pagan. Very primitive. And that's the point. But he said that it was simply a matter of vulnerability."

"Really?"

"We keep our walls up, we constantly have our defenses up, and you can't do that if you're going to do what he does."

"That's funny because it reminds me of the woman I went to in college."

"Who was that?"

"I told Dave about her. She was psychic. She really was. I don't know if you believe in that or not, but she absolutely told me things that happened later."

"No, I don't doubt it."

"And that was what she said. You have to be open to the world, otherwise nothing comes through. But you had to learn how to do it so that you don't get hurt."

"That's the way Dave's described it to me."

"Well, maybe you can tell me something that I didn't ask him."

"What's that?"

"He gave me this." Ava showed Ward the talisman. "He made it himself.

So how come he can give me this to protect me, but he can't make one to protect himself? He almost died that afternoon on the sidewalk."

"You just said it yourself. He has to remain vulnerable."

"That's what makes it work?"

"It seems very poetic to me. You want to achieve something in this world, you have to put yourself at risk, open up, be vulnerable. If he's going to be part of the universe, he can't very well do that by walking around in a suit of armor."

"I never thought of that. You're right."

"Get naked in more ways than one."

"Yeah, yeah."

"The difficult thing for me to understand," Ward said, "was to get past the notion of good and evil. That's really drilled into us. We want to think that we're good, or that we have good intentions, and that there really is evil in the world. But it's just us."

"You really think that's true?"

"I kill infections. I do whatever I can to keep you feeling well, and I do whatever I can to kill the bugs. But they're just bugs. They have as much right to be here as I do. They happened the same way I did. People we think are evil, they're the same species we are. It's hard to admit that. So I still want to think that we're basically good, that because things *exist*, that means they're basically good. It's hard to get past that."

"I can't. I don't think I can."

"But it makes sense to me the more I look at the world. Take a step back. It opens you up. I think it's because it's no longer a matter of judgment. I don't have to judge you. Maybe it all comes down to balance, anyway. Actions have consequences. Every action casts a shadow. Every thought has an echo."

"That sounds very wise."

"I think it *is* wise. That's a saying of his. Has this done you any good?"

"It has, yes."

Ward stood. "I thank you for the supper. Time to get a little sleep before facing another day and not being judgmental anymore."

"Here." Ava stepped ahead of him to lead Ward out of the kitchen and down the hall to the front foyer. She told him, "This means a lot to me, that you came by tonight."

"I'll do whatever it takes. Dave doesn't have many friends. He needs all he can get."

Ava grinned.

Ward turned to face her as he reached the door. "I'll have another sandwich if you want me to."

"I'm fine."

"Get some sleep. Hold onto that jewelry he gave you, and get some rest."

"I will," Ava promised him.

"We have to look out for this guy. All he is does is get into trouble without people like you and me to keep him honest."

Ava laughed. "I don't know where he'd be without us."

"I'd hate to think of it."

Long drives. He had usually been able to sort himself out on long trips on the highway, driving all day or, better, at night, from sundown, when life emerged from its intricacies and secrecies, to the predawn, the depressing predawn, when light returned and people and the endless things of life disguised themselves once more as presumptions, as lies.

So Neely drove through the evening, at first paying no particular attention to the direction he was taking but realizing, after some time, that he was going west, driving on Dundee Road to its intersection with state route 72. He continued on 72, past Gilbert, through Starks, on out toward New Lebanon and then Genoa. Before reaching Genoa, he turned down a series of side roads and, on a whim, stopped. He was on a gravel road with open wide fields on both sides under a cloudy sky and not much moon. The fields reminded him of all of the other fields he had sat in or slept in over the years.

Neely steered left and moved his truck off the road and through the tall grass, then braked, turned off the engine, and got out. In the settling darkness, the cool autumn air, he walked away from his truck and knelt in the grass, then lay on his back and looked up at the clouds and stars, the high stars.

What would you do if you could do anything? his brother had asked him, and the answer, of course, was, just what I'm doing now.

He thought of all those evenings he had looked up at the stars, primarily before he went to kill people, and of what he had done with his life, how his life was, just life.

What do you desire? he had been asked when he approached those who were to teach him, first the Oakleys, later the others. *What do you desire?* It was simply a way of inquiring, Who are you? Why are you alive? What would you be? Explain yourself.

Desire is the first step to be taken above mere existence and the fulfillment of raw needs. I need to live. I need to stay alive. I need food and water. I need shelter. But what do I desire? Who am I?

In studying the arts, you start upon a new way, you begin your life fresh, you are reborn into the wonder of the world without its pretensions and dishonesties, you feel the earth as it moves and breathes, you understand that all things are alive all of the time and you with them, and you understand that predator and prey belong in each other's dreams because all life is predator and prey, all life is life devouring other life, beyond good and evil, beyond reason, life eager to live and devour other life, other lives. You awaken.

So tell us who you are. Explain yourself. Why are you alive?

What do you desire?

"Revenge," he had told the Oakleys. "Revenge for my brother. A man killed my brother, and now I wish to kill him. Teach me how to kill him with deep sorcery and by whatever means necessary."

And so he, a mechanic, a man who worked in garages with automobile engines, changed his life and was reborn under the guidance of his brother, whom he dreamed of often and spoke to frequently. Arthur Neely had never had a life of his own; he had been a reflection of his parents and of his older brother, and he had been content with that. Life for some of us is quiet in that way; we reflect, we do not shine. Yet we all learn the same lessons from life.

Neely came to feel that his changed life, his new life, was in the nature of a noble calling, and he was proud of what he had learned to do. True, it was never ending. He was by instinct a man of low passions, no drive, and content to let the world move by. Now he was called upon by the murdered dead to stretch himself into new postures. This he did and was surprised to learn how many people he was, deep inside himself. Is this me? he would wonder after killing someone with gestures and incense. I am my own engine, Neely would decide after taking a soul, as formal and perfect in my way as anything mechanical ever invented. The world moved in every direction for him, full of engines and dreams and gestures and incense, and he was all of those things.

But he himself was slowly being taken apart by the doing of it. If his life was not entirely his own, well, he admitted that fact. In a peculiar way, as his brother's guardian from boyhood, Neely had been Carl's enabler, ever supporting him. Now, with his brother dead and Carl's soul caught somewhere in a mirror, or beyond candlelight, or inside Dave's head, or roaming sadly in shadows, Neely continued to enable his brother. He recognized the similarity with his enemy's life, the fact of being owned by or spoken for or held by a dead person. Dave must feel that way about his daughter. Yet are not all of us in some way spoken for or owned by the dead?

We are all held in suspension by dead people, those who came before. Life, in fact, is an echo of everything dead people have done.

And, not for the first time, looking at the stars, Neely wondered when he would die, and how, and if he himself would die soon, be killed by evil Dave Ehlert.

It was possible. In the excitement of finding Dave after many years and in the thrill of almost killing him by the most fundamental of means, Neely had indulged himself into thinking that death was for others and not for himself, always for others, with himself as the death dealer.

Yet the younger him, the young man starting on the new way, had confronted death and learned that it is life by another name, still a thing of desires, and to be borne like anything in life. The danger was in dying, in how one died, and if taken by a magician, the pain could be great, the service nearly endless, the soul in thrall.

Neely had gone so far as to discuss this with the third person he killed, an old man whose soul he took in such a way that the man took a long time dying in his hospital bed. Neely had gone to see this man, preparing himself beforehand by reciting protective spells and wearing many talismans under his clothes, but those were not necessary. The old sorcerer was weak, and out of his head. He had lived too long and had been taken in by the wonder of life laid bare and made honest. He himself had taken many ghosts, and now that Neely was killing him, those ghosts would be freed and he himself in the next life would be Neely's servant.

"How did you resist it for so long?"

The old man had told him. "When I felt it taking me in, calling me, I tried to become selfless. But when the house is burning, can I escape the fire by moving to another room? The fire found me."

"What do you feel? I'm going to use you to kill others. All of your wisdom has come to this. What do you feel?"

And looking at his killer, feeling his soul being scratched from him and pulled free like an old thread, like dirt being dug away, the old sorcerer had told Neely, "I feel relief. Life is a burden and life lived without presumptions or pretensions or lies is unendurable. The wonder makes you drunk, and the light blinds you. Wait and see."

So here he was now, Arthur Neely, automobile mechanic and sorcerer, which might as well mean that he was candlelight and rain cloud together, for all that any of these things meant.

I feel relief.

Neely decided that he did not wish to feel relief.

He wished to fulfill his need for revenge.

Kill him for me.

In trying to become like Dave, his latest hero, he had become simply more of himself. In trying to kill Nicole as a means of finding more light or becoming drunker on what he could do, Neely had learned that the best sorcerer to be was his own sorcerer.

How to do that?

The direct attack had been very much a Dave thing to do.

What is the Arthur Neely thing to do?

Do whatever everyone else does and hide and attack from far away and set things in motion and let accidents happen? Some magicians fooled themselves into thinking that they were agents of the universe by doing that.

Not Neely.

He looked at the stars, heard life all around him in the field, insects and rabbits and even deer farther out, and he thought of looking at the world again through rabbit eyes or killing the rabbit sorcerously, but then did not.

He sat up, alert, glad that he had given in to his thoughts and reflected. That had always been best for him, reflection, long drives, time to think in order to sort things out.

If his house was on fire, then who was he to deny it and tried to hide in another room? He would confront the fire.

He walked back to his truck and sat for a moment behind the wheel, then turned on the cab light and ruffled through a worn leather briefcase he kept on the passenger side floor. When he found his diary, he held it against the steering wheel and, under the weak yellow light, turned to the last couple of pages with any writing on them.

Tony Jasco, and information about him. The restaurant. Ava Beaudine. What she looked like. Where her address was on Dupont Lane in Arlington Heights.

Neely returned the diary to his briefcase, turned off the cab light, started the truck, and backed out onto the highway. Then he drove east toward Arlington Heights.

20.

She was awakened by a sound that she thought took place in her dream because, in her dream, Ava was rinsing dishes in the kitchen, which was dark except for the small light over the sink, and she heard Steve knocking on the wall to let her know he was nearby.

But when she opened her eyes, she understood that the noise in her dream was not the sound that she had heard, not Steve.

Someone was in the house.

She looked at the digital clock-radio on her nightstand. It was nearly five a.m.

Ava continued to listen. The floor boards creaked at the bottom of the stairs, and she heard the soft but definite sound of footsteps coming one by one toward her room.

Dial 9-1-1?

She sat up and reached as carefully as she could for her cell phone, which she kept on the nightstand. But as she felt for it, she knocked it into the clock-radio, and probably gave herself away if whoever was on the stairs had heard it.

Ava wondered who it could be. The man who had tried to kill Dave was the most logical assumption. Perhaps he had managed to— Neely, that was his name. Perhaps he had managed to kill Dave after all and now had come here to murder her.

Should she dial the police or try calling Dr. Ward?

What could Ward do that the police couldn't?

Still, he knew more about black magic than the police did.

But Ward was—where? Home? Where was that? At the hospital?

She opened the phone, and the light of the display bloomed. Her wallpaper was a photograph of Steve and her standing in front of the restaurant. Ava pressed the nine button, but the beep it made sounded as loud as a gunshot to her, in the silence and in her nervousness.

More footsteps, and now they were on the landing outside. Whoever it was had made it to the top of the stairs.

Damn it, what should she do?

Try to crawl under the bed? Try to move into a closet?

There was no time to get to the window and open it, she was sure of that.

Ava closed the phone but held onto it. Her hands were damp. She was not shivering but she was alert, not frightened yet but very nervous, and her hands were damp.

She slid across to the opposite side of her bed and reached for the bathrobe she'd draped over the side chair there. She had on only her panties, so whatever was going to happen, it would be best if she were covered up. She placed her feet on the floor, reached slowly for the robe, stood and draped it over her, put her arms into the sleeves—

Her door opened several inches.

She had left it ajar. Her usual habit. She never closed it tight, but she never left it wide open, either.

The room was quite dark. The bedroom was toward the back of the house, away from the streetlights and any of the motion-detection lights and other things her neighbors kept on overnight. She'd pulled down the shades at the bedroom windows, as well.

The only light on anywhere else was the little nightlight she habitually left on at the other end of the hallway. It was near the carpet, plugged into an outlet there near the bathroom.

But because of it, Ava got her first look at whoever it was who'd pushed her door open and was standing there now, looking into the bedroom.

Not Dave. Not Dr. Ward, certainly. She didn't recognize this man, and it was a man, moderately tall and with unkempt hair, rather broad in the shoulders, but no one she'd seen before.

Simply an intruder? A robber? Or a rapist?

With his left arm, he pushed the bedroom door open even wider, and Ava saw part of his face now in the weak light of the nightlight. She gasped.

It was not a whole face. It was partly a face, partly normal, with the left side burned or twisted.

Arthur Neely.

"Go on and call him."

It took her a moment. Her mouth was completely dry. She tried to swallow, but she had no saliva, no moisture. She tried again. "Call . . . him?"

"Come on."

"Call who?"

"'Who'?" He mimicked the way she said it and took a step forward, placing his hand on the door knob, then ordered her angrily, "*Call him!*"

"Okay, all right. Dear God." Ava opened the phone again, looked at

Steve, got Dave's number on the screen, and pressed Send.

"Give it to me." Neely walked toward her with his right hand extended.

Ava handed him the phone, staring at him all the time, his disfigurement.

She heard Dave's line ringing on the other end, and then his answering machine coming on.

Neely angrily closed the phone, threw it at Ava, hard. It struck her in the chest, between her breasts, and it hurt. Ava was glad she had the bathrobe on; it cushioned the hit.

"Pick it up," Neely ordered her, "and find another number for him."

"There is no other number."

"Just find one. Or we're going to be waiting here a long time."

"I know who you are."

"Quit stalling."

She opened the phone, trying to think as well as she could.

Dr. Ward. There was really no one else. She pressed his number and hoped he would answer. She sent him thought waves; maybe he'd be psychic and hear her.

"Larry Ward."

"Oh, God."

"Who is this?"

"It's Ava."

"What's the matter? You sound terrible. What time is it?"

"He's here."

"Who's here? Dave?"

"Neely."

"*Neely*?"

"He…"

Neely came forward and took the phone from her hand. "Do you know Dave Ehlert?"

"Who the hell are you?"

"Find Dave and tell him to get here."

"Where? Where are you?"

"At Ava's house. Tell him he'd better hurry."

"Wait a minute," Ward protested. "Tell me what—"

Neely closed the phone and returned it to Ava, handing it to her this time. "Come on."

"Come on where?"

"If you keep doing that," Neely said to her coldly, "asking me a question every time I tell you to do something, you're not going to live long. Now *move!*"

He grabbed her by the left sleeve of her bathrobe and pulled her toward him, then shoved her on the shoulder. She felt onto her knees on the bedroom carpet, and the top of her bathrobe fell open.

Ava hurriedly pulled the bathrobe closed, making sure that she covered up the talisman around her neck. Would it matter if he saw it? Would he take it from her? Could it possibly protect her from him?

Not that it had done such a sterling job so far.

Ava rose and limped through the doorway, then led Neely down the stairs.

"Turn a light on," he said.

She flicked the switch at the bottom of the stairs, lighting the hallway that led, on the left, toward the front entryway and, on the right, toward her living room.

Neely told her, "Wait," and retrieved his gym bag, which he'd set just around the bottom of the stairs, going toward the front entryway. Then he told Ava, "Go on. The living room. Go."

She walked ahead of him down the hall.

"You're the one got your leg banged up in a car accident," Neely said.

"Yes."

"So we're both cripples," Neely said. "Aren't we a pair?"

In the living room, she turned and faced him. Neely looked around, then walked to a lamp on an end table by the sofa and turned it on.

"Sit."

"Where?" But then, afraid that she might anger him, she seated herself on a wingback chair across from the couch.

Neely remained standing. He looked out the picture window behind Ava, looked at the darkness beginning to lighten.

Ava said to him, "I have another question."

"What?"

"What do you intend to do with me?"

"You got in the way. He'd be dead by now, only you got in the way. So let's see what happens when he gets here now."

"What if he doesn't?"

"He will." Neely looked at her so intently then that Ava turned away, could not meet his eyes. "Not that it matters, but I'd like to know how you managed to stop me."

"Stop you from what?"

"You saved his life. What did you do?"

"I did not save his life."

"Lady, you walked into the middle of this, and you did something. And you don't have a single clue about any of this, clearly. So do not lie to me. *What did you do*?"

Now Ava met his eyes as bravely as she could. "He told me what to say."

"Interesting. And what did you say?"

"I don't know. Words. Like in Latin."

"Tell me."

"Come on! I don't remember what I said!"

"*Tell me!*"

"I don't remember! I run a restaurant. I don't speak *Latin*! I do not *remember*, okay?"

Neely smiled. "Okay. I believe you. You really don't remember."

"Jesus. . . ."

The sky lightened outside, just enough for the darkness to promise that morning would begin, another day coming.

Ava said, "You should know that he doesn't care about me. You know that, right? So what if he doesn't come?"

Neely sat on the couch and, ignoring her question, said to her, "Relax."

Ava swallowed and tightened her robe around her neck.

Neely smiled. "Don't worry," he said. "Keep your clothes on. I don't care. Relax. He'll be here."

❋ ❋ ❋

Ward phoned Dave immediately. What was it, five in the morning here? It'd be six in Pittsburgh. He might even be awake.

No answer. He got the recording.

Ward pressed Dave's number again. Come on, come on . . . .

"Hello?" He sounded sleepy.

"Dave, it's Larry. This is critical."

"What is?" And like that, he already sounded more alert.

"It's Ava and the man who tried to kill you."

"Neely?"

"He's at her house. She tried to phone you. He's holding her hostage or something to that effect."

Dave made a sound— Ward had never heard anything like it before, not from Dave, not from anyone, not people dying, not people in pain. It came from the center of his soul. Incredible sound.

"He doesn't care about me..."

"What else?"

"That's all. I tried to find out more, but he hung up fast."

"I'm on my way back. Let me try to call her."

"I'm going to head over there."

"Larry, no."

"Dave, I can distract him. She needs—"

"She doesn't need you. Not at this moment. He knows what he's doing."

"I promise I'll be careful."

"You're too important a man to put yourself in jeopardy like this."

"Look who's talking," Ward said, and hung up.

Within a couple of heartbeats, his phone rang again.

Dave.

He picked it up.

Dave told him simply, "Then be very careful, and recite the prayer I gave you before you get too close."

"I will." Dave had given it to Ward years earlier, typed on a sheet of paper that the doctor had carried in his wallet ever since.

"And if your instincts tell you to get away, Larry—get the hell away."

"I will. Hurry."

※ ※ ※

The phone rang in Ava's kitchen, and Neely had no intention of letting her answer it. But he shoved her down the hall, into the kitchen, so that she couldn't try to get away.

As he reached the phone, it clicked over to take a message.

"Ava, its Dave. If you can come to the phone, tell me—"

Neely took down the handset, interrupting him. "She can't come to the phone."

"You want me back there?"

"Immediately. I finally decided that this is what I needed to do to get through to you. Am I right?"

"You intend to kill her?"

"I intend to sit here until you show up."

"You've pushed this too far. You've taken this too far."

"We'll see. Just get over here."

"I'm not close by. I'm out of town."

"So get on a plane."

"Do *nothing* until I arrive. Do you understand?"

"You just be sure you get here as soon as you can."

When they returned to the living room, Ava moved to the couch and lay there, curled up with her head on a pillow.

She told him, "I'm tired."

"Me, too. Dave's going to be a while. So relax."

"I'm asking you again. Are you going to kill me?"

"Let's wait and see what Dave does."

"You're ugly inside and out, aren't you?"

"Absolutely."

Less than twenty-four hours, Ward thought, as he accelerated his BMW, and here he is returning to Ava's house. He yawned, despite the excitement and his anger, and tried to imagine what he would do once he pulled into her driveway.

Recite the incantation or whatever it was that Dave had given him. Latin. It was in Latin. Ward hadn't read any Latin since the eighth grade.

The sky was turning lighter and traffic beginning to fill the roads. Almost quarter to six. He thought of the many other early mornings like this one, thousands of them, that he'd looked at and driven through for years, for decades. Driving to the hospital, driving to the office, leaving part of his life behind but driving to his real life, which was listening to people, listening to what they didn't say as well as to whatever they did, and putting the pieces together to make the judgment call. It hurts here. I can't do this. I'm worried about this. I don't know what I did, but now I have this, that, or the other thing. Should I be worried? Is it serious? How serious is it?

Should I be worried? Ward thought, as the sky lightened, as he got closer to Ava Beaudine's house.

He asked himself, "How serious is it, Doctor?"

He answered, "Pretty damned serious, Doctor."

He told Ava to get up from the couch, and she did so carefully, keeping her robe wrapped tightly around her. Neely told her to walk ahead of him, go down the hall and into the kitchen.

"Water, juice. Gatorade. What do you have?"

"Nothing for you."

"Hey." He grabbed her hair and painfully pulled on her so that Ava had to look into his face. "Where is it?"

"The refrigerator."

He shoved her against the counter and opened the refrigerator. There were three small plastic bottles of water and a half-gallon glass container partially filled with apple juice.

"This is it?"

"You're thirsty already? You haven't done anything yet."

"You know. You've been paying attention. Good for you. You got nothing else?"

"I've been a little too busy to get to the store."

He frowned and put the water and apple juice on the kitchen table, then demanded, "Where's the bathroom? I gotta take a leak."

"Upstairs."

"Show me."

He pushed her ahead of him, and they climbed the stairs, Ava with her bad leg, Neely hanging back a bit in case she tried something stupid.

But she didn't. The bathroom was at the end of the hall. He made sure that Ava went in first, then closed and locked the door behind him so that she couldn't easily get out. He unzipped and stepped up to the toilet, and when he was done, he pushed Ava ahead of him.

She led the way back down to the kitchen, where Neely told Ava to pick up the bottles of water and the apple juice and take them into the living room, where she set them on the coffee table and went back to the couch.

"No," Neely ordered her. "On the floor."

"What?"

"*On the freaking floor!*" he yelled, pointing toward the middle of the room.

"Okay, all right." She stood where he pointed.

"Sit. Crouch. Do something down there. *Sit.*"

She did and watched as Neely opened his gym bag, then stopped and listened.

"What?" Ava asked him.

"Shh!" Then: "Who's here?"

"Nobody."

"Dave?"

"I don't hear any—"

But now she did. She heard a car pulling into the driveway.

Neely smiled, let out a long breath, and reached into his gym bag. He took out a can of black spray paint and his long-bladed knife and turned to face Ava.

"What's the knife for?"

"What do you think we use knives for?" He smiled and walked toward her.

When Ward pulled into the driveway, he sat for a moment, trying to decide what might be the best way to approach the situation. He had parked next to a used pickup truck and assumed it to be Neely's.

Fine. Think, think, think . . . .

He took out his wallet and removed the small square of paper Dave had given him. It was more like parchment than paper; some kind of homemade paper. Ward hadn't looked at it very often, but occasionally he'd open it, wonder about it, and then put it away again. From what he remembered of his grade-school Latin, these were simply sentences asking for protection, asking for help.

Help from what?

Ward cleared his throat, then spoke the Latin words aloud.

"*Impero spiritos potentes venire mihi. Audite mihi. Conservate me.*"

He waited. Felt nothing. Heard nothing.

Refolding the paper, he returned it to his wallet, then got out of his BMW and walked quietly up the flagstone pathway to the front porch. He looked at his watch. Almost seven in the morning already. He tried to see in through the picture window behind some shrubbery, but then thought better of it.

Knock on the door? Ring the doorbell?

He tried the doorknob.

The front door fell open.

Stepping cautiously, Ward moved into the foyer and slowly pushed the door closed behind him, making sure that he turned the door handle so that the bolt wouldn't click or make a sudden sound.

But from the hallway to his left, he heard someone call, with a lisp or halt to his voice, "We're in here! Come!"

He walked down the carpet, still not moving quickly, being cautious, being careful—

Neely was standing naked in front of the coffee table inside a wide circle of black paint that had been sprayed on the carpet. Hideous man, hideous face, drooping eye, all scar tissue on his left side, and holding a knife in his right hand.

And with a surprised expression on his hideous face.

"Who the hell are you?"

Ward didn't hear him. He was looking at Ava, who was crouched on the floor, sitting in the middle of another large circle drawn with black paint, and holding her right side. Where she held her side, her robe was soaked with blood.

She was bleeding to death.

21.

ard hurried toward her, but Ava gasped to him, "Doctor, no, don't!"

He stopped. The circle. Of course.

Neely said to him, "The doctor. On the phone."

Ward told him, "At least let me get to her to check the wound."

"You know better than that. Or you *should* know better than that. Now where's Dave?"

"He'll be here."

"I heard you praying. I thought it was him. Very good. Nice trick."

"I want to help her. Let me help her."

"She's the bait."

"The 'bait.'" Ward repeated the word with utter derision. "This is between you and Dave!"

"Well, she's part of it. You, too, Doctor, if you keep this up." Neely bent forward a bit, dropped the knife on the carpet, and picked up a bottle of water. He took a sip, not removing his eyes from Ward. He asked him, "Doctor of what?"

"I'm a physician."

"Do you do plastic surgery? Because after this, I may decide on a little nip and tuck."

"Mr. Neely, let me—"

"'*Mister!*'" He laughed. "You get the award for *something* for saying that. '*Mister!*' I'm not a *mister.*"

"Give me an award for helping Ava. You, too, if you want it. Did Dave do it to you?"

"That part of your code?"

"That's right."

"We have a code, too, me and Dave. May the worst man win. That's our code."

"I know what you do."

Ava groaned, and Ward told her, "Keep pressure on it. With your hand, Ava. Keep pressing on it."

"It's too deep for that," Neely told him. "I went deep."

"You want her to die?"

"I want Dave to walk in here and find her like this. That's what I want. So where is he?"

"You don't listen well. He'll *be* here. Now let me help her."

Ava moaned again and stretched out. She closed her eyes.

Ward took a step toward her, then stopped. He felt heat from her direction, heat along the perimeter of the circle, although he saw nothing. "Ava."

She looked at him. "It's fine. I should have died with Steve, anyway."

"It's not that serious yet. Keep pressure on it."

"I don't want Dave to get hurt."

Neely laughed. "Too late for that! He should have thought about that before he killed my brother!" He took another sip of water.

Ward ordered him, "Let her go! Do whatever you have to do to get rid of the paint on the floor, whatever it is you do."

"Doctor." Neely said to him, "Just leave."

"Let her go!"

Neely smiled at him, his twisted smile.

Ward grunted. His anger came out as that sound, a grunt, and he turned and lurched out of the living room.

Ava and Neely both heard him making noise in the kitchen, knocking things around, breaking glass or something, and then spilling all of the silverware onto the floor in a loud racket.

In a moment, Ward stalked back into the living room. He was holding a carving knife, and he yelled at Neely, "*Let her go!*"

To Neely's shock, Ward threw the knife directly at him.

And Neely pulled back in his surprise, almost crossing his own barrier, the paint on the floor, as the knife hit the air above the circle.

It disappeared in a burning flash. A bright light, a sound like that of something shorting out, a crackle and hiss, and what remained of the knife fell to the carpet on Ward's side of the circle.

It was a lump, a piece of black metal, and smoking. It charred the carpet fibers, and smoke lifted. Ward wondered if it would catch the carpet on fire.

"Damn it," he whispered.

Neely laughed.

Ward's cell phone rang. He took it out of his shirt pocket immediately and flipped it open. As he talked, he kept his eyes on Neely.

"Yes," he said. "No. It's ridiculous. He's inside a circle. I can't get to him. Ava, too. He stabbed her. She's bleeding. Yes, it's serious! All right. Well, that's what it is. All right. I understand."

He closed the phone and looked at Ava.

Neely said to him, "Tell him he better hurry."

Ward didn't answer him. He said, very quietly, "Ava?"

Her eyes were closed; she opened them. "Doctor, you better leave."

"Well, I can't do that."

"You can leave. I don't want you to think you have to . . . you know, stay. You should go."

He turned to Neely.

Neely made a face, as well as he could, pursing his lips, knitting his brow in a kind of pantomime, indicating to Ward to go.

Ward was shaking. He said to Neely, "I didn't think I was capable of real hate. I didn't think I could ever hate. I thought I knew better."

"Just get out of here, Doc."

"But now I know better. I really hate you."

"Go, now!"

He did.

What else could he do?

This was utterly ridiculous and unlike anything Ward had ever experienced in his life. Absolutely ridiculous. Absolutely hateful.

He went down the hall toward the front door, opened it, went onto the porch, and sat on the steps.

He wanted to cry, his rage was so great. Wanted to scream. He could have killed Neely in that moment, easily killed him.

What am I doing here? he thought.

She was very nearly floating. Eyes closed, and she was floating. She wasn't quite talking to Steve, wasn't quite there yet. She was still in her living room, but that no longer mattered.

The funny thing was that it was not in the least how it had been when she'd suffered the car accident. That had happened so quickly that she never knew anything had happened at all. Talking to Steve one minute and, the next, this huge truck comes sliding into them, and that was it.

She'd blacked out, had been knocked unconscious, and when she came to, the earliest thing she could remember was talking to Steve and then seeing the wall of a hospital room. She had wondered, who she was visiting in the hospital? That's strange. And then she'd realized that it was she herself who was in the hospital.

Not like this at all. This was floating. This was a good dream. Chilly, she felt chilly, but it was a good dream, and all she had to do was wait, was wait, and Steve would be there, was wait.

Oh, a voice. Now she heard a voice.

Not Steve.

No. Not a voice. It *was* Steve. He was knocking, tap tap tap, their little signal. I'm here. I love you.

Only how could he knock?

But she heard the knocking , and then she heard his voice, although she barely recognized him by his voice. He didn't sound as he had when she'd seen him in the mirror. This was clearer, this voice was clearer because she was right here with him, on the other side of the mirror, in there with him, and he told her in this clear voice, "*I have to go, now, and you do, too,*" and she said to him, in her clear voice, "*I'm ready to go with you,*" and he told her, "*I'm going on alone this time. You're to stay.*"

She thought, in her clear voice, "*I'm to stay?*"

"*You're to help him.*"

"*And what happens to you?*"

"*I'm going on alone.*"

He said it, and she heard him say then, or sensed him making her aware, of something Dave had already told her: "*Don't get sentimental, Ava, my dear Ava, the spiritual world is no place for that. It's as hard as a rock.*"

He told her, as she floated, to continue pressing on the puncture in her, the bleeding wound, and with her other hand, her left hand, to hold the talisman Dave had given her because now it would help her, really help her, she was in a place now, inside the mirror, in a place as hard as a rock, where it was going to help her, and Steve told her—

"*Venite, manes.*"

She whispered, "I understand. *Wen. Eye. Tees.*"

"*Manes.*" In his clear voice.

"*May. Nees.*"

From beyond the circle, she heard Neely—was that his name? The burned man? She heard Neely screaming, "You lied to me! You lied to me!"

"*Festinate*," Steve said, in a clear voice.

"*Fes-tie-nay-tee.*"

"*Audite.*"

"You lied to me! *You know the words!*"

"*Odd-eye-tee.*"

Neely heard the car outside, or the tires at least. A taxi or a limo or something. The door slamming closed, very loudly.

The doctor's voice, and another voice.

A voice full of rage.

Good.

He came in like an animal. Unshaved. His hair uncombed. His overcoat open so that he appeared to Neely to be some sort of frontier vigilante, all angry-faced and flying-coated as if he'd just come in from the open range.

When he got to the center of the room, Dave stopped and looked at Ava and Neely could see the emotion in his eyes. Then he looked at Neely.

Rage, clear and perfect. Neely decided that he'd never before experienced anything quite like those eyes. They weren't dead; they weren't cold; they were more alive than anything he'd seen in a long, long time, and alive with rage, hate, fury.

Dave said to him, "Why this way?"

Neely replied, "You're not quite as tall as I thought you'd be. But I couldn't find a picture of you anywhere. Not even from a million years ago."

"Surprised?"

"No, no, not at all. But I had to get descriptions. And when I finally saw you, hey, I knew there was only one Dave."

"Where? How? When I killed Burkey? Or someone else?"

"Burkey."

"You're a bright fellow. Now why are we doing it like this?"

"Dave, look at it from my perspective. I've got you between a rock and a hard place. Kind of like where you left me."

"I try to save her, or I attack you, but I can't do both at the same time."

"I want to see you burn. That's all. I want to see you burn."

Dave took in a deep breath. He pressed his hands in front of him and closed his eyes for a moment in deep concentration. Then he went toward Ava and kneeled beside her, just outside the circle on the floor.

"Ava?"

She opened her eyes. Looked at him. She had one hand still pressed to her side, where all of the blood was, and the other on the talisman. She whispered to him, "Steve came. He helped me."

"Did he?"

"And I saw it all. Steve. Miranda. Neely. Everything he did, Dave."

"You know."

"I saw it all."

"You're going to live, Ava."

"Yes. Now—" She took in a breath and shuddered, then said to him, "Kill him, Dave. Take him. Him and every soul *he* ever took. Kill him."

He smiled a very cold smile and stood.

Heard footsteps behind him.

Ward.

"Doctor!" He growled it. He leaned forward, all shoulders and arms like a wolf or a bear, and he turned his head to one side like a wild dog picking up a scent. "Back up! Be ready to help her!"

Ward nodded.

Dave looked at Neely behind his circle.

"Take her and go away, and I'll go away. I'll let you take her," Neely offered.

But he was afraid, he'd said it with fear in his voice, the old fear of all victims, of every weak thing that ever gave itself up or ever was taken, in this world or others.

Dave roared. Moved to one side as though a demonic wind had lifted him and, wild, leaped the distance between Ava and Neely.

Neely once again pulled back, and there was that fear in his eyes.

"You're no smarter than your brother. I'm going to see you burn."

"If I bring this down—"

"You're not bringing anything down." Dave removed his overcoat and threw it onto the carpet, then reached into the inside pocket of his suit coat. He removed the plastic baggie Nicole had given him. "Your girlfriend gave me this."

"What girlfriend? *Nicky*?"

"Here's your problem, Neely—nobody likes you. Nobody wants you around. Nicky wants you dead. *I* want you dead. *Everybody* wants you dead."

"How do you know about her?"

"You couldn't find her, but that doesn't mean people didn't know where she was. And she had this."

"You're bluffing."

Dave took a pen from his shirt pocket, leaned over, and began tracing a circle in the carpet two feet wider than the diameter of Neely's circle.

"You ever think about why we use the circle?" he asked. "I do. It's never ending. Just like us. It goes around and around and doesn't really have a beginning and doesn't have an end. It can be a door, it can be a hole, and it can be anything. It can be a trap."

He stood, the circle completed, and moved away.

"A trap," Dave said. "You've really messed things up, son."

"I have no intention of dying this way. I will not die this way."

"Yes, you will."

Dave went to Ava's coffee table, dumped Neely's hair from the plastic bag onto the glass top of the table, and said a few words in Latin over the hair.

Neely yelled to him, "Enough!"

Dave reached into his pants pocket for a book of matches.

"You're a coward!" Neely shouted. "You won't meet me face to face. Meet me face to face!"

Dave dropped the match onto the hair, and the locks caught on fire, burning and charring in a stink.

"I will not die this way!" Neely screamed.

Dave stepped away from the coffee table and said, "Then let's see how strong you are. I did it once."

"I know that."

"And I know one other person who did. And it wasn't your brother."

"I will not die like this, Dave."

Dave smiled.

Ward was sitting on Ava's front porch steps when it happened. Dave had told the doctor to go outside because he'd be safe there, at least reasonably safe. The sound of it was loud, like a wind, like a puddle of gasoline going up all at once, and Ward instinctively ducked when the glass in the picture window to his left rattled and shot out, spraying hot fragments across the front yard.

Immediately, he stood and opened the front door.

Or tried to. A powerful wind prevented him for a moment. It was as though Dave, or somebody, were on the other side, leaning on the door to stop him from opening it.

Then it swung in, and Ward ran down the hall.

Screaming was all he heard, and when he reached the entrance to the living room, he saw Neely on the carpet, Neely charred, black, his body contracting and pulling inward, tightening and becoming hollow. Green fire. Sparks of green fire danced on him, and he had no face, eyes, mouth, nothing, he was a shell, he had dropped, and now he broke apart like ash, which is all we are, things that burn and die and scream as we go, we scream as we live, and the pieces of him, black and tinged with green fire, scattered across Ava's living room carpet, a thing easily broken at last, a human being of screams and anger easily broken at last.

Dave, holding Ava, looked up as Ward came in. He pleaded, "Please."

Ward came to them and gently pushed Ava back, examined the side of her, all wet and red, her robe soaked. But she was breathing, and she had a smile, her wonderful smile. Ward had wanted to tell her from the beginning what a charming smile she had, and here it was, and she was alive.

He directed Dave, "Help me," and together they carried her as gently but as quickly as they could outside, into the driveway, and laid her there.

Dave took out his cell phone and pressed 9-1-1 while Ward opened the trunk of his car to remove a spare blanket he had there. Ava was in shock, whether she knew it or not, and Ward put the blanket around her and then crouched there, holding her, whispering to her.

He said a prayer to her, not an incantation, nothing in Latin, simply a prayer that his grandmother had taught him in church when he was a little boy.

While Dave stood watching the house as the fire took it.

Orange fire, now. No more green fire, but fire all the same, an emergency but not hellfire, taking Ava's house and whatever she had in there, her life, what her life had been.

Ward felt tears fill his eyes as he watched his friend, his strange friend, strange Dave, evil Dave, alone, tired, watching the burning house, and now with how many more souls crowding his own dark soul, burning souls, angry souls, weeping souls.

And the fire burned.

22.

ave was gone by the time the ambulance arrived to take Ava to Northwest Community and by the time the fire trucks and personnel came to put out the fire. Ward rode in the ambulance with Ava and signed her into the emergency department before getting the phone call from his receptionist reminding him that he had, after all, a professional life to fulfill. But throughout the day, as he attended to his appointments with his regular patients, he phoned the hospital regularly to check on Ava's progress.

Dave was there, in any event. He had gotten to the hospital ahead of the ambulance; he told Ward when he phoned the doctor later that morning. Dave had cleaned himself up as well as he could in a hospital restroom, then asked at the desk how Ava was doing, and waited throughout the morning until the surgery was completed—quite successfully, Dave was told.

He remained there throughout the day, eating little but making many trips to the cafeteria to buy many bottles of water and juice. He seemed to subsist only on liquids the entire day.

And that evening, when Ward came in to check up on Ava, both men found her doing well in her room, sitting up and feeling oddly . . . revitalized, she told them. Revitalized and very thirsty.

She couldn't drink enough water, apparently, or fruit juice to quench her thirst.

But she rested well that night, after Dave and Ward left, and when Dave came by the following afternoon, it was to find Ava in conversation with her insurance adjuster. Everything was in order, he told Ava, although the cause of the fire had not yet been ascertained. The body of the man found there—it was still proving difficult to identify him, almost nothing was left of him, although sooner or later, without doubt, the police would know who he was. The knife Ava mentioned had been found in the remains of her house, so her story that this madman, whoever he was, had broken in to attack her—clearly, that was what had happened. Thank God her doctor had been nearby and able to reach her before she, too, had died in the fire.

And whatever the cause of the fire, Ava was covered for the full value of her cottage, so she should concentrate, the adjuster told her, on getting better and planning on what she wished to do next with her life.

Interesting, isn't it, Dave whispered to Ava, out of earshot of her roommate, once the insurance adjuster had gone, how people can look right at something and not want to admit what it is they're seeing, so they make up something else and choose to believe that instead of what's right in front of their eyes.

Such as, Ava asked, fires that burn much faster than normal? Taking out a whole house in a matter of minutes?

Precisely, Dave said.

As well as sorcerers killing themselves by starting something they should never have gotten involved with in the first place, and burning themselves so completely that hardly any bones are left, nothing is left, at least not in this world.

❈ ❈ ❈

That evening, when Dave and Ward came by again, Ava was doing so remarkably well that she was walking the halls, and her surgeon had told her that she would be sent home very soon.

"Which," Ava said to her friends, "for the time being, is the motel room the insurance company is kindly providing."

Ward looked at Dave, who was watching Ava.

Dave said, "No."

Ava asked him, "No, what?"

"Stay at my place if you like."

She frowned, considering it. "It's certainly nicer than a motel room."

"Take your time," Dave told her. "I think you should relax. You can always build your new house."

"You're not still worried, are you?"

He shrugged but admitted, "I'd feel better doing it this way for the time being."

Ward said to her, "Here—what would you do if you could do whatever you wanted? Being completely selfish?"

"Completely selfish?" Ava smiled. "Me? Hmm. I'd relax in a hot bath for the next year."

"Well, consider it," Dave said. "You've helped me."

"We've helped each other."

"True."

They looked at each with deep understanding, and Ward saw it in their eyes, something between them now, a bond, the life each of them was beginning now.

"Maybe she can do something with that ugly room you always make me stay in."

Ava grinned. "It needs new drapes. It definitely needs something bright on the walls."

"Something bright," Ward said, and looked at Dave. "That would be refreshing. And a nice change."

Dave glanced at both of them, shook his head, and allowed a smile to come through.

The bath that Ava enjoyed the first morning she woke up at Dave's house was not, after all, a year long, but it was sufficient for her to relax, relax completely, so completely that she . . . floated.

And was no longer afraid.

"I saw it all. Steve. Miranda. Neely."

"You know."

"I saw it all."

"You're going to live, Ava."

"Yes. Now—"

Yes. Now . . . .

As she recuperated, she and Dave began taking walks together, at first simply around the outside of his house, as large as it was, and then into the wide, deep woods he owned. They had many talks, good talks. He explained further about the protective talismans he had, and they discussed the possibility of Ava herself perhaps trying to learn some of the arts.

She wasn't sure that she wanted to, that she ever wanted to.

But she did want to be aware enough that she could assist him whenever he might need it.

"You really need to have somebody around. Larry and I have discussed this."

"Have you?"

"He's not always going to be there."

"And you are?"

She lifted an eyebrow. "I'm giving it serious consideration."

And she did do some improvements to the upstairs room, as well. Decided to put new paint on the walls, a lighter color. And new drapes. New throw rugs.

The framed photographs? The old toys?

They disappeared overnight one night without Dave's saying a word to her. Where they went or what he did with them, Ava did not know and, for the time being, did not inquire.

But she did ask Dave what had occurred during a brief ceremony he had held in his attic a couple of weeks after Ava had moved in. He had performed the ritual to see whether he could reach the dead Neely, or both Arthur and his brother.

He caught Carl briefly, a glimpse of him, chattering like an insane monkey, really, but there was nothing of Arthur, whose soul must surely have been even less coherent than Carl's.

Dave had spoken with Miranda again. She appeared in the mirror, floating, beautiful, white, as pure as a sylph, cool, bright-eyed, hovering and suspended, his living memory. And she reminded him, as though he needed to be reminded of it, they were to help each other.

And he glimpsed Steve, as well. Smiling. Steve somewhere far back in the depths of the mirror, pleased, and complete now, this life complete.

When Dave came downstairs after performing that ritual, he found Ava in the kitchen, preparing him a meal of scrambled eggs, with plenty of juice set out.

"I saw Steve," he said and explained what he had felt.

She finished making his breakfast and set it out for him, not sad, although not smiling, and as Dave ate and drank, famished, Ava told him, very quietly, "Thank you," and reached across the table to touch his hand.

A few weeks later, Ava and Dave and Ward relaxed on Dave's patio on a cool autumn evening. They were drinking coffee, not wine, not replenishing water or juice, and had fallen silent from whatever they had been discussing, small talk, when Ava looked at a bird flying across the dusk.

She thought, for the first time in what felt like a lifetime, of her old business card, embossed blue ink on bright white stock, and with an embossed silhouette of a bird in flight.

Dave asked her, "You're thinking of the bird?"

"Yes." She nodded but didn't look at him. "The bird and everything else."

Discussions in libraries, and talismans, and evil men, and people burning alive. Black paint or tar, or what remained of souls, smeared across a glass window. And floating. And her dead husband, still alive. Everything remains alive, no matter how evil, because maybe there is no evil after all, just us and an entire universe full of living things, other things, not evil, but alive, not like us, but alive.

And ultimately, all of our lives touch, and everything is an echo of what has come before.

Dave, looking at the purple sky drawing down the dark, said to Ward, "I haven't said this until now, but . . . thank you for going over there."

"Yes!" Ava echoed.

Ward made a sound of disgust. "I have never in my life felt anything as abhorrent as that man."

"He felt he was justified," Dave said.

Ava and Ward both looked at him. The tone of his voice— Dave was speaking to them from his depths. They each felt it.

He said, "I admit, Ava, that when I first saw you there . . . my fear was that you were dead."

"I almost was."

"It made me very afraid because it reminded me of something from very long ago."

There was prolonged silence until at last Ward asked, "Is it proper for us to inquire?"

"My fear was that it was the same way Evelyn died."

Ava asked, "Evelyn?"

"My wife."

She and Ward shared a glance.

"It was self-sacrifice. She did it to protect me. She gave up her life."

Ward said, "I had no idea."

"The same with Miranda. It was my fault that the ritual went wrong. I should have died myself, or been pulled in, but Miranda interfered, and she did it deliberately. There are so many ways for things to go wrong. You lose your concentration, you step across the line, you open one door instead of another—" He looked at Ava, then at Ward. "Why did you decide to study medicine, Larry?"

Ward thought it an odd question, but he answered it. "I have an aptitude. I like science. Part of it was that I wanted to show the world what I was capable of, and prove it to myself, too. And I wanted control. That's what it is for a lot of personalities in medicine. Make sense of the world, influence it, affect it, maybe do some good, or at least what we perceive to be good."

Dave told him, "When you enter into the arts, the people who welcome you and initiate you ask you a question. 'What do you desire?' That's the question."

"And what did you tell them?"

"I told them, 'I want to know what the truth is in life.'"

"Really?"

"We had come through the Great War, and the effect of the war was enormous. Most people simply turned away from it. They wanted to be done with it. But there was also a search for meaning. Many of us wanted to know that life means something, and we were willing to go all the way down, however far it went, to find out. You go to war, you're dealing with absolutes. You come through the war, now you understand that there are no absolutes. Yet that's exactly what we want."

"You make a very good point."

"We're in the world—we *are* the world—and I'm a young man, I've married a beautiful, intelligent woman, yet we know that everything around us perishes, everything changes. What does it all come down to?"

"Did you get an answer? Is that what the initiation was about?"

"My answer was that life is loss. The truth is that life is about loss. We're given so much, and yet it's taken away, it's taken back, or we lose it while we live our lives."

"I disagree," Ward told him. "I think life is about change. I wouldn't call it loss."

Dave shook his head. "When you're initiated, the question you ask, what you desire—that becomes your path in life. That's what you become. You become the answer to your question."

"You're saying that your life is about loss."

"It's the path I chose."

"But not intentionally."

"How much more intentional could I be? This is my desire, knowing the truth of life, and I embody that. I live it. That's what the arts are for."

"What about Neely?"

"Whatever his desire was—revenge, probably, for his brother—he learned what it is to live that life, a life fulfilled by revenge."

Ava suggested, "But there's always some gain. It can't always be about loss."

"True," Dave agreed. "And that's part of the truth that I've come to learn. The things I've lost . . . there's been—" he searched for a word "—not restitution or wholeness, but balance."

"Balance," Ava asked him, "like a state of grace?"

"Perhaps. If I've earned it. Perhaps it's simply to earn . . . moments like these."

"Perhaps," Ava said, "we save each other's lives in more ways than one."

Ward turned his attention to her. He saw that Ava, not looking at Dave, reached her left hand out for him and found him. Dave took her left hand with his right, and they held onto each other that way in the dark, holding hands.

Ward looked to see where that bird had flown against the purple of the night, but the night was complete now, and the bird gone.

He smiled.

THE END

ABOUT THE CREATORS

AUTHOR –

DAVID C. SMITH – was born on August 10, 1952, in Youngstown, Ohio. In addition to many essays and short stories, he is the author of twenty published novels, primarily in the sword-and-sorcery, horror, and suspense genres. These include a series featuring the character Oron (1978-1983) set on the prehistoric island-continent of Attluma, the fantasy trilogy The Fall of the First World (1983), and two occult suspense novels featuring the character David Trevisan (1989, 1991), as well as a literary coming-of-age novel, *Seasons of the Moon*, set in the rural matriarchal village of Weyburn, Ohio (2005). Smith has written or coauthored eight pastiches based on Robert E. Howard characters, including the series of six fantasy novels featuring Red Sonja (1981-1983) coauthored with Richard L. Tierney. The five Attluman novels, *The Fall of the First World*, and the two occult suspense novels are due to be reprinted by Wildside Press.

Aside from writing fiction, Smith has worked as an advertising copyeditor and English teacher and for more than twenty years as a scholarly medical editor. He has served on the staff of *Neurology,* was the editorial production manager of the *American Journal of Ophthalmology*, and for more than ten years has been the managing editor of the *Journal of the American Academy of Orthopaedic Surgeons*.

Smith, his wife, Janine, and their daughter, Lily, live in Palatine, Illinois, just outside Chicago.

Further information about David C. Smith and his writing is available on his website (http://blog.davidcsmith.net/) and in his entry on Wikipedia [http://en.wikipedia.org/wiki/David_C._Smith_(author)].

INTERIOR ILLUSTRATOR –

MARK SAXTON – was born in 1965 in Northern California, and has professionally been selling his work since the age of 9. He currently resides in Southern Oregon, and has done illustrations for comic books (as well as being writer or co-writer on a few), t-shirt designs, advertising design, children's illustrations, and a variety of other art projects. He is versed in a multitude of artistic and creative media, and enjoys his free time with fantasy role playing games, or playing his guitar or drum set.

COVER ARTIST –

BRYAN FOWLER – is a painter and illustrator who resides in North Carolina with his wife and a crazy Alaskan Malamute. You can see more of his work on his website at http://www.bfowler.com.

In 1190, two years after wresting the crown from his father, Henry II, Richard the Lionhearted departed France for the Holy Lands and the Third Crusade. He left behind regents, Hugh, Bishop of Durham and his chancellor, William de Longchamp. But his younger brother, Prince John, lusted after the crown and saw Richard's absence as a golden opportunity to seize control. John began a program of heavy taxation that threatened to destroy the social-economic stability of England.

While the royals conspired against each other, it was the people of the land who suffered. Working under inhumane laws, they became no more than indentured slaves to the landed gentry. Amidst this age of turmoil and pain, there arose a man with the courage to challenge the aristocracy and fight for the weak and helpless. He was an outlaw named Robin of Loxley and how he became the champion of the people is a timeworn legend that has entertained readers young and old.

Now J.A. Watson brings his own vivid imagination to the saga, setting it against the backdrop of history but maintaining the iconic elements that have endeared the tale of Robin Hood to readers throughout the ages. It is a fresh and rousing retelling of an old legend, imbuing it with a modern sensibility readers will applaud.

Making Pulp History!

From the heart of Africa to the streets of Harlem, a new hero is born sworn to support and protect Americans of all races and creeds; he is Damballa and he strikes from the shadows. When the reigning black heavy weight boxing champion of the world agrees to defend his crown against a German fighter representing Hitler's Nazi regime, the ring becomes the stage for a greater political contest. The Nazis' agenda is to humble the American champion and prove the superiority of their pure-blood Aryan heritage. To achieve this end, they employ an unscrupulous scientist capable of transforming their warrior into a superhuman killing machine.

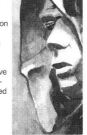

Can the mysterious Damballa unravel their insidious plot before it is too late to save a brave and noble man? Airship 27 Productions and Cornerstone Book Publishers are proud to introduce pulpdom's first ever 1930s African-American pulp hero as created by the acclaimed author, Charles Saunders.

Move over Doc Savage and Captain Hazzard, here comes America's newest pulp hero - CHALLENGER STORM

The sole survivor of a senseless tragedy, the heir to a massive fortune devotes himself to a life protecting the innocent and punishing the guilty. From his base of operations at the Miami Aerodrome Research & Development Laboratories, he and his colorful associates brave any danger to bring justice to those in need.

His name is Clifton Storm... the world will call him "Challenger."

When a wealthy aviation tycoon asks Storm to help return his kidnapped daughter, the MARDL crew is plunged into a rescue-mission on the tiny island-nation of La Isla de Sangre. From the sunny streets of Miami to the assault on a guerrilla enclave & the ruins of a lost-city deep in the jungle, the action is non-stop in this debut pulp thriller. Can Storm rid La Isla de Sangre from the vicious warlords known as the Villalobos Brothers and defeat the mysterious Goddess of Death?

Writer Don Gates and legendary graphic artist, Michael Kaluta join forces to unleash this exciting and original new pulp hero guaranteed to provide pulp fans with explosive thrill-a-minute entertainment.

AIRSHIP 27 PRODUCTIONS
PULP FICTION FOR A NEW GENERATION
AVAILABLE ONLINE AT AIRSHIP27HANGAR.COM